Praise for the Novels of Katie MacAlister

"Smart, sexy, and laugh-out-loud funny!"
—Christine Feehan

"A nonstop thrill ride." —A Romance Review

"Crazy paranormal high jinks, delightful characters, and simmering romance." —Booklist

"Who knows where she will take us next? . . . [A] fascinating and fun writer." —The Best Reviews

"You get mystery and great chemistry from the characters." —Romance Junkies

"A fun and witty paranormal romance . . . an entertaining and engrossing read . . . engaging and memorable." —BookLoons

"Witty banter that sparkles with humor and a plot that zips along make even the most outlandish situation seem perfectly reasonable. MacAlister is a rare talent." —Romantic Times (4½ stars)

Ghost of a Chance

Katie MacAlister

Writing As

Kate Marsh

AN OBSIDIAN MYSTERY

OBSIDIAN
Published by New American Library, a division of
Penguin Group (USA) Inc., 375 Hudson Street,
New York, New York 10014, USA
Penguin Group (Canada), 90 Eglinton Avenue East, Suite 700, Toronto,
Ontario M4P 2Y3, Canada (a division of Pearson Penguin Canada Inc.)
Penguin Books Ltd., 80 Strand, London WC2R 0RL, England
Penguin Ireland, 25 St. Stephen's Green, Dublin 2,
Ireland (a division of Penguin Books Ltd.)
Penguin Group (Australia), 250 Camberwell Road, Camberwell, Victoria 3124,
Australia (a division of Pearson Australia Group Pty. Ltd.)
Penguin Books India Pvt. Ltd., 11 Community Centre, Panchsheel Park,
New Delhi - 110 017, India
Penguin Group (NZ), 67 Apollo Drive, Rosedale, North Shore 0632,
New Zealand (a division of Pearson New Zealand Ltd.)
Penguin Books (South Africa) (Pty.) Ltd., 24 Sturdee Avenue,
Rosebank, Johannesburg 2196, South Africa

Penguin Books Ltd., Registered Offices:
80 Strand, London WC2R 0RL, England

First published by Obsidian, an imprint of New American Library,
a division of Penguin Group (USA) Inc.

First Printing, February 2008
10 9 8 7 6 5 4 3 2 1

Copyright © Marthe Arends, 2008
All rights reserved

OBSIDIAN and logo are trademarks of Penguin Group (USA) Inc.

Printed in the United States of America

This book is dedicated to my mother, Shirley, with much gratitude for all the years of hauling me to the library, letting me confiscate her blue tweed Nancy Drews, and instilling in me a lifelong love of mysteries.

1

"Hi there! You've reached Spider and Karma's house, but we're busy showing some lovely homes at affordable prices to charming and attractive people, so we can't come to the phone right now. Ha-ha, just kidding. We're really having wild monkey sex on the bathroom floor. Since that'll keep us busy for a while, go ahead and leave us a message, and we'll get to you when we can."

"Um . . . hi. I'm looking for Karma? I heard Marcy at the Quick Stop Java Shop talking about you, and I thought I'd see if you were available to help me. I'm looking for someone to take care of a problem in my house—"

The answering machine clicked off in the middle of the message as I grabbed the phone. "Hi. Sorry about that message; it's my husband's idea of a joke. I'm Karma. What did you need?" The groceries made an unpleasant clunking sound as I set the bag down to adjust the phone. A splash of latte hit my knuckles from one of the two cups I held in a cardboard drink carrier.

"Oh, hi. That's OK. My partner has a horrible

sense of humor, too. You wouldn't believe the sort of things she says in front of other people. I was told that you . . . um . . . clean houses?"

"Not in the usual sense," I said cautiously, setting down the lattes to wrestle a can of soup from the small yellow creature that had grabbed it as it had rolled out of the bag. "I don't actually do cleaning, per se. My work is a little more specialized than that."

"Specialized?"

There was a puzzled pause. I used it to snatch a pint of melting Ben & Jerry's from two yellow imps that charged out from behind the toaster, and I stuffed the ice cream into the freezer before shooing the imps back into their home. They *eek-eek*ed at me. I ignored them and used a magazine to push them back into the stainless steel flour drawer, then closed the door firmly and secured it with a bungee cord to keep them from opening it.

"Um . . . does that mean you don't do windows?"

I sighed to myself as I gathered up a carton of juice, a couple of containers of yogurt, and a bag of grapefruits and ferried them to the refrigerator while clamping the phone between my ear and shoulder. Obviously this caller didn't know the nature of my cleaning services, which was fine with me. "Sorry, no windows. And no floors, and no dishes, and no dusting, for that matter."

A domovoi shimmered into view. "Did you remember the Quaker Oats?"

I covered the mouthpiece of the phone so the woman on the other end wouldn't hear me. "On the counter. Did you let the imps out again?"

The domovoi wrinkled his nose. "They got out while I was cleaning their cupboard, but I put them all back."

"I see," the woman said slowly. I doubted she did, but I wasn't in the mood to clue her in.

"Next time, put the bungee on the door, or they'll just push it open again. Have you done the bathroom?"

"On my way." The domovoi, a Russian house spirit named Sergei, who spent his time being helpful, took the carton of oats, which were his main source of food, and disappeared.

"What exactly *do* you clean, then?" the woman on the phone asked.

"I'm more of an exterminator than a housekeeping service," I answered, grabbing an armful of canned goods as I headed to the pantry.

"Good morning, Karma." Cardea sat cross-legged in the pantry reading a *Cosmo*, glancing up at me as I put the cans on the shelf.

"Morning," I said, putting my hand over the phone again. "I don't suppose you'd like to go for a walk or something? It's a nice day out."

"And leave the pantry?" she asked, looking a bit wild about the eyes. "Oh, no, I don't think I'm ready for that."

"Ah. Well, I don't have any bugs in my house," the woman on the phone said.

"Maybe another day," I told Cardea, and made a mental note to find someone, *anyone*, who was willing to work with an ancient Roman goddess of door hinges and thresholds with agoraphobia so intense it kept her locked inside my house.

"But my brother has a rodent problem. What sort of exterminator are you? Do you do rats and mice, or just bugs?"

I dumped a couple of packages of pasta on the shelf and made a face as one of them moved back toward me. An imp leaped out from behind it and tried to fling itself upon me. I grabbed it by the scruff of its neck and took it back to the flour drawer, where its brethren lived. "The technical name is transmortis anomaly exterminator."

The silence that followed that announcement wasn't unusual or unexpected. "OK. That went right over my head."

"Don't worry. It went over mine the first time I heard it, too," I said, laughing. "It's just a fancy name, nothing more. I'm sorry I can't help clean your house, but I appreciate the call."

A couple of bags of salad greens were all that remained from the morning's trip to the store. I stuffed them into the vegetable bin, smiling at the dada (vegetable spirit) as it exclaimed happily, "Oh, good, you got the kind with arugula. I love arugula!"

"Is there something else I can help you with?" I asked when the woman on the phone didn't make the polite good-bye noises I expected.

" 'Mortis' means death, doesn't it?" Her voice was soft and somewhat rushed, as if she was trying to speak without being overheard.

"Yes, it does." The fine hairs on my arm stood on end as Sergei drifted through me.

"I thought so. Transmortis anomaly—that's across-death deviation from the norm, isn't it?"

Damn. She was getting close to the truth. "That's one interpretation, yes."

"And you're an exterminator, so that means you get rid of something that deviates from what's normal, and whatever that is, it's already dead?"

I folded the cloth carrier bag and crammed it into a nearby drawer, swearing under my breath at the pair of imps that ran through the kitchen, chasing a tennis ball. "Something like that."

"Oh!" The woman sucked in a startled gasp. "You're a ghost buster?"

"No, I am not," I answered, allowing myself a moment of teeth grinding over the much-hated term before deciding it was useless to keep mum about something the woman was so clearly determined to ferret out. "I don't *bust* anything. I simply clean houses of any unwanted Otherworld spirits, beings, or entities. So unless you have an imp infestation, or are bothered by a troublesome ancestral spirit, I'm afraid I can't help you."

"Good lord. People really buy into that hogwash?" the woman asked, her voice rife with dismissal.

I held my tongue. There were two kinds of people in the world—those who knew about the Otherworld and those who lived in blissful ignorance of it. I found it was better to leave the latter group alone.

"What happens to the ghosts you clean? Do you kill them?" asked the woman, a slight mocking note evident.

A small herd of imps thundered in from the dining room, running right over the top of my foot. I caught three by their tails, and another two by a couple of their arms, and hurriedly dropped them into the flour drawer. Annoyed, tired, and with a suspicious notion that another migraine was about to hit, I spoke without thinking. "You can't kill something that's already dead. When spirits are exorcised from a house, they are sent to the Akasha."

"The what?"

"Akasha. The Akashic Plain is the proper name, but around here we just call it Akasha. Basically, it's limbo. The beings there dwell in perpetual torment until they're released."

"And you send them there?" the woman asked.

A lone rogue imp scampered toward me from the dining room, raised all four of its arms to me, then swooned in the best dramatic fashion.

"Er . . . not always. Sometimes I relocate them."

"Busy, honey?" My father walked into the room, carefully stepping over the fallen imp. "What's wrong with him?"

I covered the phone again. "He's having a moment. I'm really going to have to limit their soap opera consumption. They're starting to get out of hand."

"Ah, yes. Ooh, two lattes? Is one for me?"

I nodded. He took the cardboard latte cup in both hands, reaching for the cookie jar, where I kept his favorite ginger cookies.

"People like you ought to be ashamed of yourselves. I've heard all about your type—you prey on people who've lost someone, and give them false hope. I do *not* want you cleaning my house."

A beep on the phone gave me the perfect excuse to end the conversation. "I'm sure it's better if I don't. I have another call, so thanks for venting your spleen on me. Bye-bye."

"Not a client?" my dad asked as I pressed the call-waiting button.

"No, thank god. Hello?"

"Karma Marx, please."

"Speaking." I accepted the latte my father handed me.

"This is Carol Beckett, director at the Home for Innocents. I just wanted to let you know that Pixie O'Hara will be arriving this morning at ten. Please be sure to adhere to the schedule that Pixie will have with her; she's notoriously bad about keeping her counseling sessions, and Dr. Wellbottom feels strongly that Pixie needs a firm hand in her life."

"Pixie O'Hara? I'm sorry, Ms. Beckett, but I don't have the slightest idea what you're talking about." My father flitted over to the window and began rearranging my collection of ceramic parrots.

"You *are* Karma Marx?"

"Yes." Dad moved on to the dining room, where I could see him moving around, straightening chairs.

The sound of papers shuffling could plainly be heard over the phone. "It says here that you were contacted last week about your offer to help with wayward teens."

"I'm sorry, but I wasn't. I don't know anything about it. And now isn't really a good time—"

"The notes say that the caseworker spoke with . . ." More paper shuffling. "Mr. Marx on Tuesday the seventeenth at ten twenty-three a.m. Arrangements for the custodial care of Pixie were agreed to then."

"Tuesday?" I rubbed my forehead, trying to remember where Spider had been on Tuesday. It didn't make any sense. Spider would never consent to having someone live with us, especially a troubled teen. When he'd found out I had signed up as a foster volunteer with the children's home, we'd had a huge fight, which had ended with him storming out of the house. So for him to be changing his mind without talking to me . . . A thought burst into my brain. I wrapped my hand around the bottom of the phone and leaned into the dining room. "Why the hell did you tell the local children's home that I would take one of their teens?"

"Hmm?" Dad was apparently engrossed in re-shelving by height the books in the bookcase. "I have no idea what you're talking about."

"I'm not buying that at all. You're in serious trouble, buster," I said before uncovering the phone and speaking to the woman at the other end. "I'm sorry; there's been a slight mix-up. My . . . er . . . husband forgot that this is a particularly bad week for visitors, so regrettably, we—"

"The arrangements were made last week," the woman said brusquely, shoving aside my excuse. "Pixie will stay with you for a month. During that time you are to see to her general health and well-being, and make sure that she attends her counseling appointments."

"But you don't understand—"

"No, *you* don't understand!" I held the phone a few inches away from my ear at the outburst. "Arrangements were made! You cannot simply wait until the last minute and say it's not convenient! This organization is run on strict rules, and as a volunteer, you have sworn to uphold those rules."

"But—"

"I need not remind you, I'm sure, of the importance of steady, reliable volunteers who fulfill the commitments they make. For them to do otherwise would have grave repercussions."

My jaw dropped open a smidgen. "Are you threatening me?"

"Of course not. I wouldn't dream of doing anything so reprehensible. I'm simply pointing out that someone who holds the position of responsibility and respect that you hold with the Akashic League should think long and hard before she endangers that position. Especially someone who is working off wergeld."

"Son of a—" I bit off the oath, grinding my teeth. She had me by the short and curlies, and I suspect she knew that very well. My job with the League was not one I held by desire, but it was better than the alternative, something of which anyone who knew my history, as this woman did, would be aware. I was trapped, good and proper; I had absolutely no choice but to continue working for the League, but there was going to be hell to pay if Spider discovered we'd taken in a needy teen for a month or more.

I sighed. When it came down to a choice between Spider and the League, there was only one answer. "Fine. I'll take the girl."

"I knew you'd see reason," she said with smug amusement. "Pixie will be there shortly. At the end of the month, your fitness as a foster parent will be reevaluated. Until then, good luck."

"Problems?" Dad asked as I hung up the phone.

"Just an insurmountable one, thanks to you." A little burble of frothed milk poked out the top of the latte lid. I licked it off, ignoring the patter of little feet as a flash of yellow *eek-eek*ed across the kitchen floor.

"Imp," Dad said helpfully.

"Don't you 'imp' me! How dare you pretend to be Spider on the phone! What on earth were you thinking? Spider is going to have a cow when he finds out I've taken in a teenager for a month."

"I wouldn't be so sure of that," Dad said softly, avoiding my gaze.

I took a deep breath, ignored the headache that threatened to blossom, and chewed my father up one side and down the other. By the time I was done, he was positively dancing with the need to get out of the room.

"Well, the damage is done," I said, slumping against the counter. "The girl is on her way. I have no idea what I'm going to say to Spider, though."

"You're a smart girl; you'll think of something. There's another imp," he pointed out. "You seem to have a problem with them."

I savored a sip of latte. "That's the understatement of the day. They think I'm their mother. They're like a plague. I can't seem to get rid of them. I drop them off in the woods, and they find their way back here. I take them to the beach, and they come back. I even left them in the Hoh Rain Forest . . . and the next day the whole troop of them showed up wet and covered in moss. Whoever heard of homing imps?"

He gave me a sour look. "If you wouldn't mess with powers beyond your abilities, you wouldn't have such strife."

"Not again. Please, Dad, not today." I took my latte with me to the tiny dining room, which looked out on a mundane bit of backyard. The headache that had been threatening me since I'd woken up burst into glorious being. I rubbed my forehead and wondered whether a handful of ibuprofen would be enough to take care of it or if I'd have to go in for the hard-core migraine meds.

"You wouldn't get those headaches if you left well enough alone," he said, gesturing toward my head. "What you're doing is wrong, Karma. Taking spirits from their natural habitats and banishing them to the Akasha is cruel. I raised you better than that."

"You didn't raise me at all," I pointed out, deciding ibu wasn't going to cut it. I snagged my purse and dug around in it until I found a prescription bottle, then washed down a couple of pills with a swig of latte.

"Now you're being pedantic," he answered, taking a stance at the head of the table, his hands on his hips. "Just because I had the foresight to realize you would be better off living with your mother while you grew up is no reason to be snarky. Besides, it has nothing to do with the fact that what you are doing is wrong on many, many levels. As you well know."

"It may be wrong, but someone has to do it. Would you rather it be someone who doesn't rescue as many beings as she can? Someone who doesn't care about them at all?" I rubbed my forehead again, tired even though it was early morning.

"I'd rather no one exterminated beings at all," he said.

"Tell that to the Akashic League; they're the ones who insisted I do this job."

He was silent for a moment, his eyes sad. "How much longer until you've worked off the wergeld?"

"I told you before: I don't know. It's up to the League. And you can stop looking at me like that!"

"Like what?"

"Like I just killed your best friend."

"I'm not—"

I shoved myself to my feet, my head swimming. "You think I don't recognize that look? You're wrong there, Dad. Dead wrong. I'm the one who killed her own best friend, remember?"

2

"Karma, I won't have you talking like that. What happened wasn't your fault."

I sat down again, fighting to hold on to a shred or two of sanity. "I know it wasn't. But sometimes, I could swear I see things in people's eyes. . . . Oh, forget it. I can't help having been born with the skill to banish spirits any more than you can help the ablities you were born with."

"You look awful," he said, changing subjects with the same lightning-fast speed that was characteristic of all he did. "What have you been doing? Up late? Exterminating? Watching Spider's latest orgy?"

"I'll go touch up the paint in the study," Sergei said as he drifted through me, the dining room table, and a small potted palm on his way to the far end of the house.

I waved him on, rustling up enough energy to frown at my father as he moved restlessly around the room. He never could stand still in one place for very long. "Up late, yes. No exterminating, no orgies, just a restless night."

"Aw, munchkin," he said, coming around behind

me, giving me a little hug. "I'm sorry. You're still mourning your cousin, aren't you?"

I leaned back against him for a moment and closed my eyes, wishing I could be five years old again, comforted by the embrace of a father I believed could make all the evils of the world go away.

Now I knew better. "Yes, I'm still mourning Bethany. She was only fifteen. She was bright, and charming, and loved life. . . ." Tears pricked hot behind my eyes. I blinked them away, too tired even to cry. "Did Aunt Chris tell you about the postmortem?"

"No, I haven't talked to Chris lately. It's all been so distressing."

"The police said . . ." I swallowed back a painful lump. "They said that she killed herself. The marks on her hand suggested she used a piece of glass to cut her own throat."

Dad looked appalled. I hated to have to be the one to tell him all this, but it was better he understood the full tragedy that had occurred. "*Killed herself?* But why?"

"She was raped. The police are speculating that she was so traumatized by that, she chose to end her life."

"So sad. So young," my father said, shaking his head. "And for someone to physically abuse her, driving her to take her own life . . . horrible. Just horrible. I'll call Chris later."

My hands tightened into fists. "I don't care what the police say. She didn't kill herself; she was driven to it by whoever kidnapped her and raped her just as certainly as if he'd cut her throat himself. I just wish I knew who the monster was so I could string him up by his balls."

"I know, honey, I know."

We spent a few minutes in uncomfortable silence. Dad flitted around the room. I willed the pain away and wondered how I was going to explain a troubled teenager to Spider.

"Is this just one of your usual morning visits?" I finally asked, feeling as if I were a couple of hundred years old instead of thirty-eight. "You seem edgier than normal. Is something going on?"

"Well, now that you mention it . . . I do have a little something for you."

I took the large manila envelope he handed me, a feeling of dread welling up as I undid the clasp. "What's this?"

He gestured toward it. "Open."

I bit my lip, hesitant. I had an idea of what I'd find in there, and although I knew I had to see it, sanity urged me not to look. "Dad, you haven't been following Spider around again, have you?"

"Open!" he said, more loudly.

"Because you know that's illegal, right?"

He just looked at me.

"I don't know what good you think this will do. I've told you before that I know Spider is a philadering bastard."

"Then why are you still married to him? There's no reason you can't get a divorce," he answered.

"There's every reason." I ran my hands through my hair, remembering when I was young and foolish and naively believed everything Spider told me. "He was so charming when we first met, he just swept me off my feet. I was thrilled when he asked me to marry him. I thought it was the answer to all my problems."

Dad snorted, aligning the dining room chairs an infinitesimal fraction to the left.

"Yeah, well . . ." I slid my hand across the envelope. "By the time I figured out the truth, I was stuck. I couldn't leave him, couldn't support myself with the wergeld bound on me."

"You could have moved in with me," Dad pointed out.

I smiled. "We'd have driven each other insane in less than a day. And it wasn't so bad, at least at first. Spider did his own thing, with the realty agency and his speculations of fixing up homes and reselling them. I had the League to take up my time. We just kind of drifted into a relationship of . . . oh, I don't know, more roommates than husband and wife."

"All the more reason to be rid of him," Dad said, nodding at the envelope. "Open it." I hesitated for a moment, then opened it and allowed the photos inside to slide out onto the table. "Just so you're aware that it's an invasion of privacy to take pictures of people without them knowing. Especially—holy hellhounds!"

"You see?" Dad nodded, peering over my shoulder. "I thought they turned out pretty well, considering the material I had to work with."

The pictures were of three people, at least two of whom were human. One looked like a poltergeist, although it was hard to tell at the odd angle from which the pictures were snapped.

"See the backlighting in that one? I like the corona it gives the redhead. Kind of a Madonna effect, huh?"

"Hardly that," I said, blinking at the positions the

three people were twisted into. Odd that I shouldn't be more upset about seeing them. Fidelity had always been important to me, not a concept I took lightly. So why weren't the pictures bothering me? Why could I look at them with only mild interest, an appreciation for the limberness of the females in the picture, and the realization that Spider needed a haircut? I shook my head, flinching when a throb of pain had me almost barfing. Careful not to move my head, I slid the pictures back into the envelope. "All right. You gave them to me. I saw. Happy now?"

"Happy that your husband is cheating on you? No. But yes, I'm happy you now admit the truth rather than living in denial."

I massaged my temples. "I wasn't in denial. I've known all along Spider has been fooling around."

"Then why the hell haven't you gelded him yet, girl?" Dad stomped around the table, his footsteps stabbing into my head.

"Because I didn't have any hard proof." I waved a hand toward the envelope. "Not until now. And . . . well, you know how it is. Sometimes it's just easier to maintain the status quo. Spider is hardly ever here, and what chance do I have of getting a job to support myself with the League calling me in at the drop of a hat?"

"You could ask them for a leave."

"That would only be temporary," I said, sighing.

"You can't go on like this, Karma," he pointed out.

I glanced at the envelope again. "No, I can't."

"I think you're going to have to revist the subject of divorce," Dad said.

I shrugged. "I suppose. I don't know how I'm

going to handle a job in addition to the League, but that's something I'll just have to work out. I guess I should grit my teeth and start the divorce process."

"You'll be better off without him," my father said, giving my shoulder a comforting squeeze. "You have no idea what a slimewad he—"

"Spider's home!" Sergei's voice cut across my father's as he zipped out of the study, racing through the house as if he were some sort of ghostly Russian Paul Revere. "Spider's home! Everyone hide! Spider is here!"

"Crap, the imp," I muttered, leaping to my feet to catch the imp that I heard still rustling around the kitchen. My headache exploded at my sudden movement, leaving me clutching the back of the chair.

"I'll get it," my father said, shooting me an unreadable look as he went to catch the rogue imp. "Although I'd like to point out once again that you wouldn't have the problem of hiding houseguests from your husband if you would banish him to the Akasha."

I slumped back into my chair, rubbing my head, wishing there was a way to hurry up the migraine medicine.

"I'm home for a few minutes, darling," Spider said. "Oh. Matthew. You here again? Didn't you just see Karma yesterday?"

My father and I had an agreement to keep his daily morning visits quiet. Spider wasn't a control freak or anything like that, but the two of them didn't get along very well, what with the differences in their beliefs.

"A father has a right to visit his daughter whenever he likes," Dad said stiffly.

"Hmmph," Spider said, pulling off his tie and his

shirt as he headed to our bedroom. "Where are you, Kar?"

I watched him dispassionately for a moment. Blond, with laughing blue eyes, a dimpled chin, and a body that I knew from firsthand experience was impressive, Spider wore his forty-six years well. He had the handsome boy-next-door good looks that left so many women sighing with desire.

It was the ones who did more than sigh who I took issue with.

"I'm in the dining room. I thought you were closing on a house today," I said loudly enough for him to hear me down the hall. He emerged from our room wearing a new shirt and holding up two ties. "Which goes best?"

"The one on the left."

"I like the one on the right," he said, tossing my choice on the couch as he wrapped the silk around his neck. I bit back all sorts of unkind comments and waited to see what he wanted. Spider never popped home unless it was important. "And yes, I'm closing on a house today. Very exciting stuff, and actually, that's why I'm here. You're not busy tonight?"

My father appeared in the doorway and made a crude two-handed gesture. I ignored him. "Not exactly, although there's something I need to talk to you about. We're going to have a visitor for a short while—"

"Another family member?" He shot my father a seething look.

"No, not a family member. It's a girl from the children's home—"

"Just keep her out of my way," he interrupted. "I need you to clean a house for me tonight."

"No."

"It's the old Walsh house out on Tamsin Road. You know, the one that looks like something left over from a *Psycho* movie? Great location, five bedrooms, three baths, twelve rooms altogether."

"No."

"It needs fixing up, of course. It's fifty years out of code, there's all sorts of wood rot, termites, the basement is bound to be flooded when it rains, the roof is covered in moss—"

"No, Spider. No cleaning."

"—and it has that horrible asbestos insulation, but I'll get a few itinerants in to fix it up. The place will make us a fortune."

"He's not listening to you," my father said, still in the doorway.

"He seldom does," I answered.

"Karma." Spider yanked my chair sideways, taking my hand as he squatted next to me. "I know you don't like cleaning houses, but this is important, love."

I started laughing. I couldn't help myself. Only someone with Spider's immense ego would believe he could have a threesome with two other women and still be able to sweet-talk me into doing something for him. I pulled my hand from his and gave him the envelope as I got to my feet. The pain meds were starting to work, making my head feel oddly numb. "No. No cleaning. Not tonight, not ever. We're through, Spider, through with everything—the marriage, cleaning, us."

"What?" Spider asked, doing a good impression of a startled husband. "What are you saying? Why are we through?"

I pulled one of the pictures out of the envelope he held. "This, for one."

He barely glanced at it. "Darling, I can explain that—"

"I'm sure you can. But it's not going to work this time."

"This time?" my father asked. "You mean there have been others?"

Spider opened his mouth to protest, then closed it quickly as a hard look came into his eyes. "All right. I thought there would be need for your particular talents for some time to come, but recently, I've begun rethinking that strategy."

"Strategy?" I asked. "Do my abilities have something to do with why you said no to the divorce last year?"

The mocking glint in his eyes as he gave me a once-over left me feeling soiled. "You don't think I said no to the divorce simply because I couldn't be parted from you?" He laughed, but there was no humor in it. "Sweetheart, you had value to me, but not between the sheets. Now, do you want that divorce or not?"

"I think that would be best," I said, the numbness seeping from my head down to the rest of me. Not even his cruel words had the ability to hurt me anymore.

"You can have it on one condition."

"I don't need your permission to divorce you," I said, welcoming the dulling sensation. "This is 2008, not 1908. I can do it without your consent."

"But it will be easier if I don't create a fuss, won't it?" he asked, a small smile curling his lips. I hated that smile. It always made my palm itch. "After all, you don't want certain . . . *truths* coming out, do you?"

"You bastard!" Dad started forward. I held him back with an upraised hand.

"What condition?" I asked my hopefully soon-to-be ex-husband.

His smiled deepened. I had to clench my hands to keep from slapping it off his face. "You clean the Walsh house for me, and I won't contest a divorce. I won't fight an equitable settlement, and won't argue over the division of our assets. I'll even let you keep this place," he said, glancing around the dining room with a look of distaste.

I hesitated. Oh, part of me wanted to tell him just where he could shove his precious Walsh house, but the other part of me, the part that knew full well I had a faerie's chance in Abaddon of finding gainful employment of the mundane variety, prodded me into considering his offer. It was just one house, one cleaning. I wouldn't have to send whatever was there into the Akasha. . . . Despite my father's accusations to the contrary, I had banished only a couple of nasty house spirits. The rest I'd acquired as roommates, and with Spider gone, at least they wouldn't have to hide. "How many entities are there?"

"How the hell should I know?" He shrugged. "It's an old house, built by one of the timber lords a hundred or so years ago. It's got a few creepy crawlies in it. I just want them gone so I can get the place turning a profit. Tell you what: I'll give you a cut of the first six months' profit. Ten percent. That ought to keep you living pretty high on the hog for a long time."

"First six months?"

His smile changed slightly. "I'm going to use the house for a little moneymaking venture."

"Oh." I thought about what he was asking, what it took out of me to exterminate a house, what it would mean living with even more Otherworld beings. Then I thought about the alternative.

"All right," I said, ignoring my father's horrified gasp. "I'll do it. I'll clean the house for you, and then you're out of my life."

"Forever," Spider promised with yet another of his smug smiles.

Ironically, it was one of the rare times in his life when Spider actually spoke the truth.

3

"So, what, you expect me to be your slave or something? Like my life isn't hell enough, now I have to play cozy family with you? I don't even know you!"

I slammed shut the car door, giving the dog crate inside another quick glance to make sure it was escape-proof before turning to my surly companion. "Listen, Pixie—"

"I told you, my name is *Desdemona*! Desdemona Macabre!"

The girl had a world-record pout; I'd give her that. The rest of her . . . well, that wasn't quite so perfect. She radiated hostility and anger, her hands fluttering madly to emphasize words when she spoke. Dark, distrustful eyes peered out from brows pulled together in a seemingly perpetual scowl. If her roots and fair coloring were anything to go by, she was a natural blonde, but she'd dyed her hair a dull black, no doubt to match her Goth ensemble of a long black opera cape, a black lace skirt, black and white–striped leggings, a black and red–striped bustier, black fingerless gloves, and a knee-length scarlet gauze scarf.

"I realize that you'd much rather be left alone, but unfortunately you're only fifteen, and the League home has asked that I take care of you for a bit while things are sorted out. So why don't we try to make this month as drama free as possible?"

"*Deus!* You just don't understand!" She stomped around to the far side of the car and flung herself into the passenger seat.

"Quite possibly, that's true," I agreed, surprising her enough to shoot me a puzzled glance. I slid into the driver's seat, praying for the strength to get through the next month. "I'm sorry to rush you out like this when you just got here, but I have an appointment I must keep. Why don't we use the time to get to know each other a little better? Were both your parents polters?"

"I knew it! I knew you were going to start grilling me the second I got here!" she snarled. "My parents aren't any of your business!"

"Whoa, calm down. I just asked a polite question. You don't have to answer it."

"Oh, sure, you say that now, but what happens if I don't answer? Are you going to send me back to the home?"

I slid her a curious look. She was really upset about this. "Of course not. I was just trying to make conversation, not pry into your life. I'm sorry. I guess I forgot just how emotional everything is at your age."

"Age discrimination! I knew it!" she said with a triumphant glare.

I sighed. "That's not what I meant."

"Oh, right." She stared out the front window, bristling with hostility. "Well, go on. Is there anything *else* you want to know about my life, Mrs. Nosy? Like when I had my last *period*; or if I'm still a *virgin*, or what size *shoes* I wear?"

"The League worker who brought you said that your parents died as a result of a drunk driver. I'm very sorry that you've had to endure such a tragedy, but as I just said, I didn't intend to pry, so please lower the hostility level a few notches. Let's move on to something a little less personal. . . . The League woman said you were working on a novel; maybe you'd like to tell me about that."

"No one listens to me!" she said, looking pointedly out the window. "I am a *poet*! I write *poetry*! And no, you can't read any of it. It's *personal*."

I rubbed the back of my neck, where the muscles were beginning to tense up despite the lovely migraine meds. I had a horrible foreboding that the next month was going to be one long drama . . . as though I needed any more of that in my life. "What else are you interested in? Boys? Books? Movies?"

"What is this, the third degree? I don't have to answer your questions!"

"No, you don't, but a little common courtesy wouldn't be amiss here. We have to spend the next month together, Pixie. Let's just try to get through that without drawing any blood, all right?"

"My *name* is Desdemona Macabre," she said, grinding the words out between her teeth.

"I'll make a deal with you: I won't call you Pixie if you promise to be civil."

"Define 'civil,'" she said quickly.

I smiled to myself as I turned onto the highway that would take us to a small resort town an hour's drive away. She might not be the most pleasant teen in the world, but she seemed intelligent and, despite the defensive posturing, needy. For some inexplicable reason, I empathized with her. I certainly knew what it was like to not belong. "It must be my biological clock. Nothing else would explain it," I said to myself.

"*Deus*, you're old enough to have a biological clock?" she asked, looking at me as if I was some sort of scaly monster.

"We will leave my age out of it," I answered. " 'Civil' in this instance means making an effort to get along. That includes participation in conversation, keeping your room relatively clean, and generally staying out of trouble."

She tossed her head, still refusing to look my way. After a few minutes of silence, she finally capitulated. "All right. I will recognize your dictatorship, but you have to call me by my *proper* name, respect my privacy, and not intrude in my life any more than you already have."

"I agree to the first two terms, and will do my best on the last within reason."

An uneasy peace was reached. I kept silent for most of the ride, preferring to let her have a little time to sort through her no doubt tangled emotions.

"Where exactly are you dragging me?" she asked, breaking the silence forty-five minutes later as we exited the highway and headed down a narrow country road.

"Otherworld petting zoo. The owner is a summoner, and said she wouldn't mind if my imps ran free on her acreage. There should be a sign somewhere around here pointing the way. . . . Ah, there it is."

"Ew. Imps. They light fires and things. Why don't you just kill them?"

"These aren't common imps. They're Australian House Imps; they're quite friendly, and not in the least bit destructive, as normal imps are, unless they are mistreated."

"An imp is an imp is an imp," she muttered, directing her frown to the back, where the dog crate sat. "How come you're taking them to live outside if they are house imps?"

"They'll have a nice imp shelter to snuggle into when they are done romping around outside," I answered with confidence, more to convince myself than her. I wasn't sure how the imps would take to life on a farm open to the public, but Simone, the summoner, assured me that they would have the run of a distant pasture and bordering woods, and a chicken coop that had been specially customized for imps. They certainly seemed cheerful enough as I let them free from the dog crate. They *eek-eek*ed happily without a glance back at me as they scampered off to explore their new home.

"Let's hope they stay there this time," I said after telling Simone good-bye.

"This time?" Pixie asked as we bounced our way down the long unpaved driveway.

I was pleased. She hadn't said a word the whole time we were releasing the imps, contenting herself to stand behind me like a big unhappy black and red rain cloud. This was the first thing she'd said that didn't concern just how miserable she was.

"I've tried to set them free two other times. Each

time they found me. I really hope they stay where they are safe; my life is complicated enough without having a dozen imps trying to wreak havoc whenever they can."

"That servant said he let them loose. You should fire him."

"Sergei isn't a servant. He's a domovoi, and domovois help out because they want to, not because they're being paid anything. Well, anything other than oats and the occasional package of Pop Rocks."

She shot me an inquisitive glance, clearly struggling with the need to appear aloof and a natural curiosity about her new—if temporary—home. "Why do you have a Russian ghost? And the little thing in the refrigerator?"

"Sergei is there because he needed a home. The same applies to the dada; I found him in a restaurant. He's harmless, and very sensitive to noises, so if you could keep from screaming at the top of your lungs when you see him, I'd be grateful."

"He *scared* me!" she said, bristling with indignation. "I wasn't expecting to find *living things* in the veggie bin!"

"You have yet to meet Cardea. She's very shy, but if you're gentle with her, she'll prove to be an entertaining companion."

"That's the goddess who lives in closets?"

I nodded.

"You're really weird," was her verdict upon consideration of the other members of the household. "No wonder your husband left you."

"Ouch. You're big on judgments, aren't you? My husband isn't important, and won't be around to be a part of home life."

"Whatever. So, how many spirits and things have you killed?"

I wondered if she'd overheard anything from the League home people.

"Technically, you can't kill something that is already dead, but I have banished to the Akasha only two spirits, and they certainly had it coming. The rest I've taken in, and they will stay with me for as long as they like." The sight of the dog crate in the rearview mirror caught my eye. "Well, other than the imps, that is."

She mouthed another "ew."

Silence reigned for ten minutes before she broke it with "Margo said you were working off wergeld, and you had to foster me or else you'd get in trouble. What's wergeld?"

I jerked convulsively, causing the car to veer onto the shoulder. With a mental scold at the overreaction, I tried to calm my wildly beating heart. "Who is Margo?"

"The woman who brought me to your house," she said in a tone that dripped disbelief that I could be so clueless.

"Ah. I didn't catch her name. As it happens, Margo is correct about the wergeld, although no one forced me to take you in." A little white lie wouldn't hurt and might make her feel wanted. I had a hunch that particular emotion was a stranger to Pixie. "My situation is a bit complex, and I'm not sure if I can explain it quickly. Wergeld is a payment someone makes when they have inadvertently caused the death of someone else."

She gave me a long, thoughtful perusal. "You killed someone? Really killed them? Someone mortal?"

"No. And to be perfectly honest, this isn't a subject I'm comfortable discussing. Since we're allowing limits in conversational topics, I'd like to move on to something else."

"Afraid to talk about it?"

What an annoying girl. No wonder the League home was having difficulty finding her a foster home. "I'm not afraid, no. I just don't wish to discuss the situation with you, just as you don't wish to discuss your parents with me. It really has nothing to do with you and me, so I think we can let it drop."

"Maybe," she said with a cryptic look, then continued her silent examination of the passing scenery.

I bit my lip, trying to think of the best way to deal with my unexpected charge with regard to the evening's activities. "As long as we're dealing with unpleasant subjects, there is something I have to do tonight, a job I've promised to do for my husband."

"A job? A killing-ghosts sort of job?"

I refused to give her the satisfaction of a reaction. "A cleaning, yes."

She looked at me with as much indignation as my father did. Despite my better intentions, it put me on the defensive. "I don't like the job any better than you do, but I *am* the only licensed TAE in the area, and there are extenuating circumstances."

"Suuure," she drawled. "So how many spirits will you be killing tonight? I get to watch, right?"

"For someone who professes such abhorrence of the subject of cleaning, you certainly are jumping on the opportunity to watch."

"They used to have public executions, you know. My foster dad said they were really popular."

I reminded myself that she would be with me only

a month and, more importantly, that I'd survived worse calamities. "I have no idea how many beings there will be; that's why we're going out to check the house now. I need to see who and what is there to be cleaned . . . if anything. As for you coming along . . ." I paused for a moment. "We'll see."

Pixie pulled out an iPod and dismissed me as we drove back to town.

Although the Olympic Peninsula was best known to tourists for its spooky rain forests, glorious mountain range, and fiercely beautiful coastline, the shallow, quiet inlets were what I loved best. Short stretches of smooth sand dotted with sandpipers and other shorebirds were tucked away between jagged edges of coast. The calm, protected waters in which waterfowl paddled around with contented pleasure provided a peaceful haven. Sea lions sunned themselves on the sandbars while overhead gulls and terns dipped and rose on the air currents, singing a harsh song of life on the water. I breathed deeply of the sharp tang of the sea air as we followed a narrow road along the shoreline, a stubby spit of land curving in a half-moon to create a small calm lagoon populated by birds and wildlife. Above it, a dull red Victorian house sat hulking against the skyline.

"It looks haunted," Pixie said in a voice rich with perverted satisfaction. "Very haunted. With, like, really evil spirits and things."

"You should know better than to make such gross generalizations. Regardless, it's hardly something we can tell until we get there," I said calmly, although my heart rate sped up as the car climbed a twisting road that finally emerged at the crown of the hill. I was pathetically aware of the undertone of worry in my voice.

The house was even more impressive when viewed close-up. Built to last, it had a wide covered verandah that ran around three-quarters of it, cupolas fringed with delicate gingerbread trim, and, at the top, a widow's walk that must have commanded a tremendous view of the Strait of Juan de Fuca.

"*Deus!* What's that? It's *horrible!*"

I looked to where Pixie was pointing. A woman strolled around from the far side of the verandah. She looked like something from a Fleetwood Mac video, dressed in a long, filmy gown, a flower garland on her head, ribbons fluttering in waist-length golden hair that fell in long ringlets.

"Don't worry, Pix . . . er . . . Desdemona. She's not a spirit."

"I *know* that. But it's still horrible! She's all *flowery!* It's positively *ghastly!*"

"To each his own," I said, unable to keep from shooting a pointed look at Pixie's lace skirt and black and white–striped leggings, visible below the bottom of her cape. "Do you have a glamour handy?"

She shook her head, a mulish look on her face. "Mrs. Beckett said it's bad to rely on glamours, and we should work on other techniques to blend into the mortal world."

"Yeah, well, sometimes a polter has no other choice but to use a glamour to hide the extra arms. Since you don't have one, and I have no idea who this is, keep your cape on, just in case it's someone unaware of the Otherworld."

"Oh, I'm very good at hiding the truth about myself."

I didn't have time to wonder what on earth she meant before the woman spotted us. The woman called out a cheerful hello, hurrying toward us with a wave and a smile. "Are you both here for the sitting? I'm afraid that isn't until midnight. Witching hour, you know. Hi, I'm Savannah. And you are . . . ?"

A faint buzzing noise was barely audible. I glanced around quickly but didn't see a bee or a hive nearby.

"Um . . . hello?"

"Sorry. I was just distracted for a moment. Do you hear a weak sort of buzz? Kind of like a distant bee or an electrical box?"

"A bee? No, I don't hear anything."

"Ah. Must just be a side effect from the migraine I had earlier." I shook the offered hand, returning the woman's smile. "I'm Karma Marx. This is a friend of mine, Pixie, although she prefers to be called Desdemona. I'm afraid you must have us confused with someone else; we're just here to take a peek at the house. Er . . . you're having a sitting tonight? A séance?"

"Yes! Isn't it exciting? We've been dying to get into this house for ever so long, and it's just recently been sold, so now at last we can go inside and document the entities within. I was just taking a look at the house to see where we should concentrate." Her smile brightened. She was around my age, mid- to late thirties, with a sunny nature that fit her name.

"I see. Does the new owner know that you plan to hold a séance here tonight?" I asked, wondering if Spider was pulling some sort of trick on me.

For a moment, her cheerful, happy-puppy-dog exuberance was dimmed. "Well . . . I did ask my control, Jebediah—he's a Quaker, you know, and *very* honest—and he said it would be all right, that the new owner was very sympathetic to those who had gone beyond the misty veil. And I do have a key from the Realtor."

"A *Quaker!*" Pixie gawked at Savannah in apparent shock.

I knew how she felt, although for another reason. If there was a man alive less tolerant of things Otherworld than my husband, I had yet to meet him.

"I see," I said again, at a loss as to how to explain the reality of the situation. I was a bit confused about why Spider had let her have a key, but I assumed he had some purpose in doing so. Unfortunately, the purpose that came foremost to mind involved adultery. I pushed it away and kept my face as placid as possible. "Did you talk to the owner himself, or just get the key from the agency?"

"Oh, my husband got it for me. He knows the Realtor, so all he did was make a call and one of the realty secretaries let me have the keys. I took a peek inside. It's just perfect! Positively ripe with entities! I have high hopes we'll make contact tonight."

Pixie's perpetual frown cleared. "That sounds *creepy*. I want to go."

"Hmm." I didn't pay her much attention, still mulling over Spider's unusual action and finally deciding that without realizing someone had an ulterior motive, he'd given instructions for the keys to be handed over to interested persons. Usually one of the agents showed people the houses for sale, but occasionally Spider allowed people he felt trustworthy to examine property by themselves. "I hate to be the bearer of bad tidings, but I believe it would be best if you were to talk to the realty agency before holding a séance. I'm sure they don't have a problem with people viewing the house, but holding a group meeting there is another matter."

"What do you have against séances?" Pixie demanded. "You don't want me to have *any* fun, do you?"

"Oh, surely no one could object to us documenting the entities!" Savannah said at the same time. "This house is unique! Everyone knows it's the most haunted building on the Olympic Peninsula! It's a fabulous resource that has been kept from true researchers like those of us in PMS for far too long. Now at last we have a chance to do some serious investigation, and Jebediah assures me that our work will be fruitful."

"PMS?" I couldn't help asking.

"Psychical Mysteries Society. Silly acronym, isn't it? It's a lovely group, though, and very scientific. We seek to solve the age-old mysteries of life after death, hauntings, demonic possessions, clairvoyance, and poltergeists."

"Poltergeists?" Pixie asked, her face a frozen mask.

Savannah turned her smile on the girl. "Yes. That's German for 'noisy ghosts.' Poltergeists are known for their disruptive and malicious behavior. I'm particularly interested in them because I had a poltergeist experience in my teens that I've never forgotten. It darned near scared the life out of me! I have high hopes we can call one tonight."

"I think you'll find that most of what you've read about polters is fabrication, created to sensationalize rather than inform," I said quickly.

" 'Polters' being poltergeists?" Savannah's brow furrowed.

"Sorry, yes."

Her frown cleared. "Oh, are you interested in them, as well?"

Pixie sent me a warning glare. It was unnecessary: I had no intention of allowing the woman before us to see the extra set of arms that Pixie kept hidden beneath the cape. The kid had enough problems without having her heritage exposed. "I'm familiar with the history of poltergeists, yes."

"Excellent! I knew you were a fellow enthusiast!"

"*Enthusiast* might be an overstatement. About this séance tonight—I happen to know the new owner of the house, and I'm sorry to say that I really don't think he'd be overly pleased to have people traipsing around inside. From what I understand, it needs quite a bit of work, so it could actually be dangerous to go in there—"

"You *know* the owner?" she interrupted.

"Well . . . yes. He's my husband, actually."

Her face lit up with happiness. "You're the owner's wife? Oh, that's wonderful! There will be no problem, then, if you're along with us!"

"Oh, I'm not here to join your group—"

"But you just said you're interested in poltergeists, so of course you must come!" She beamed at me as she gave my hand a little squeeze before moving off to her car. "Both of you!"

"I'll come," Pixie said quickly with a defiant glance my way.

"Regardless of my interest, my husband isn't going to be pleased with the idea of people holding a séance in a house he's about to sell."

That stopped Savannah dead in her tracks. She whirled around to face me. "Sell? Your husband is going to sell this fabulous resource?"

"I'm not privy to his thoughts, but I believe that is his intention, yes."

She rushed back over to me, her face clouded. "But you can't let him! This house is absolutely unique! There's not another like it on the entire peninsula! There have been hauntings here for the last one hundred and ten years! If new owners come along . . . who knows what they will do with it! They may not provide an environment in which the spirits will thrive!"

"Or perhaps the new owners will be as enthusiastic as you to have the house investigated," I pointed out.

Her eyes narrowed on nothing for a few moments while she thought. "No," she said, shaking her head and marching back toward her car. "I can't allow that. This house is too important. My husband will talk to the owner and make him see reason."

I didn't bother telling her that the person who could change Spider's mind once he had made it up hadn't been born. Instead, I murmured polite, noncommittal noises of vague agreement.

Savannah's frown lightened when she rolled down her window and waved at me. "We'll start the investigations proper at eleven, so I hope you are up for a late night. The séance is at midnight, as I mentioned earlier. I'm so pleased you'll be joining PMS!"

"I . . . but I . . . I don't— You haven't listened to me at all, have you?"

"Wear something old that you don't mind getting dirty," she called as she pulled away. "We're bound to have an evening to remember!"

"I have a horrible feeling those are going to be famous last words," I told Pixie as the SUV bearing the perpetually cheerful Savannah made its way down the winding drive.

"Yeah, and I can guess who they'll apply to," she said with a dark implication before stalking off to the verandah.

I had a nasty feeling she was right.

"This house is . . ." I paused, not for dramatic effect, but to try to put into the words the sensation that skittered down my back.

"Clean?" Pixie asked, drifting past me to a bow-front window that looked over a short bit of scraggly lawn.

"Hardly that."

"Yuck. Flowers. That's probably where the bees were."

A mouse dashed out in front of me, froze when it spotted me, nose and tail twitching.

"It looks like Spider will need to contact the real sort of exterminators. What I was going to say was that the house is . . . different."

The mouse ran off to hide behind a love seat when I stamped on the floor.

"Different as in *deadly*? Filled with toxic fumes, do you mean? Carcinogens leaching into the air, the kind that seep deep into your healthy pink lung tissue, *corrupting* and *destroying* every healthy cell in their path?"

"You are the strangest child!" I said, giving her a look that should have scared her silly.

She shrugged. "Strange is what I do best."

"Evidently."

"And I'm *not* a child. I'm almost *sixteen*."

"What I meant was different as in . . . well, *different*. Or not, given the present company. Take that picture, for example."

Pixie stalked over to the wall opposite me and stood with two hands on her hips, the other two arms crossed over her chest, an obstinate look on her face.

We were in what must have been the house's parlor, a sunny room that overlooked a small garden that had been allowed to run wild. Faded heavy maroon curtains dated it to at least a hundred years in the past, and the thick, dark mahogany furniture couldn't have been much newer. Several uninspired, muddy watercolors hung on the dusty yellow and cream wallpaper, occasional squares of brighter color indicating where pictures had been removed.

But there was nary a spirit to be seen.

"What? What's wrong with it? It's just a picture of some boring old people," Pixie said, her eyes lighting up at the sight of a sharp letter opener that had been thrust into a small bud vase.

"Take a closer look at it."

She sighed the sigh of the put-upon and gave the picture another glimpse. "It's just some Victorian people. A family. OK? Can we go now?"

"Not just yet. How many people are in the picture?"

Pixie glanced back at it, frowning slightly as she

noticed what I'd seen straightaway. "Four. Oh, I see. So now, what, you're a bigot or something?"

"Don't be ridiculous," I said, moving closer to the picture. It was indeed a standard Victorian family portrait, with two men standing behind a seated woman, a small girl leaning on her knee. . . . Except the woman clearly had four arms. "I wonder how a picture of a polter's family found its way into this house? And are they all polters, or just the one?"

"No way to tell," she said, dismissing the picture and wandering around the room.

"Not unless one of them hadn't lost her extra limbs yet," I said, squinting at the child in the picture. "Interesting. I might be able to tell in person if someone was a polter, although my Otherworld radar isn't the best. My father's is much better. Does the child have an extra arm hidden in her pinafore, do you think?"

"Who cares? They don't live here, do they?"

"I doubt it. Some mortal families knew about the polters who lived with them, but I doubt if they'd include them in family photos unless there was a blood tie." I straightened up and glanced at the other pictures. No other family portraits were displayed. "Just out of curiosity—how old were your parents when they died?"

She spun around and glared at me. "You *are* a bigot! You're a polter bigot!"

"Don't be ridiculous. Would I have offered to take you in if I was?"

"Then why do you keep *asking* me and *asking* me and *asking* me about my parents? What does it matter how old my parents were?"

"Calm down! Polter genetics interests me. The

child in that picture has only three arms, but the woman has four."

"She does? Oh. She does. Maybe she's not related or something."

Well, now, that was odd. Polters grew up knowing the ins and outs of basic polter genetics. There were many times when children had fewer arms than their more-than-two-armed parents, mixed parentage being the primary reason. But Pixie didn't seem to know that . . . which was very strange.

"I was just curious if one of your parents was human, or half-blooded," I said slowly, doing a little gentle probing.

"*Deus!* My parents are dead, OK? *Dead!* Will you stop harassing me about them?"

"Sorry," I apologized, letting the subject drop. Some polters were very touchy about their heritage, especially those who didn't have the protection of the Akashic League and had to make their own way in the mundane world. "Back to the picture—I think it's a safe bet to say that the family who used to live here was made up at least partially of poltergeists. I wonder what happened to them."

"They were driven away by the endless curiosity of the local townspeople," a deep voice said behind me.

Pixie's startled jump was almost as high as mine, although hers had a horizontal element that ended up sending her across the room, leaving me in apparent solitude with the large dark-haired man who all but filled the doorway.

"Who are you?" I asked, reaching behind me for something I could use as a weapon. My hand closed around something smooth and cold.

"I was about to ask you the same question. Please don't steal that greyhound. It's very old, and a favorite of mine."

I held tight to the small but heavy statue of a sitting dog that I remembered seeing below the picture of the polter family. "Steal? I'm not stealing anything. For one thing, my husband owns this house. For another, I don't steal."

He moved into the room in just a few strides, making it feel suddenly small and cramped and extremely full of an evidently angry large man. "You what? You're not my wife."

I frowned, pulling the dog statue around to my front, hoping he wasn't so deranged that I had to bean him with it. "I never said I was!"

He stopped in front of me, his arms crossed over a broad chest. Somewhat dimmed beams of sunlight worked their way through the grime-streaked windows, falling on his face and revealing that angry, deranged, and largely intimidating though he might be, he was also incredibly handsome. I think it was the combination of black-as-sin hair and pale blue eyes.

"You did. You said you were married to the owner. That would be me."

"No, that is my husband, Spider. Who are you?"

The man joined me in a round of frowning. "Adam Dirgesinger."

"Dirgesinger?" That was a polter name. I looked him over carefully, but there were no signs of a poltergeist heritage. He had the normal number of arms and didn't display the restlessness that was common even in the most human-looking polters. "That's your family in the photo?"

"My grandparents, yes." His eyes narrowed.

"So you're a third-generation polter?"

His frown deepened. "What concern is that of yours?"

"None, really," I said with a faint shrug. "I'm just a bit surprised to hear you acknowledge it. Most people wouldn't admit to a polter ancestry to strangers."

"Would you?" he asked, a challenge in his voice.

I summoned up a smile I didn't in the least feel. "I suppose it would depend on the circumstances."

"All right, Mrs. Whatever-Your-Name-Is . . ."

I straightened my shoulders and tried to look down my nose at him, something I couldn't quite pull off, since he had a good six inches on me. "It's Marx. Karma Marx. That's Pixie, but she prefers Desdemona."

"*Deus*, do you have to keep saying it like that?" Pixie glared at both Adam and me.

"Fine, Karma Marx—would you like to tell me just why you feel free to rummage around my house without my permission?"

I pointed the statue at him. "You keep saying that. It's not true. My husband bought this house a few days ago. I'm sorry if the house went into foreclosure or whatever happened to cause you to lose it, but ignoring reality isn't going to do anything to make the situation change."

"You're lying," he said, his eyes filled with disbelief.

I sighed. "Look, Mr. Dirgesinger—"

"Adam," the man interrupted.

"I beg your pardon?" I asked.

"Adam. Call me Adam. I seldom use my last name."

How very odd. For a brief moment, I wondered why he wanted to disown his surname when he was so willing to admit to his ancestry. "Very well. I'm not lying. I don't lie. I'm sorry I don't have the title papers on me, but I assure you that I am entirely serious when I say that my husband now owns this house."

"I find that difficult to believe when I haven't put the house up for sale."

"It's dirty and run down and looks like it's going to fall into the sea," Pixie said, looking around the room. "I like it."

"Hush, you. You're not helping." I took a firmer grip on the dog statue. "My husband bought the house at some sort of a foreclosure sale, I believe. A couple of days ago."

"I haven't even been home for the last ten days, so I don't see how . . ." The sentence petered out as a look of horror crept into Adam's eyes. Without another word, he ran out of the room, loud footsteps quickly fading into nothing.

I sat down heavily on the nearest chair, a sick feeling of sympathy gripping my stomach. I no longer had on any blinders to the less-than-sterling morals of my husband. It was entirely possible that he had bought the house out from under Adam, without so much as giving him time to clear out his belongings.

A moment later, Adam burst back into the room, shaking a paper beneath my nose and yelling in a way that was anatomically impossible, even for a third-generation polter.

After allowing him to rage at me for a few minutes, I managed to pry the paper out of his fisted hand. "That bastard! That royal bastard." He stormed, pacing up and down the length of the sitting room.

I smoothed the paper on my knee and gave it a quick once-over before looking up at where he now loomed over me, his face dark with emotion.

Pixie leaned over my shoulder to read it. "Foreclosure. That's not good, is it?"

"No." I watched Adam for a moment. "Where did you find this?"

"It was in my mailbox. Look at the date!"

I glanced back at the foreclosure notice. It was dated six months before. "I gather from your colorful suggestions of what your mortgage company can do with themselves that this is the first you've heard of foreclosure proceedings?"

"It is!" He snarled an obscenity and stomped over ro a small keyhole desk, then yanked a phone book from a drawer. "This is bullshit. I may have been late on a few mortgage payments, but not foreclosure late. No one at the bank ever mentioned that I was at risk to lose the house—no one! I've certainly never had any letters stating the house was going into foreclosure."

The sick feeling in my gut grew. "Perhaps there's been some massive mix-up. . . ."

"Like hell there is," he said, his eyes cold with fury as he snatched up the phone. "Meredith had better tell me what's going on if he knows what's good for him."

"Meredith?" I asked, the sick feeling in my belly turning to outright horror. "Meredith Bane?"

The look Adam turned on me would have likely

sent any sane person screaming from the room, but I was not known for my rationalness. "You know him?"

"No, not personally. But I've heard his name mentioned. He's my husband's business partner. Meredith runs the local bank. . . . Oh. Pixie, come over here."

"Des-de-mona! It's not that hard to remember!"

Slowly, Adam hung up the phone, his face a frozen mask. I got to my feet, my hand on Pixie's arm, prepared to shove her out the door and race for the car if Adam took even so much as one threatening step toward us. "Karma . . . *Marx*. Your husband is Spider Marx, the real estate agent?"

I pushed Pixie behind me, backing us up three steps toward the door. "I believe we'll be on our way now. I have a few things to do before tonight—" My lips clamped down on the sentence. I had a feeling Adam wouldn't appreciate hearing about Spider's plan for the house that night.

"Like finding an outfit to wear at the séance," Pixie said from behind me.

"What?" Adam asked, still coming toward us, his face red with anger. "What séance? What the hell are you talking about?"

"Run, you idiot," I said, spinning around and shoving Pixie none too gently out the door. She must have decided it was wiser to lip off to me than Adam, because she raced for the car.

"You can tell your husband that it'll be a cold day in hell before I let the likes of him take possession of my home!" Adam bellowed from the verandah.

Despite his anger, I felt an odd sort of kinship with Adam. I knew what it was like to be on the recipient end of Spider's immoral actions. Although Adam's problems weren't mine, a horribly annoying compulsion to help him refused to be squashed.

I stopped in front of the car and looked back at him. "Look, I'm really very sorry about this whole mess. Clearly something is going on that's not at all right. I don't know what I can do, but I will be happy to talk to Spider about it—"

"You can talk all you like! The house is mine, and it's going to stay mine!" he yelled, his eyes blazing with a cold blue anger.

"You're understandably angry now, but if we could just sit down and talk this out—"

"There is nothing to talk about. I'll warn you right now, Karma Marx: I protect what is mine. Stay out of my house!"

"That's going to be a little difficult considering she's supposed to be cleaning the house tonight," Pixie pointed out from the safety of the car.

I wanted to strangle her on the spot.

"Clean? You want to clean my hou—" Understanding dawned in his eyes, chased by rage. "You're a damned exterminator, aren't you? You're here to destroy my wards!"

The use of the word "ward" was interesting. It told me there was more to the man in front of me than was readily apparent.

"It's not my choice," I said simply, meeting his furious glare with one that I hoped expressed sympathy. "I will see if there's something that can be done to straighten up this mess. I don't know what I can do, but I will try. Perhaps if you talked to Spider—"

"I don't need your damned help! If your husband tries to step foot in my house, he'll regret it. So help me god, you'll both regret it!" he bellowed, marching back into the house and slamming the door.

Pixie looked thoughtfully at the house as I got into the car. "He really was pissed, huh?"

"Understatement of the year," I murmured as I turned the car around.

She sat back with a faint, satisfied little smile. "Tonight's going to rock. I can't wait to see what he does to the flower chick."

5

Spider was home when we returned an hour later.

"Keep your cape on until you're in your room," I warned Pixie in a low voice before she got out of the car.

"Why. Is he another bigot?"

"Spider can be extremely unpleasant when he puts his mind to it. I'd rather you were under his radar."

She pursed her lips, but nodded.

"Leaving so soon?" I couldn't help asking as Spider carried two large suitcases out to his car. I leaned against the garage door, suddenly too tired to move.

Spider ignored Pixie, who clutched her cape around herself as she hurried past him to the guest room I'd given over to her.

"I thought it would be best, given our agreement. Or perhaps you've changed your mind about that?" he asked, pulling me into an embrace. He rubbed his hips against me and murmured suggestive words as he nibbled a spot on my neck. "Could it be you realize what you'll be missing by giving me up?"

The headache that had been drugged into submission pulsed to life again. I put both hands on Spider's chest and pushed him back, idly wondering if the nausea that accompanied the migraine was entirely due to the pain or if my husband wasn't the cause of at least some of it. In fact, lately, the headaches seemed to increase intensity, too, whenever he was around. "Stop it, Spider. Despite your wishes, I will be quite happy on my own. This may come as a shock to you, but you're not irresistible anymore."

"Just because you don't get wet at the sight of me doesn't mean there aren't plenty of women who do." He laughed as he slapped me on the behind before reentering the house. "Who's the prime bit in black?"

I dug my knuckles into the pressure points between my eyebrows, praying the migraine didn't flare up into its full glory. After a few seconds, the pain faded enough for me to make my way into the house. "I told you I was taking in a girl from the children's home. Her name is Pixie, and she is just fifteen, hardly old enough to be considered a 'prime bit.' "

"You'd be surprised," he said, waggling his eyebrows at me. "If I'd known you meant such a sweet young thing when you said 'girl,' I wouldn't have been so quick to leave."

"That's not even remotely amusing," I snapped, slamming down my things onto the hall table.

Spider disappeared into the bedroom. I leaned against the door frame, watching as he emptied the contents of a dresser into a large duffel bag. "I went out to the Walsh house today."

"It's a mess, isn't it? But it's going to make us a lot of money. A few fixes here and there, a bit of polish, and it'll do."

The pain and nausea were back. I slid along the

wall to a chair that sat a few feet from the door. "The owner isn't very pleased, you know."

"Owner?" He looked up from arranging socks. "The previous one, you mean?"

"Yes. He didn't know the house was in danger of being foreclosed upon."

Spider shrugged. "His loss, not mine. He should have paid closer attention to his affairs."

"He swore you wouldn't take the house from him, Spider. He sounded like he meant it." My sense of fair play demanded that I warn Spider of Adam's intention. Fat lot of good that did me. Spider just laughed it off.

"He's all bark and no bite. Don't you worry your pretty little head about old Spider. I can take care of myself."

I flinched when he tried to pat my cheek. My head throbbed so horribly for a few seconds I seriously thought I was going to pass out. When the feeling lessened, I followed Spider out to the living room, where he had packed up various trophies and awards from his sporting days. I collapsed onto the couch, using my knuckles to hit every pressure point on my head that I could recall. "Did you somehow steal the house from him?"

" 'Steal' is such a very nasty word," Spider said, pausing before our wedding picture. He shook his head and passed on, moving behind the entertainment center to begin unplugging the stereo equipment. "For six months I've made him very attractive offers on the house—offers that far exceeded what the antique junk pile is worth. He refused to negotiate."

The feeling of dread returned to my belly. I had a suspicion I didn't want to hear what Spider was going to say next.

"Did he tell you that he'd been late with or missed several house payments? The bank has the right to foreclose after so many missed payments, you know. They also have the right to sell the mortgage to others. There was nothing illegal in what I did; I simply waited until his carelessness left the property in a position where I could acquire his mortgage in an expedient manner, then did so. And before you accuse me of conducting any more illegal acts, I did send him the legal notice informing him of the change. I even went so far as to say that unless he paid the past-due amount on the house, I would have no recourse but to foreclose."

I thought seriously of vomiting on him but knew that would provide only temporary satisfaction. "You did all this when? While he was out of town and unable to respond? Unable to save his house? How much time did you give him to pay you? A week? A day?"

Spider grinned. "He had the legal forty-eight hours to respond. He chose not to do so."

"You're an evil man, but you know that."

"It's not evil to be savvy, darling. Be a love and grab the DVD player, would you?"

I gritted my teeth against the pain, picking up the DVD player and following him out to his car. I hated to see the electronics go, since movies and music were two of my few pleasures, but it was worth losing them to see the last of the monster I'd married twelve years before.

"What are you looking so down in the dumps

about?" he asked when I silently handed him the player. "You're getting everything you demanded."

"At the expense of an innocent man, who is going to lose his beloved home."

Spider rolled his eyes and tossed the duffel bag into the car. "He'll find another. I'm doing him a favor, really. The house is a dump, and it's full of evil spirits. Better to get it cleaned out and taken care of than let it rot. Besides, you know who used to live there?"

I followed him back into the house.

"Poltergeists." He made a face as if he'd bitten something sour.

"What's wrong with polters?"

"They're evil." He looked around the house, clearly scanning for anything else he wanted to take with him.

"Judging by the pictures my father took of your nocturnal activities, I'd have thought you had an affection for polters, not hated them."

He grinned again, giving my butt a squeeze. I slapped his hand away and moved to the other side of the dining room table. "Just because I'm not blind to their true nature doesn't mean I hate them. There are many times when it's quite the opposite. The young ones are particularly delectable. Naomi—she's the redhead in the picture—was as limber as the rest of the poltergeists I've known. And just as insatiable. Lots of energy. She just kept going and going and going. Oh yes, they can be *very* tasty in the right circumstances."

"You really are contemptible; you know that, right?"

"Jealous?" he asked with a loathsome leer.

"Hardly. My tastes don't run to eighteen-year-olds the way yours do. I just hope that someday you'll be caught by an irate father."

"Won't happen, sweetheart. I'm very, very careful. I don't leave loose ends."

I frowned, wondering what the hell that meant. I'd known for the last few months that some of Spider's lovers had been inappropriately young for him, but I assumed they had been just as willing as he had. Certainly the participants in the photos my father had shown me looked enthusiastic.

"Do you have everything?" I asked, changing the subject.

"I've probably forgotten something, but I'll come back later for the things I've left." He glanced around the room one more time, his gaze narrowing on my purse and a manila envelope I'd put on the table. "What's this?"

Before I could snatch the envelope from him, he opened it and was quickly scanning the documents. He turned the envelope over and read the name stamped in the corner. "Akashic League? What were you doing there?"

"A little research on your house," I answered, seizing the papers from his hands.

He gave me an odd look before dismissively shrugging. He checked his watch and grabbed his keys. "How you waste your time is no longer my business. Be at the house at eight."

"Spider, wait." I bit my lip, hesitating to tell him about the planned séance. Part of me wanted to see Savannah pulling something over on Spider, but the realist in me pointed out that few people have ever managed to do that. "There's a ghost-hunting group who plans on investigating the Walsh house—"

"I know all about them," he interrupted with yet another smarmy smile. "There's not going to be anything for them to investigate by the time you're done, now, is there?"

"But—"

"Don't be late. I want that house cleaned by no later than ten." The slam of the car door shot through my head like a red-hot bolt. I didn't so much close the door as slump against it, collapsing to the floor in a giant puddle of pain-racked goo.

Sergei's concerned face and the sound of the phone were the first things I became aware of when I returned to consciousness several hours later. Somehow I'd been carried over to the couch.

"You all right?" Sergei asked me. "You look bad."

"Migraine," I croaked, the very act of speaking enough to bring on waves of pain and nausea.

He drifted over with my purse and the phone, silently handing both to me. I took the purse, dug through it for the pain meds, then downed them before collapsing back onto the couch. "Let the machine answer it."

A tinny male voice came from the kitchen as the answering machine kicked in, but I was too out of it to listen. Twenty minutes later I swam up from the blessed numbing action of the medicine and carefully sat up.

Sergei hovered in front of me, holding a handful of papers. "These were on the floor. You want? Or recycle?"

"I want them. Thank you for tidying up so

quickly." I put the papers back into the envelope. Sergei continued to hover in front of me, a worried expression twisting his face. "Is there something else?"

He pointed at the envelope. "It says Akashic League."

I stared silently at him, unable to work out in my fuzzy brain what it was he was so concerned about.

"You going to banish me?"

"Oh," I said, the light finally dawning. "No, the League hasn't ordered me to banish you. I was simply using their library to do some research on the house I'm going to clean tonight. Speaking of that, what time is it?"

Sergei moved so I could see the clock above the mantel.

"Oh, no! How could you let me sleep so long? I only have twenty minutes to get to the house. . . . Urgh."

"You look horrible. More horrible than you did earlier when you fainted," a voice said from the doorway." Pixie stood watching me with arms crossed over her chest. "Are you going to barf?"

"I don't think so. I'm sorry if I frightened you." I pushed damp hair back from my forehead, trying to think. My head was woozy and felt like it was filled with molasses, making my thoughts thick and slow-moving. I shook it in an attempt to clear it.

"I wasn't scared," she said as she strolled into the room, trying hard for nonchalance in her voice, but I heard an undertone of relief that warmed my heart. "There was a turkey sandwich in the fridge. I ate it."

"That's fine. I'm sorry I was so out of it. This has been some first day for you."

She shrugged. "I've had worse."

"I'm sorry to hear that. And I'm sorry to have to leave you, but I need to go. Will you be all right by yourself? There's food, and the TV, and I'll have my father check on you to make sure—"

"I'm *not* an *infant*!" Her back stiffened with indignation. "I can be left by *myself*, you know."

I rubbed my numb head. "I'm sorry, Desdemona—"

"Obsidian Angel," she interrupted.

"What?" I wondered if the drugs were making me hallucinate. "Obsidian what?"

"Angel. It's my new name. I'm done with Desdemona. You may now call me Obsidian Angel."

I stared at her for a second, wondering if the repayment for my sin was worth having Pixie in my life. "We'll talk about that later, OK? Right now I need to get going. Sergei, can you please get my bag of tricks?"

Sergei toddled off to get the bag in which I kept my tools. I tried to get to my feet, gritting my teeth to keep the waves of nausea roiling around inside me from coming to fruition. "Can you help me get up, Pixie . . . er . . . Des . . . oh, whoever you are? I think once I'm on my feet I'll be OK."

"I doubt it," she said, hauling me to my feet. I stood weaving for a second, my vision swimming

"Thanks. Sergei? Where are . . . What's wrong with you?"

The domovoi was a dim figure in the darkness of the hallway. He was evidently struggling to pull together enough energy to move my bag from the other room. That surprised me. "Why are you so wiped out?"

Sergei left the bag halfway down the hall and floated into the living room. "I did the windows while you were gone. And vacuumed, and dusted in the attic, and washed the kitchen floor, and then there was a rattling in the dryer, so I took it apart to find the bit that was loose, and after that I—"

"Oh, please stop," I said, rubbing my head. "I feel guilty enough that you're working around here without knowing you're a virtual slave to housecleaning."

"I like it," Sergei insisted. "I am sorry I did so much today. If I'd known you were going to need me—"

"It's not a big deal. I can do this. . . ." I ignored the groan forced out as I bent to retrieve my bag from the floor.

"You're going to wrap yourself around a tree or something if you go out like that," Pixie said, watching me with a dispassionate eye.

"I'm OK. Just a bit woozy. It'll pass in a minute."

"The young lady with many arms is right," Sergei said slowly. "It would not be safe for you to drive as you are. Cardea must help you."

He hurried to the kitchen before I could protest, and returned with a worried-looking Cardea.

"Sergei says you need me?"

"I'm fine," I repeated, my vision slowly clearing. I took a tentative step forward. "He's overreacting."

"Just look at her," Sergei said, gesturing toward me. "You must drive her to the house she is to clean tonight."

Cardea glanced back toward the kitchen. "You know I would be happy to help you, Karma, but I really do have much to do in the pantry. There're all those cans of soup to be organized, and some of the potatoes are growing eyes, and I thought I would arrange the pasta by expiration date rather than shape, as they are now."

"You must put your own desires aside for the mistress," Sergei said.

I slowly bent to retrieve my jacket, pausing a moment to breathe deeply as a wave of red wooziness washed over me.

Cardea bit her lip. When I had first discovered her, she had been haunting a small dank basement. The owners of the house had sympathy for the agoraphobic goddess but wished to finish the basement to house their growing family.

"I'll be OK," I said, slipping into my jacket and staggering toward my tool bag. "I just need to take things slowly. Well, as slowly as I can, which isn't very slow at all, but what the hell. Spider can just deal with me being a little late."

"You are going to clean a house?" Cardea asked, panic rising in her pretty green eyes. Her hands fluttered around helplessly. "Oh, I couldn't leave here; I just couldn't!"

"Someone must take her," Sergei insisted. "She isn't safe to drive as she is."

"But . . . I couldn't . . . so many people . . ."

"*Deus!* I'll drive!" Pixie snatched the keys from the hall table, grabbing her cape and a black leather messenger bag before stalking toward the garage.

Sergei frowned. "You're not old enough to drive, are you?"

"Hel-*lo*! Driver's ed? I so passed that months ago," she told him with an impatient gesture.

"Do you have a license?" I asked, unable to believe I was seriously considering letting her drive me anywhere.

"I had the highest score in the class," she said, tossing her head.

"Which means you don't have a license." I sighed. I'd just have to get myself to the house on my own.

"I have a permit! It says I can drive with an adult present, and since you're, like, *ancient*, that means I can drive you."

I hesitated, weighing the hell it would be driving myself against the concern of bringing Pixie with me to an environment that was hostile, if not downright dangerous.

"Come on, Karma," she said, her dark eyes curiously vulnerable. "I'm a good driver. My last foster mom used to have me drive her to the liquor store all the time."

I winced. "All right. But only on my conditions!" I said, holding her back when she leaped for the door leading to the garage. "You have to promise me you'll do as I say when we get to the house. If Spider or any of the ghost people are around, keep your cape on. Damn, I wish I'd thought of sending my dad out for a glamour."

"Mrs. Beckett says glamours give you brain cancer if you use them too much."

"That's just an old wives' tale." I fretted for a few moments more about taking Pixie with me but didn't see a way around it.

"Do you think the flower chick would freak out at a real live polter?" she asked, waving her arms around in an exaggerated manner.

"I have no idea how she or the other ghost hunters

would react. Some people have no issues with the Otherworld; others refuse to believe the truth. Until I can judge which group they fall into, I want you to keep a low profile."

"*Maximus deus!*" she swore, rolling her eyes. "Fine! Have it your way! I'll keep my cape on, OK?"

"OK," I said, going against my better judgment. I kept one hand on the wall for support as I walked to the car.

"It's automatic, right? I can't drive a stick. My foster dad was going to show me how, but he was arrested for DUI."

"What lovely people they must have been," I murmured, then gave her instructions on where we were headed.

To my surprise, Sergei followed us.

"You need me," Sergei said by way of explanation.

"I do?"

"I would come with you, but I have all this pantry rearranging to do," Cardea called from the doorway, giving us a little wave. "Have fun!"

"You need me," Sergei repeated, shimmering into nothing as he melted into the backseat of the car.

There wasn't much I could say to that. I didn't have the energy to fight a determined spirit, so I gave in with as much grace as I could muster. Before we reached the car, the phone rang. I hesitated, looking at the garage phone for a moment, assessing my need to leave against the possibility of a phone call I shouldn't miss. "Just a second, guys. I'd better see who it is."

"Probably your father," Sergei said as I picked up the phone. "He called earlier and left a message saying he wanted to see you immediately."

"Karma? I forbid you to go out to that house," my father said even before I could say hello.

"Dad, I really don't have time for this. I'm late, and I have a killer headache."

"It's payback for what you're about to do," he snapped.

"I'm sorry; I really have to go. Can we have this argument another time?"

"No! This is important, Karma. I can't let you destroy any more spirits! It's wrong—wrong on a cosmic scale. I will not have a daughter of mine being the angel of death!"

I would have rolled my eyes at my father's dramatics but didn't have the energy. "I'm hanging up now. I'll talk to you tomorrow."

"I'm coming out to the house!"

"Like hell you are! Spider will have the hissy fit to end all hissy fits if he sees you there. Not to mention ghost hunters are going to be there. Just stay home, and we'll work it out tomorrow."

"Don't do anything until I get there and can talk some reason into you!" he shouted into the phone as I hung up the receiver and turned to face three inquisitive expressions.

"Honestly, there are times when I wish I could divorce my father. Pixie, I need to get to the Walsh house as fast as legally possible."

"Obsidian Angel!"

"Sorry." I took the passenger seat, buckling myself in as I shied away from the thought of what Spider would have to say about my father's showing up.

"Let's see . . . R for 'forward'?" Pixie started the car and immediately hit the accelerator. We shot backward into a series of shelves that lined the back wall of the garage, boxes of Christmas decorations perched on the beams overhead tumbling down onto the car.

I glared at her. "R for forward?"

"Heh-heh. Little joke." She smiled. I continued to glare until she made a face and put the car into the proper gear.

"I will clean it later," Sergei reassured me as I slowly turned to look out the back window at the spilled garlands of gold and silver, the tinsel fluttering to the ground on either side of the car, and the soft stuffed Santa that tangled itself on the car's antenna. The shelves looked a little worse for wear, but not totally destroyed.

The car jerked forward four feet. My forehead hit the padded dash.

"Sorry. This car is a little different from my foster mom's. I have it now."

We shot out of the garage, trailing tinsel and garlands, some of it flying off the car as we careened around the corner on what felt like only two wheels. I clutched the dashboard with both hands, mute with horror.

"Gotta have tunes while I'm driving," Pixie said, fiddling with the radio. I screamed and pointed. She jerked the car back into our lane, narrowly missing plowing headlong into a semitrailer. "It's not what I normally listen to, but it'll have to do."

Rap exploded from the radio.

I closed my eyes and prayed to every deity I could think of to just get us to the house without anyone being maimed or killed.

6

"Well, *that* doesn't look good."

As I got out of the car, a large shadow arose from a settee on the verandah and stood at the top of the steps. It was Adam, and he was holding a shotgun.

"Wow. He's really pissed-looking." Pixie eyed Adam for a moment before waving me ahead. "You go first."

"It is not proper that Karma be exposed to such danger. I will go first," Sergei said, floating to the front of our little group.

"He's not going to shoot me," I assured my sweet domovoi. "He's just trying to make a statement."

"Yeah. A statement like a herkin' big hole blown through your head," Pixie added in a suspiciously cheerful voice.

"You are a morbid little girl," Sergei told her.

"At least I'm alive, and I'm not a slave," she snapped back.

"I am a domovoi! I am not a slave—"

"Knock it off, you two," I interrupted, squaring my shoulders and starting up the flagged pathway.

"This is difficult enough without you going at it. If you all could be quiet and let me deal with the situation, I'd appreciate it. Hello, Adam."

"I told you that you were not welcome on my property," Adam called down from the verandah. "I meant it, Karma. You will step foot in my house over my dead body."

I ignored the fact that he made an impressively threatening figure—with or without the gun—and slowly climbed the stairs until I was directly in front of him. Pixie trailed behind me. Sergei was beside her, materializing only enough to be vaguely visible. "That's going to be a little difficult given that you're a polter, isn't it?"

Even in the failing light, I could read the irritation that flashed through his eyes. "My heritage has nothing to do with the situation."

"No? I have always believed that orthodox polters were bound to their domiciles, guardians of their homes, unable and unwilling to leave them so long as they stood. That sounds to me like very good motivation for not wanting to face the reality of the loss of your property."

His face tightened. "You've been busy. Looked me up, did you?"

I smiled. "I work for the Akashic League. Their records are extremely extensive when it comes to Otherworld citizens, so it wasn't difficult to find a background on you. You're an orthodox polter, born 1902—which means you've had long enough to drop the extra arms, and you work in the mundane world as a U.S. marshal. Your family has guarded this house since it was built, although it wasn't until the

1990s that you bought it outright and took over ownership from the mortal family who inhabited it. I believe those are all the pertinent facts."

"Not quite all," he said, shifting the shotgun to his left hand. I fought the urge to back up a step or two at the hard look on his face. "You missed one: I, too, work for the Akashic League."

That took me aback for a moment. "You do? In what capacity?"

"I am a member of the watch," he said with a smile that was far from reassuring.

"He's a watch?" Pixie asked in a puzzled whisper. "How can you be a *member* of a watch?"

I didn't have time to do more than wonder why she wasn't aware of the Otherworld police system. Evidently Sergei filled her in, because it wasn't a few seconds later that she said, "Oh, great, he's a cop. They were always arresting my foster dad. Although he had it coming a couple of times."

" 'Mad, bad, and dangerous to know,' " I quoted softly.

Adam all but smirked. "I'm not Lord Byron, but it fits well enough. And you aren't the only one who used the League's archives to look things up. I know all about the wergeld."

I narrowed my eyes at him, considering his unspoken threat.

"You know? Who did Karma kill? She won't tell me anything!" Pixie complained.

I prayed for patience. "Many people know about my history. It's not relevant right now, however. My husband, who is due here at any minute, *is* relevant. He will have little respect for the fact that you're a marshal, and none for the fact that you're a member of the Otherworld's elite police force. You're going to have to face that legally he owns your house, Adam. He's mortal. You're not. By the laws that govern the League, you can't do anything to seriously harm him."

"Except in self-defense," he corrected, taking up an aggressive stance. "I have no doubt he will attempt to attack me, at which point I will legally be able to defend myself and my home."

"You don't know Spider," I said, shaking my head. "He's—"

"Oooh, guests! Adam, you didn't tell me we were to have *guests*! And me without mint juleps or fresh gingerbread. A domovoi! And merciful Scot, another polter!"

Pixie, who had been loudly chewing gum, stopped to eye the young man with long blond curls, clad in what seemed to be late-Victorian garb, as he appeared in front of her. He wore a highly anachronistic bright yellow apron bearing the words IS THAT A SAUSAGE ON MY GRILL, OR AM I JUST HAPPY TO SEE YOU? "Not more bigots!"

The spirit squealed. "Not in the least, my dear girl! We positively love polters here! Adam, why didn't you tell me we were going to have guests?"

"Get back in the house!" For a moment, Adam looked disconcerted as he attempted to shoo the spirit back through the front door. "I told you it wasn't safe out here!"

"Don't be ridiculous; these lovely ladies wouldn't dream of harming anyone! Julie! You simply have to come out here! We have guests!"

"No," Adam said, throwing himself across the front door. "No one else—"

"This had better be important, because my egg whites aren't even close to stiff yet, and you know what a disaster limp whites can be. . . . Sweet St. Peter and all the saints! Lady visitors!" The spirit of a second young man swept right through Adam, stopping next to his friend. He was likewise dressed in Victorian clothing, although his waistcoat was a shimmering turquoise, while the first spirit's was a gorgeous patterned silver and green. "Welcome to our home. It's been forever and a day since anyone has paid us a call. We must warn Amanita."

"Oh yes, absolutely," the first spirit agreed.

Adam banged his forehead on the door frame a few times. "Why don't you listen to me? Why does no one listen to me?"

"The younger one is a polter," the first spirit whispered loudly to the second after Sergei introduced himself. "I think she's what they call a punk rocker."

"I'm not into punk!" Pixie said with a toss of her black hair. "I'm a Goth!"

The spirits peered at her. "Are you sure?" the one named Julie asked. "You look like the people on the TV we saw a few decades back. All black leather and chains and spiky dyed black hair."

"I'm fifteen, not a million years old! I'm a *Goth*!"

"I talk. I know I'm talking, because I can hear my voice, but no one listens." Adam whumped his head on the door a few more times.

"Goth? As in Visigoth? Is it some sort of alternative lifestyle?"

"We're all over alternative lifestyles," the first spirit said, nodding.

Pixie heaved a dramatic sigh. I smiled at Adam. He banged his forehead twice more.

"It's not an alternative lifestyle. Goth is . . ." Pixie's hands gestured while she tried to put into words her outlook on life. "It's . . . oh, it's hard to explain. It's dark. It's all about darkness and evil and twisted reality."

"Now you've lost me," Julie said.

I took pity on the ghosts. "It's a somewhat popular movement wherein members express via creative means the duality of man's nature, exploring everything dark and nightmarish, often through music, poetry, books, and dress style."

"There's more to it than that!" Pixie said, outrage dripping from her words.

"Yes, but we only have so long before Adam is going to give himself a concussion," I said with a nod toward him.

He glared at me in return.

"Well, whatever you are, it's a look that works," the second spirit told Pixie, totally ignoring Adam. "I am Jules, and this is my domestic partner, Antony. Please, all of you, do come in and make yourselves comfortable. I don't think we've ever had a Goth in before. We'll open a bottle of champagne to celebrate!"

"I don't like champagne," Pixie said with a regal inclination of her head as she marched in the door. "I'd prefer absinthe."

"Do you have any oats?" Sergei asked as he drifted after her.

"You're not having anything alcoholic—" I said, but was cut off almost immediately.

"This is ridiculous!" Adam shouted, blocking the door again so I couldn't follow Pixie. He swung around to face his spirits, his arms outstretched to bar the entrance. "You don't know who you're talking to. These people are not here on a social visit. They're dangerous to you all!"

"Ignore Adam. He's so melodramatic," Jules told Pixie.

I ducked under Adam's right arm and squeezed into the room before he could grab me.

"I am not melodramatic! I have never been melodramatic a day in my life! I am the least melodramatic person I know, and I know a lot of people! Now, will you be quiet and listen to me? I'm trying to save your rotten hides!"

"It's like living with a drama queen," the spirit named Antony said in a confiding tone as he escorted Pixie to a chair. "He's been very cranky today because some evil assassin is on his way here to destroy us. Now, you just sit right there. Serge, darling, you must think us utter pigs for allowing you into a room in such a state, but it's simply impossible to get good help these days. It's all Julie and I can do to keep the kitchen running. But that's another story, isn't it? Everyone relax, and make yourselves comfy. We'll be back with a little something to celebrate your visit."

Tony started across the room but stopped when his partner grabbed his arm and nodded toward me.

"Oh, I beg your pardon," Tony said, hustling to offer me a hand, his body suddenly changing from translucent to solid. "I'm the rudest thing ever, aren't I! Please, do come in."

"Stop! You have no idea who she is!" Adam warned.

Tony waved away the objection as I shook his hand. "Pfft. Any friend of Adam's is a friend of ours. How d'ye do? I'm Antony."

"Karma," I said, shaking his hand.

"She's the exterminator come to send you and the others to the Akasha," Adam growled behind me.

Tony's eyes widened, his face freezing. Beyond him, Jules stopped dead, an identical look of horror on his face.

"The assassin is here?" a voice squeaked from behind the door. A petite woman with white-blond hair that stuck out in odd clumps burst out, her large gray eyes dark with fear. She threw her hands over her head, shrieking, "Eeek! I don't want to die looking like this!"

The woman raced across the polished wooden floor and disappeared up the stairs. The two spirits vanished. Pixie plopped herself down on the sofa and pulled out her iPod. Sergei faded a few notches until he was just barely visible.

I turned to face Adam, who was standing with a belligerent look on his face, the shotgun still clutched in his hands.

"Was that woman what I think she was?"

"Amanita is a unicorn, yes. She's having a bad hair day. You're not going to send the ghosts or her to the Akasha." His voice was deep and full of threat.

"No, I'm not," I agreed, taking him by surprise. I smiled and waved my hand somewhat wearily toward the Sergei. "How do you think I ended up with a Russian domovoi?"

"And the imps," Sergei said, a glint of humor in his eye. "And Peter the dada."

One of Adam's eyebrows rose as he considered me. "You have a vegetable spirit?"

"Doesn't everyone?"

He just stared at me.

I sighed. "Yes, I have a dada, and imps, although I released them into the wild earlier today, and Sergei, and as you can see, a teenage polter named Pixie."

"Obsidian Angel!"

"I thought it was Desdemona," Adam said, momentarily distracted.

Pixie looked down her nose at him, not an easy task given his height and the fact that she was sitting down. "I *changed* it! It's Obsidian Angel now!"

"I know you think I'm the devil himself," I said, turning back to Adam. "But I'm not. I'm not going to send your charges to the Akasha; I promise. I will, however, have to relocate them."

"No," Adam said, his face growing dark.

I sighed again and took his non-shotgun hand, pulling him over to the settee across from Pixie. "Look, I know you don't want to go over this again, but we literally are out of time. Spider will be here any minute. I'm surprised he wasn't here to meet me, actually. This house legally belongs to him." I held up my hand to stop the protest. "I know, I know, he got it from you by trickery, but legally, it belongs to him. He has made a deal with me to clean it. If he shows up and the spirits and your unicorn are not gone, there will be hell to pay."

"You made a deal to clean my house?" Adam asked, anger flaring to life in his beautiful light blue eyes. "How much is he paying you?"

"He's giving me a divorce," I said, ignoring the sarcastic tone. "You said you looked into my background. If so, you'll know I'm licensed by the League to perform exterminations when a property's owner requests it, so there's no legal grounds for you—

either in the mundane world or the Otherworld—to stop the extermination from being carried out. What I am offering you is the best compromise possible: I will relocate your charges to the location of your desire. Your spirits and the unicorn will be safe, Spider will never know the difference, and you can get on with your life."

"No," Adam said, shaking his head. "I won't allow it. They belong at Walsh House, just as I do. None of us will be leaving."

Outside the house, the sounds of voices and car doors closing could be heard.

"You have about ten seconds to change your mind," I warned, nodding toward the window. "It sounds like the ghost hunters are here early, and that man shouting is my husband."

"No one is leaving the house," Adam repeated, giving me a curiously unreadable look.

A man rushed through the door, but it wasn't who I was expecting. "Karma! Tell me you haven't done anything rash! Tell me it's not too late to reason with you!"

I cast my eyes heavenward for a moment, praying yet again for patience. "Dad, I told you not to come here. I may be drugged up to the eyeballs, but I know I told you not to come."

"*Dad?*" A familiar blond woman stepped into the house behind my father. She glanced from him to me, her eyes growing huge with wonder and delight. "This is your father? He . . . he has three arms!"

Dad gave her a haughty look. "Haven't you ever seen a polter before?"

I thought Savannah was going to pass out from excitement. She positively danced in place. "Goddess above! You're a poltergeist? A real poltergeist? But you look so normal!"

"My father is a real, honest-to-goodness poltergeist, yes," I said, rubbing my forehead. Despite the potent migraine medicines, pain was beginning to blossom again. Not only that, the faint buzzing noise had started up again. I wondered vaguely if Adam had a faulty electrical connection somewhere. "Complete with three arms, the inability to sit down for more than five minutes, and an annoying tendency to ignore everything I say."

"Not everything, honey. Just the foolish parts."

"Then you're a poltergeist, too? Oh, merciful goddess!" Savannah seemed almost to clap her hands with joy. "I never knew that poltergeists could manifest themselves to look human, but I'm thrilled, thrilled to death! Oh, this is perfect! Two poltergeists for our meeting!"

"Try four," I said wearily. Pixie had instinctively grabbed for her cape when people had rushed into the room, but there was little reason to keep her heritage a secret when everyone else's was out in the open.

I thought Savannah's eyes were going to bug out when she saw Pixie. "This is the greatest day of my life," she whispered, a look of utter delight on her face. "She has four arms! But you only have two, and your father has three? Is it a family trait?"

Pixie rolled her eyes, turned up the volume on her iPod, and, pulling out a book, ignored everyone.

"Um . . . no. It has to do with the age of the polter. It's kind of complicated. My father can explain it better than I can."

"I would very much appreciate an explanation. I'd

love to interview you both. But . . ." Savannah looked around the room. Sergei had disappeared completely at their entrance. "Where is the fourth poltergeist?"

I smiled and tipped my head toward Adam. He shot me a look. I shot it right back at him. If I was going to be the sacrificial lamb for the ghost-hunting group, he was going to be the mint jelly. "I should point out I'm only half polter. My mother is mortal."

Savannah transferred her gawk from the scowling Adam to me. "Four poltergeists! This is unprecedented! I can't wait to tell the others; they should be here soon. I came a little early to get things set up, but I never in my wildest dreams expected to find poltergeists here! I do hope you'll participate in the evening's events."

"There will be no events, not tonight or any other night," a voice said from the doorway. Spider stepped into the room. "This house is scheduled to be cleaned tonight. Your group will have to find somewhere else to meet."

Adam growled something very rude and lunged at Spider, who sidestepped nimbly away, holding up a sheaf of stapled papers. "Need I remind you who is owner here, Dirgesinger?"

"You bastard—"

A faint, familiar sound reached my ears. I frowned, turning my head to try to catch it.

A tall, thin man stepped between Adam and Spider just as Adam launched himself forward. "Now, now, there's no need for violence, Adam."

"Meredith," Adam snarled, his teeth bared. "How much did it take to buy your favors? How much did it take to betray me?"

The noise grew. It was high-pitched, like the sound of distant gulls . . . only much more ominous.

Spider caught sight of Pixie. His eyebrows rose; a lascivious look was in his eyes. "You took in a polter? My, my, if you'd only told me earlier . . . I would have been happy to make the young lady . . . *welcome*."

My skin crawled at the tone of his voice. Pixie evidently heard him, because she stuffed her book and her iPod into her bag and moved over to stand behind me.

"Goodness. What's going on here?" Savannah leaned close to ask, her eyes on the three men standing in the center of the room.

My father flitted around the edge of the room, clearly so wound up that he wouldn't be able to stand still. I pinched the bridge of my nose, praying the pain in my head would lessen enough to let me cope with the situation quickly spinning out of control.

The noise outside increased. My father listened for a moment, then turned to me with a question in his eyes.

I sighed and braced myself for the onslaught. "Adam is the owner of the house. Or he was until Spider bought it. I gather that the other man is Meredith Bane. He's the crooked banker who helped Spider steal Adam's house while he was away."

Savannah stiffened, her gaze sharp. "Meredith happens to be my husband. He is not crooked!"

"Your husband? Oy. I'm sorry."

"Meredith!" She dismissed me with a cool nod and swept over to her husband, trailing a long gauze scarf that hung down her back. "There is much discord in the house. It will disturb the spirits greatly."

The middle-aged, slightly balding man leaned his head down to that of his wife, evidently cooing reassuring words in her ear.

"That's all well and fine," she said, pointing at Spider, "but that man said the house is going to be cleaned. That's a euphemism for exorcism! The house is of no use to us whatsoever if the spirits are driven from it!"

"No one is going to exorcise anything," Adam said loudly. "Isn't that right, Karma?"

Everyone turned to look at me. I avoided meeting Spider's gaze. "I have agreed to Spider's request for me to remove any entities in the house. I will honor that agreement."

A wave of yellow rolled through the front door, the high-pitched *eek-eek* causing everyone to turn and stare as a herd of six imps—dirty, smelling to high heaven, and clearly near exhaustion—limped over to me. The group leader stopped in front of me, hiccupped, and, with a dramatic flair that would have done a diva proud, staggered two steps before fainting onto my foot.

I cleared my throat and carefully pushed the unconscious imp to the side. "I'll throw in imp removal for no extra charge."

"Goddess above. Can it be? Meredith, do you see?"

"Yes," he said, a nonplussed look on his face as he watched the other five imps hug my ankle before collapsing. "They look like little yellow rodents."

"With six arms! Merciful heaven, they have six arms! Do you know what they are?"

"Imps," I answered, sighing as I gathered up the mostly comatose creatures. "Very determined ones at that. I have no idea how they found me, but they should be confined or they'll be in our way."

Adam didn't look any too pleased. "You brought imps with you to my house?"

"No. I moved these guys to a farm. They refuse to leave me. Somehow, I'm imprinted on them as their mother." I gestured with one of the limp imps. "Try as I might, I just can't seem to get rid of the little buggers."

"I'll get a box," Adam said, heading for a nearby closet.

"Will you please stick to the matter at hand and stop waving those nasty little yellow rats around!" Spider moved into my field of vision, his dark eyes narrowed with suspicion. "You told me you'd clean the house."

"And I intend to."

"Karma, honey, don't do it! You have a higher authority to answer to!" my father shouted.

Spider shot him a look of loathing before turning back to me. "You said you'd exterminate the spirits."

"I said I would remove them from the house, and I will do so. Thank you, Adam. Do you have a cord I can tie the box shut with? They'll get out otherwise."

"There's some in the drawer." He nodded toward a sideboard.

I cut off a long piece of cord and wrapped it carefully around the box after making sure there were enough gaps in the cardboard to allow airflow. The last thing I needed was for the imps to add to my troubles.

"You can't send the spirits away," Savannah

pleaded, coming forward to take my hands after I had deposited the imps underneath the sideboard. "You just can't! They belong here."

"It is awfully mean, Karma," Pixie said with a look around the room. "This house is pretty cool."

"Pixie—"

"Obsidian Angel!"

"Seen and not heard," I told her. She harrumphed and threw herself down onto the sofa.

"That's right, listen to the nice blond lady," my father said, nodding. "She knows what she's talking about."

Savannah turned to her husband. "Meredith, tell her that she can't do it. This house is a gold mine of spirits! It would be a tragedy to lose them simply because that man wants them gone!"

"You're not going to clean the house?" Spider asked me, his eyes glittering dangerously.

I thought carefully about what I was going to say. It was tricky dealing with Spider at any time— doubly so when he was in a mood. "The spirits will be removed."

"Relocated," my dad said, sighing in relief as he slumped onto a nearby armchair. "She means to relocate them rather than exterminate them. I live in fear she'll do otherwise, but thank the gods she has finally figured out what is right."

"I had a feeling you would try something like this," Spider said, reaching into his jacket pocket.

For one brief, horrifying moment, I thought he was going to pull out a gun and shoot me.

What he did was much, much worse. The object he held in his hand was small, made of black plastic, bearing a gauge on the top. It looked like a slim-line version of an electronic tape measure or stud finder. But as he pressed a couple of buttons on it, pain exploded in my head, sending me to my knees.

"Karma? What is it?" my father asked, hurrying to me. Red agony washed over me, so great it almost blinded me, driving every thought from my head but ceaseless, unending anguish.

Next to Spider, a figure appeared, writhing in pain. I didn't know how Spider was able to summon Sergei, but I could see Sergei was suffering as much as—if not more than—I was.

"Stop it," I tried to shriek at my husband, but all that came out of my mouth was a howl. "Make him stop it."

Adam took a step forward as Spider pointed the little black torture device at Sergei.

"Meredith!" Savannah gasped. "Look! Ghosts! Honest-to-goddess ghosts! Where's my camera?"

"Let's see if this really works as advertised," Spider drawled, pressing a button. Sergei's being exploded into a million pieces, his scream of torment hanging on the air long seconds after he had been destroyed.

The silence that followed was filled with horror. I was so stunned I forgot the pain for a moment to try to grasp the fact that Spider had destroyed Sergei right before my eyes.

"Excellent work," Spider said, turning to Meredith. "You were right about it being extremely efficient. We won't need Karma at all to clean any ghosts we don't want. Your little device will take care of that problem once and for all."

I lunged at Spider, intending to do god knows what to him, but my legs refused to cooperate. I stumbled over my father, arms and legs tangling with his. Pixie tried to help me up.

Savannah yelled at Meredith, hitting him with a beaded bag while accusing him of ruining everything.

"Bunch of noise over nothing," Spider grunted, turning the machine on my father. "Let's just see if the polter setting works; then I can clean whatever else is hiding in the house."

"No!" I shrieked, trying to kick my feet free so I could crawl over to Spider and stop him before he destroyed anyone else.

"There will be no more!" Adam's voice was so loud it literally rattled the window. A couple of apports, shiny white pebbles that were warm to the touch, dropped from the ceiling.

"What on earth—" Savannah gasped, picking up one of the pebbles.

"It's an apport," my dad explained to her as I staggered to my feet, one arm around Pixie both for support and to protect her. "In times of stress, we tend to manifest them. It's a little embarrassing, actually. You shouldn't make a big deal about it."

"By my authority as an officer of the watch of the Akashic League, I seal this house!" Adam bellowed. A little tingle ran down my back, like a faint electrical shock.

"Are you still here?" Spider asked, giving Adam an obnoxious glance. "You've overstayed your welcome, Dirgesinger. Get the hell out of my house, and off my property."

"No one is leaving," Adam said, his breath coming hard.

"Honey?" My father and Pixie helped me to a

chair. Every inch of my body felt like it had been pounded with a sledgehammer. "Are you all right?"

I watched, praying Adam had the power he appeared to have, as Spider aimed the little machine at us.

The machine clicked. Dad turned to glare at Spider. I slumped back in the chair, thanking every deity I could think of.

"What the hell? It isn't working!" Spider said, his voice filled with accusation. He clicked the button a couple more times, but nothing happened. "I put it on the poltergeist setting. Why isn't this working?"

"I don't know. It was working before," Meredith said, taking the machine and popping the back off to look at the guts. "It looks fine. Maybe you weren't using it right."

"Adam has sealed the house," I said, digging my knuckles into my temples.

"Nothing that filthy polter can do is any concern of mine," Spider said as he looked over Meredith's shoulder.

"It should be. He has more power than you can imagine." I used two of my father's arms and one of Pixie's as leverage, rather shakily getting to my feet.

Adam stood silent in the middle of the room, his eyes bright but distrustful.

Meredith half turned toward his wife but, at a glare from her, prodded the machine in his hand. "There was a wire loose, I think," he said, snapping the cover onto the back of it. "Give it a try now."

"Over my dead body!"

I'll say this for my father: he's fast. As used to his polter quickness as I am, even I couldn't see him move. One moment he was behind me; the next he was across the room, having snatched up the small black machine en route. He threw it down and slammed his boot into the plastic, grinding it into the throw rug before any of us had the time to do more than blink.

Spider lunged at my father as soon as he realized what Dad had done. Meredith swore. Savannah wrung her hands and moaned about everything going wrong. Pixie looked thoughtful. I yelled and threw myself forward, but for once, my intervention wasn't necessary. Adam plucked Spider off my father, separating the two men with an ominous growl. "There will be no fighting in my house!"

"It's not your house," Spider snapped (somewhat predictably, I thought), jerking himself out of Adam's hold. He straightened his shirt and tie with exaggerated, hostile motions.

Adam crossed his arms and looked immovable.

"You'll pay for that, Matthew," Spider warned as my father hustled over to stand at my side.

"It will be worth any price to ensure my ethereal brothers and sisters are free from your evil plans," Dad retorted.

"I have a spare one at home," Meredith told Spider as the former headed for the front door. "I'll go get it."

My father smiled. Adam smiled. Pixie's brow smoothed. Meredith looked confused when he tried to open the door but couldn't get it to budge. "Who locked this damned door?"

"It's not locked," Spider said, going over to lend a hand. The doorknob turned freely, but the door itself wouldn't open. "It's stuck. Wood must be swollen or something. The whole place needs to be torn down."

Although the pain was receding gradually, my head throbbed with every beat of my heart. I needed to lie down. Badly. The sooner Spider understood the situation, the sooner I could beg Adam for the use of a dark, quiet room. With an almost inhuman effort, I managed to get to a chair before collapsing. "You're wasting your time trying to get the door open. The house is sealed. Nothing can get in or out. Not so much as a mosquito will be able to pass through the seal for twelve hours, or more if Adam renews the seal before it is released. In other words, soon-to-be-ex-husband"—my lips curled as the irony of the situation struck me fully—"we're trapped here. All of us. *Together*."

"I think I'm going to be sick," Savannah said, sinking bonelessly into the nearest chair.

I knew just how she felt.

7

"This is a lot more interesting than anything my last foster family ever did." Pixie squatted next to me, her frown back in place as she looked at the spot on the rug where Sergei had writhed in agony before being destroyed. "Although I have to say, your husband is a dickwad."

"All that and so much more," I agreed. I leaned toward her to add in a soft voice, "I don't want you to be alone with Spider, OK?"

Her dark eyes examined me for a moment.

"He's not safe to be around by yourself," I said, sick at the thought of her being soiled by Spider's filth. "Just promise me you won't go off with him anywhere."

"Normally I don't take orders, but this time . . ." Her gaze flickered over to Spider before dropping. "He's really evil, isn't he?"

"Yes, I believe he is. If I'm not around, stay with Adam or my father, all right?"

She nodded.

I heaved myself from the chair. "I hate to be a party pooper, but my head is killing me, and I need to lie down in a dark room for a few minutes. Adam, would you mind if I borrowed a bedroom?"

"Upstairs, second door on the left," he said, his eyes a dangerous icy blue. "Take your shoes off before you lay down. My grandmother made the quilt on the bed."

"I'll help you up the stairs, darling," Spider said, his voice filled with threat despite the endearment. He grabbed my elbow and half pushed me up the stairs. "There are a few things I'd like to say to you."

"I have a fair number of items to discuss with you, too," I muttered under my breath. I didn't particularly care if anyone knew that Spider and I were arguing, but there were some things I would rather not say in front of witnesses.

Pixie started to follow us, but I waved her back. My father flitted over to introduce himself. I knew between him and Adam she would be safe from Spider's disgusting attentions.

Spider shoved me up the last few stairs with a couple of choice swear words.

"Take your hands off me," I snarled when we were out of everyone's sight. I jerked my arm away from him, but he just grabbed my wrist and hauled me into the room Adam had indicated.

"I'll touch you whenever and wherever I want," he spat, flinging me against the wall. I saw stars for a moment as my head cracked against it, but Spider's rubbing himself suggestively against me was what raised the nausea in my belly. "Don't pretend you don't want it. I know how hot you polter bitches are."

I swore under my breath, put both hands on his chest, and shoved as hard as I could. He stumbled backward and landed on the bed. He laughed and patted the bedspread. "See? Can't wait to get me into bed, can you?"

"Why did you bring that god-awful machine?" I asked, ignoring the taunts. "Why would you bring it if you arranged for me to clean the house?"

"Because I knew you wouldn't do it. I knew you'd simply move whatever parasites are living here to our house rather than destroy them as you should. Don't look so surprised; you don't seriously think you can pull anything over on me, do you? I've known all along about your little friends that you keep hidden whenever I'm around. I let you keep them because I knew the day would come when we'd need to test Meredith's machine."

"Why is it so important the entities be destroyed?" I asked, my arms wrapped around me to keep the pain and the guilt at bay. "The end result of a cleaning is the same: the house is empty of all Otherworld entities. Why does it matter *what* I do with the spirits I transport?"

"Because they're filthy, evil things," he said, slowly getting off the bed and stalking toward me. "They're unnatural freaks, just like you. The spirits are worthless, and the others, the poltergeists, like you and your family, are good only for one thing."

"Why did you ever marry me if you hate polters so much?" I couldn't help asking. I didn't want to get sidetracked by a discussion about our relationship, but I was genuinely curious. "I explained to you about my father before we were engaged. Why did you propose if you think I'm such a freak?"

He grabbed my hips before I could move, rubbing himself against me. "I told you, Karma: polters are hot. Very hot. The younger, the better, and you were very young when I met you. Not quite as succulent as that sweet little cousin of yours turned out to be, but still, enough to keep me happy for a bit."

"You bastard!" Rage unlike anything I'd ever felt filled me. I shoved him away, escaping to the other side of the room, the realization of what he was saying making me physically ill. "You had sex with Bethany? That's illegal!"

"She wasn't human. There's nothing in the laws that says minor polters can't have sex."

I swear to god, I was about to vomit on him. "She was fifteen, Spider! *Fifteen!* She was just a child!"

"Mmm." A repulsive smile curled his lips. "A very *sweet* fifteen. So limber. Limber enough for two, as Meredith and I found out."

I stared at him in horror, my skin crawling with the realization of what he was implying. "You mean that both of you . . ."

"Oh yes, both of us. Didn't you know? Meredith is my partner in all things, and he shares my taste in young polter flesh. You wouldn't believe the things your cousin did with us. We had a lot of fun, the three of us together. . . . But then she went and slit her throat. Stupid bitch."

I fell to the floor, retching up the contents of my stomach. I wanted to hide from what Spider was saying, but each word pierced my body with blade-like accuracy.

"You've looked better," he commented, strolling to the door. "Since you don't seem to be in the mood to talk, we will continue this discussion later. Meredith and I need to figure out what the hell we're going to do with this polter who thinks he can get the better of us. When will your kind learn who your masters are?"

I waited until the door closed before vomiting again.

"You look worse than ever," a female voice said from the shadows at the end of the corridor. The darkness parted as Pixie stepped forward. "Worse than roadkill, even."

"Thank you, that makes me feel infinitely better. Fortunately, the migraine has receded, so I can live with looking like roadkill. What are you doing hiding in the shadows?"

Her face was inscrutable as she approached me. "I dunno. I just seem to like them."

Most polters had an innate ability to blend into shadowed areas, making themselves all but invisible to mortal eyes . . . but somehow Pixie didn't seem to be aware of that. "Is there something you want to tell me?"

"Tell you?" She was the very picture of innocence. It redoubled my suspicion that something was up with her. "Like what? You're not going to third-degree me again, are you?"

"I've never third-degreed anyone, and I certainly wouldn't you, but I did want you to know that if there was something you wanted to tell me about yourself, I promise I wouldn't be judgmental."

She looked for a moment like she was going to speak, then shook her head. "You get to have your secrets, so I get to have mine, too."

"Fair enough. What have you been doing while I was out of things?"

"*Deus*, you just *said* you weren't going to question

me! I wasn't doing anything, all right? I was over there in the shadows!"

An icy chill, spiked with guilt so thick it choked me, gripped my guts. "Did Spider follow you?"

"No." Her eyes avoided mine, but she flitted around in a manner that said she was agitated about something. "You're an exterminator, right? Can you do the reverse? Can you bring Sergei back?"

A shaft of pain cut through me—but not the familiar pain of a migraine. This was sadness and remorse, heavily painted with guilt. "I don't know. It depends on what that machine that Spider had did to him; if it sent Sergei to the Akasha, then there is a chance he can be retrieved. If it actually destroyed him . . ." I sighed.

"That'll suck if you can't. Sergei was kinda cool, even if he was a grunt."

"He wasn't a grunt, and yes, he was cool." I looked at the towel twisted between my hands, forcing myself to relax them and toss the towel into a hamper. "If it makes you feel any better, Spider will pay for what he's done."

"That's a given," Pixie said, an odd look on her face that cleared quickly when she realized I was watching her. "So, what now?"

"Now we go down and see how we can clear up this mess. Where is everyone? What's been going on?" I walked quickly to the stairs, then paused at the top to listen for sounds of arguing. To my surprise, there were none.

"Do I look like some sort of personal-information slave?" Pixie flounced past me down the stairs. "They're down there, I guess. I came up to escape the Monster from the Planet Flower Child. Oh, by the way, your dad is cool."

I stopped at the bottom of the stairs. "He is?"

"Yeah." She twirled a strand of long black hair around her fingers and peeked at me from the corner of her eye. "He told me if she gets too nosy, I can flash at her."

My jaw dropped a hair. "Flash?"

"Yeah, you know, turn on and off really fast. Matthew says it unnerves mortals."

"You mean flicker?" I put my arm on hers, stopping her for a second. "Pixie, what's going on here?"

She pulled her arm away, a wary look on her face. "I don't know what's with you, but you're acting weird."

"I'm acting weird? I'm not the one who doesn't understand basic polter abilities like flickering and shadow melding. You act as if you don't know anything about being a polter."

"*Deus!* You're so nosy! I hate it here! I just want to be left alone! Why can't you leave me alone?"

The anguish in her voice—genuine anguish, not the normal put-upon teen whine—stopped me from pursuing the issue. "I'm sorry. I seem to be pushing a lot of your buttons tonight, don't I? We'll leave it for now, all right? As to the flickering—no. Savannah is bad enough without you displaying the more showstopping polter abilities."

"Matthew said you'd say that," she answered, apparently appeased by my apology. "He said that it's against my civil rights for you to tell me I can't celebrate my heritage by flickering."

"Oh, for god's sake . . ." I grabbed her arm and

stopped her before she could reenter the living room. "My father is not responsible for you; I am. At least . . . well, we'll worry about that later. I'm in charge, and I say no flickering. Got it?"

She tipped her head to the side. "When are we going to leave?"

I blinked at the change of subject. "I don't know. It depends on Adam, I guess. Do you want to leave?"

She watched me silently for a moment.

"We'll go as soon as it's possible, OK? And . . . er . . . about the future . . . I know you're supposed to stay with me a month while we see how we suit each other, but I'm afraid that's not going to happen."

Her eyes narrowed, filled with suspicion and pain. "You don't want me, do you? No one ever does. It's OK. I'm used to it," she said with an attempt at an indifferent shrug.

I felt about as low as a snail's belly. The poor kid desperately needed to find a permanent home, but the sooner she realized that couldn't be with me, the happier we'd all be. "It has nothing to do with not wanting you to live with me. It's just that things are a bit complicated right now, and what with Spider . . . well, you're not going to be able to stay. I'm very sorry. I'll talk to Mrs. Beckett as soon as the seal is lifted."

"Whatever," she said with another shrug.

Guilt, anguish, dread, and many other emotions that had been stirred up in the last few hours made my stomach roil, but there was nothing I could do.

"Thank god you're here," a low male voice rumbled from behind, distracting me from my personal hell.

Pixie turned her attention to the man marching toward us, his jaw set, his light eyes flashing pale blue. "He looks pissed again."

"He certainly does. It seems to be a normal state for him."

Pixie snickered as Adam stopped in front of us. "Your father I can deal with; I know how to keep him occupied. But that woman—" He waved a hand toward the closed double doors in front of us. "You're not going to believe what she wants to do."

"That bad, is it?" I asked, raising my eyebrows.

"Yes. I had to order the ghosts and Amanita to stay hidden so she wouldn't see them. Not that they're of a mind to come out while an exterminator is present." He paused, eyeing me carefully. "You didn't rest for long. Did it help your headache?"

"Incredibly so. Oh, before I forget: I owe you for a towel. I'm afraid I was sick in the bedroom, and I threw away the towel I used to clean up."

"Yuck!" Pixie said.

"I have bigger things to worry about than a towel," Adam said grimly.

"Oh, there you are!" Savannah slid open the double doors and hurried over to us. "Head better? You look much more animated, and not nearly so pale. You're just in time, too. We need to get started in the next three minutes. Obsidian Angel, you must join us, as well."

Savannah's hand clamped around my wrist as she dragged me into the large living room that took up the entire width of the house. The decor was the same as in the sitting room—clunky, uncomfortable-looking Victorian furniture, lots of china, muddy paintings on the wall, and dark, heavy velvet curtains at the windows. It was slightly less dusty in here than in the sitting room, but it clearly hadn't seen a good spring cleaning in a few years.

"I'm just in time for what?"

"You sit here, Karma, next to me. Obsidian, on Karma's left. Matthew . . . Now where did he go? Matthew?"

My father, his eyes avoiding mine, flitted in through the far door, wearing an air of suppressed excitement. I wondered what he'd been up to. "Right here. I wanted to have a look around the place." A faint pattering followed my father as he hurried over to us.

Adam bent to pick up a small smooth stone, looking at it curiously before narrowing his eyes at Dad. I did the same. My father normally had unusually good control over things like apports.

"Excellent. Now we just need Meredith and Spider, and we can get the séance started. Matthew, you're on my right. I've never had a real poltergeist in my circle before, so I expect great things with three and a half polters!" she said, beaming at us all.

My father beamed back at her, taking her hand in two of his own. "I am honored."

"We can even call one of your kind, if you like! Wouldn't that be an experience!"

"I suppose, although I can't think of anyone I'd like to see right now," Dad said after a moment's consideration.

She squeezed his hands, then moved to the doorway and opened the door to bellow toward the stairs, "Meredith! Séance! Bring Mr. Marx!" before turning back to us with another of her sunny smiles. "Meredith should be right along. Shall we take our places?"

"I'm not sure a séance is really such a good idea," I said, not wanting to participate, but not sure how to avoid it without offending her.

"Sit!" she ordered.

I gave in and sat. Hopefully it would be over quickly.

"Adam, if you could sit across from me, that would be lovely."

"Er . . . you don't really need me, since you already have the others," Adam said, clearly trying to get out of the séance.

"Nonsense! I don't know much about poltergeists, but I am guessing that the more of you we have, the better our chances at making contact," Savannah said, giving him such a pointed look he reluctantly pulled out one of the dining room chairs she'd set around a large round table.

"Misery loves company," I murmured to him as I sat to the left of Savannah's place. "I'm surprised you're giving in to her, though."

"I think she'll continue to nag if I don't," he answered, then cocked an eyebrow as he asked, "What's got you looking so confused?"

"I don't exactly know. I've got a horrible feeling that Savannah just said something I should have paid attention to, but I can't figure out what it is."

"What was the something about?"

I shook my head. "I don't know. It's just . . . have you ever had a feeling like something important was said, but you missed it?"

"No."

"Then you're lucky. Somehow, I feel like she said something that I wanted to think about, but I was distracted, and now it's gone."

"It'll come back to you." He watched Savannah at the door for a moment. "Will you come with me when I try to talk to your husband?"

"Sure, although I doubt it will do any good. He seldom listens to me in the best of circumstances."

He gave me a long look with his icy blue eyes.

"Spider is extremely stubborn; I'm just warning you of that."

"I intend to make him see reason."

"Well, we can but try. Pixie, what on earth are you doing?"

"It's *Obsidian Angel*! *Deus*, you have the memory of an *ice cube*!"

"Fine, Obsidian Angel, what are you doing with that bar of soap?"

"Drawing a circle, *obviously*." The look she gave me said in no uncertain terms what she thought of my IQ. "So we can summon a ghoul. I'd give *anything* to be able to talk to a real ghoul."

"You wouldn't get much talking done before it tried to strip the flesh off your bones," Adam said under his breath. "Stop rubbing soap on my floor."

She threw down the bar of soap with a muttered oath. "You people are Nazis! First you question me; now you're telling me what to do! What's next, the rack? Hot irons? Bamboo under my fingernails?"

"That's tempting . . . ," Adam said, giving her a gimlet eye.

She threw herself into a chair, arms crossed, her expression hostile.

"Honestly, men! And they say women take forever. Shall I go over the procedures while we wait for Meredith and Mr. Marx?" Savannah asked, coming back to the table. I stopped fidgeting and tried to put a pleasant expression on my face, but judging by the sympathetic looks my father was sending my way, I was afraid my reluctance was all too apparent.

Savannah chatted for a few moments about the sé-ance, what she would be doing, along with our role in the proceedings.

"It sounds pretty straightforward. Does your group do many séances?" A thought struck me. I glanced at my watch.

"Only when we have a truly promising location, like this wonderful house."

"Ah. Um . . . what happened to your group?"

She blinked at me. "I beg your pardon?"

"Your group, the PMSers. You said they were due here at eleven, yes? It's a quarter to midnight. They must have discovered by now that they can't get into the house, and are probably worried sick about your safety."

"Oh!" She beamed a happy smile at me. "You're sweet to worry, but there's absolutely no need. I called Mac—he's the vice president—a little bit ago and told him the event was canceled."

"Ah. You must have a cell phone?"

She made a little face. "Goddess, no! I am a complete technophobe. No cell phone or computer for me. I prefer to do things the old-fashioned way. I used Adam's phone to call Mac." She leaned toward me, lowering her voice. "I didn't think it was wise to tell them *everything* that's happened here."

"I'm sure that's for the best. Things are confusing enough." I met Adam's gaze. He raised both eyebrows, indicating he'd caught Savannah's lie. The sealing he had enacted affected the structure of the house—including the landline. A cell phone could get out, but not a phone with lines physically inside the house.

She clearly didn't know that, but her ignorance highlighted the question of why on earth she had lied about phoning someone. Evidently Adam didn't think it was a big deal. I wondered if her group could be quite as enthusiastic as she was. Perhaps no one had shown up, and she decided to cover up that fact by making it seem she'd sent them away.

Then again, maybe she had an ulterior motive for making us think she was a member of a psychic group when she wasn't. . . . I shook my head at such unfounded suspicions. I'd been around my father too long and was obviously seeing mysteries where there were none.

After a desultory bit of conversation dropped off entirely, Savannah tsked at her watch and frowned at the door. "Where can they be? You said they couldn't get out?"

"No. The house is sealed," Adam said. "No one will get in or out until Spider agrees to go to a mediator about the house."

"I hope you have plenty of food stocked up, because that could be a very long time," I warned.

"I'm working on it. I've got a call in to my lawyer."

"Well, just so long as this sealing is finished by morning, I'm fine with it," Savannah said, blithely unaware of the glances Adam and I were exchanging. Clearly she had no concept of just what Adam had done.

"Do you want to tell her, or should I?" I asked him.

"Tell me what?" she asked, looking from me to Adam.

"This ought to be good," Pixie told my father as

he returned from the bathroom. He just smiled happily at her.

Adam cleared his throat. "You'll probably do it better than me. I'm not good with explanations."

"That's a cop-out if I ever heard one," my father said.

Unable to sit next to Savannah while I worked out a way to tell her what was going on, I got out of the chair and went over to the fireplace, then fiddled with the porcelain figurines on the mantelpiece.

"What are you talking about?" Savannah asked. "What do you need to tell me? Why is Karma so nervous?"

"I'm not nervous, I'm just . . . oh, never mind. The sealing that Adam has conducted won't be over in a few hours," I said, moving on to the window. "Adam is a member of a powerful group of people in the Otherworld."

"Otherworld?" She frowned.

I tidied up a collection of postcards in a bowl on the sideboard. "It's a collective name for those people who aren't mortal. There's a French term for it, too, but I can never pronounce it. Most people call it the Otherworld. Adam is a part of that, and as such, he has powers that go beyond those of mortal people. Seals last for twelve hours."

"But I have appointments in the morning!" Savannah said hotly. "I have things to do! I can't stay here in this house for another ten or eleven hours! Why can't this Otherworld place make Spider give back the house?"

"I'm hoping we can clear this up by mundane legal means, without involving the Otherworld any fur-

ther," Adam said with a frown at me as he re-
arranged the things I had just tidied.

She didn't looked soothed by his words. "I don't
care. I'm not going to stay here once the sun is up.
My husband will have something to say about that,
as well. Meredith! *Meredith!* Oh, where is that
man . . . ?" She jumped up and headed out the door,
calling for her husband.

"We aren't going to have the séance?" Pixie asked,
pouting just a little.

"Apparently we have to wait for the two men,"
Dad said.

"Dammit," Adam said. He got up and started after
Savannah. "They'd better not be doing anything to
harm the house, or there *will* be hell to pay."

"I don't want to miss this," my father said, leaping
up to follow Adam. Pixie sighed, tucked away her
iPod, and ran to the stairs leading to the basement.

I grabbed the back of my father's shirt just before
he reached the stairs, and whispered in his ear, "I
want to have a couple of words with you."

"About what?" he asked, still not meeting my
eyes. He fairly twitched at being in my grip. I released him, frowning.

"What's wrong with you? What have you been
up to?"

"Why do I have to be up to anything?" he asked,
straightening his shirt with exaggerated care.

"Because you're nervous as a scalded toad. You
can't stand still, your eyes are shifty, and you were
apporting earlier when you came into the room.
What were you doing when I came downstairs?"

"You are not the police. I do not have to answer

your questions," my father said, tossing his head and inching toward the top stair.

I grabbed his arm to keep him from continuing. "No, but Adam is, and he's suspicious enough from me telling him you're up to mischief."

"I have better things to do than submit to your inquisition." He yanked his arm from my grasp and hurried down the stairs to the basement.

I was right behind him. "That's only part of what I wanted to talk to you about. Spider said something earlier that I think is important."

"Spider did?" He stopped so quickly, I ran into his back.

"Yes. Did you know he was having sex with Bethany?"

The horrified expression on my father's face said it all.

I nodded. "I think the police would like to know about that."

Dad swore in Poltern, the half-knocking, half-clicking poltergeist language that was so often mistaken by mortals as spirit rapping.

"I agree one hundred percent, Dad. But . . . do you think we should leave it for the mundane police? We could bring in the watch, since it involved Bethany, and you know as well as I do that the watch would take a much sterner view of the situation, since they have fewer legal issues to work through. If we could let Adam deal with the situation, it might be quicker and easier."

"We won't have to wait for Adam or the rest of the watch. Your uncle will geld Spider," Dad whispered as we stepped into a dimly lit long L-shaped room.

"He'll have to get in line. I plan on doing a little neutering myself," I said, the need to see justice done leaving an acid taste in my mouth.

"Meredith? What on earth are you doing down here?" Ahead of us Savannah stood with hands on hips as she peered around the cluttered basement. Two naked bulbs dangled from the ceiling, casting not very much light on the area. The basement seemed to be filled with the detritus of the house's lifetime: a modern washer and dryer were next to the door, but beyond them I could see an old-fashioned washer and wring board, a winepress, several broken wooden chairs, wooden crates stacked to the ceiling, lawn equipment, and assorted large bulky bits of furniture.

My father nodded toward a rusty scythe that was held against the wall by a stack of boxes bearing bricks, old weight-lifting equipment, and several iron fireplace implements. "Just the thing for a neutering."

"Tempting," I whispered back to him. "I think we should tell Adam what Spider was doing with Bethany, and let the watch deal with the whole thing."

Dad shook his head. "I'm not sure it would do any good. Adam seems a bit preoccupied with his own problems. Besides which, would he see sex with a minor polter as just cause to tackle a mortal? It's difficult enough for the Akashic League to punish one of them; perhaps he wouldn't want to get involved in that."

"They will take on mortals if the situation warrants their intervention, and I definitely think this does," I said quietly, my heart filled with so much anguish I wanted to sit down and sob. "Adam's going to be our only hope. We have to make him understand what happened, so he can see that justice is done."

"I don't think there will be any problem in finding people who have a score to settle with Spider," Dad replied as he trailed after me.

Ahead of us, Adam, Savannah, and Pixie paused, looking around the room. There was no one else to be seen.

"I like this basement," Pixie said, examining a large stuffed vulture that lurched drunkenly on a metal seaman's trunk. "There are some nice things here."

"Are you sure they're down here?" Savannah asked Adam. "Maybe they slipped out the back way?"

"No one can enter or leave," Adam answered, his eyes narrowing as he pushed past a stack of boxes. "There's a door on the other side. If they broke it trying to get out . . ."

"Meredith?" Savannah picked her way around miscellaneous boxes to the part of the room kitty-corner to us. "I insist that you come out from wherever you're hiding. Are you over he— Oh, dear goddess! Nooo!"

There wasn't much room to move in the basement. Adam stopped next to a small rowboat that leaned against the wall, his large body blocking the view. I hurried up behind him, peering over his shoulder, gasping in surprise at the sight before us.

Savannah was on her knees, pulling large black bound books off the body of her husband, her sobs alternating with a chantlike prayer.

"Good lord. Is he all right?" I asked, squatting next to her when Adam moved to the other side. A huge dark bookcase lay on the floor, propped up by a small mountain of books. "Dad, use my cell phone to call an aid unit. Pixie, go upstairs. Here, Savannah, let me help you. . . ."

It took us only a few seconds to clear off Meredith. Although the books themselves were heavy—they looked to be an ancient set of encyclopedias—he hadn't been struck with the bookcase itself.

"Is he dead?" Pixie's voice sounded strained.

I shot a frown at her over my shoulder. "This is no place for you. Go upstairs, please."

"I'm *not* a *child*! Besides, I've seen dead bodies before."

"You *what*? When?"

She wore her inscrutable look. "I've seen a lot of reality shows about homicides and stuff."

"Thank the goddess, he's alive," Savannah said, her voice choked as she wiped blood off her husband's face.

I pulled my attention from Pixie to the man lying before us. "I've had some first aid training. Let me just have a quick look at him so we can inform the paramedics of his injuries."

Meredith's eyes opened at that point.

"What the hell is going on?" he asked, his face twisted in pain, as he raised a hand to his head. "Dammit, what hit me?"

I lifted a volume of the encyclopedia. "Belize to Byzantine, I think. Do you hurt anywhere other than your head?"

"No. Stop fussing over me, woman," he said, pushing Savannah back as he sat up. She ignored him and continued to wipe off his face as he snarled at the rest of us, "What the hell happened? The last thing I remember is trying to open that damned door, then someone walloped me on the head."

My father hurried into the room. "Which paramedics do I call? Mortal, or Otherworld? Will they be able to get in with the house sealed?"

I sat on my heels, my fingers on Meredith's wrist as I eyed his head. There was a cut above his eyebrow that no doubt was the cause of all the blood, but his pulse was strong and steady. "Are you seeing double? Do you feel nauseous at all?"

"I'm fine, or I would be if everyone would stop hovering around me. I have a hell of a headache is all."

"Karma," Adam said from where he squatted next to the downed bookcase.

"Just a sec. I'm just making sure Meredith is OK. Squeeze my hand," I said, shoving my hand into his. He squeezed it hard enough to cause me to wince. "I don't think you have a concussion, but you should probably see your doctor, anyway. You may need a stitch or two in that cut on your forehead."

"So I'm not calling the paramedics?" Dad asked, looking from me to Meredith, who was getting to his feet with the assistance of Savannah.

"Karma, come over here," Adam said.

"Luckily, I don't think there's a need for one," I told my father, standing up and dusting my knees. The basement wasn't filthy, but the books were dusty enough to have my nose wrinkling. I looked around that corner of the basement. The door that Adam had mentioned was visible behind an old-fashioned icebox, but it didn't appear to have been opened in several decades. "Where did Spider go?"

"I swear to god, I'm going to get a bullhorn to

make people listen to me," Adam groused from the other side of the room.

"Oh. Sorry," I said, carefully stepping over stacks of fallen encyclopedias to go to him. "What did you want?"

"Does this look familiar?" he asked, gesturing toward a mound of books.

A hand could be glimpsed amongst them, a hand wearing a familiar gold watch. A chill swept down my spine as I realized what it was I was looking at. "That's . . . that's Spider's watch."

"Yes." Adam's icy blue eyes were unreadable. He gently touched Spider's wrist. "There's no pulse. Your husband is dead."

Pixie's gaze shifted from Spider's hand to me, her eyebrows upraised.

"The hell he is!" Meredith said, sitting down abruptly in an old cane rocker.

Savannah gasped and wrung her hands.

"Thank god," my father said softly.

I said nothing, just stared at the hand and wondered how the world could change with just a few words.

9

A peculiar, distant sort of numbness set in as I looked down at Spider. Pixie stood next to me, the picture of silent unhappiness, her arms wrapped around herself. I wanted to get her out of there, to shield her from the ugliness of Spider's death, but I seemed to be unable to stir myself.

My father and Adam had no problem in hoisting the huge bookcase off Spider's remains.

"That thing must weigh five hundred pounds," Meredith commented from his chair. Savannah, once she had ascertained there was nothing to be done for Spider, had run upstairs for some water to wash the blood from her husband's face. She knelt next to him now, dabbing at the cut on his forehead.

"They're poltergeists," I said absently.

"So?"

"Hmm? Oh, sorry." I gave him a quick wry smile. "Polters can summon brief spurts of great strength if needed. It's sort of a racial trait."

"The question is," my father said in Poltern as he

lifted one end of the bookcase, "did it fall over itself, or did he pull it down?"

I didn't answer. The three of us who could understand my father all glanced with speculation at Meredith, however.

A handful of small pebbles fell from the ceiling as Adam grunted with effort when he and my father shoved the now upright bookcase against the wall.

"Apports?" Savannah asked as I gathered up the tiny rocks. Half were white; half were grayish granite-colored, flecked with silver. I looked around the room, depositing them in an ugly urn that sat on a shelf next to antiquated kitchen appliances. "I'm sorry; this probably isn't the time to ask, but can I—?"

"Sure." I gave her the urn, hesitating at the sight of the mound of books. Now that the heavy bookcase was off it, parts of Spider were visible beneath the volumes.

"Oooh, these are pretty. I assume the different colors come from different poltergeists?" Savannah asked, having poured the apports into her hand.

I frowned. I really didn't want to talk with Savannah as if nothing momentous had just happened, but I knew that people reacted differently to stress. Clearly she was in the "distract yourself" camp when faced with a dead man. "Yes. My father's are the silver ones. Adam's are white. Each are unique to their owner."

"Fascinating. I like the jade green ones. Do you mind if I keep them for research purposes?"

"Go right ahead." I steeled myself to approach Spider's body. I didn't have the luxury of avoiding the reality of the situation.

"Is he going to be all bloody and guts spilling out and brains bashed in when you take the books off him?" Pixie asked in a hushed voice.

Guilt spiked through the odd numbness that held me in its grip. "Pixie, I'm sorry. This really isn't something you should see." I gave her a little hug, gently escorting her to the turning in the room. "Why don't you go upstairs?"

"Are you kidding?" She pulled away from me, giving me a look that questioned my sanity. "This is *great*! I've never seen a dead body in person before! I've always wanted to, and now you're trying to *ruin* my life! You can't make me leave! I'll tell Mrs. Beckett that you're abusing me if you do!"

"Now, that is one strange kid," Meredith said from the depths of a battered, paint-splattered leather chair.

I just gawked at the teenager for a few moments, then shook my head. "I can't imagine how seeing my dead husband is going to fulfill a life's ambition, but if you're truly not horrified about what's happened, I guess you can stay."

"Why would I be horrified? It's just like the TV shows. Besides, your husband was mean. It's like justice that he got killed after he killed Sergei. It's . . . karma."

Five pairs of eyes turned to look at me.

"So to speak," she said with a tepid smile.

I took a deep breath and knelt to pull books off Spider's body.

"Honey?" My father gently touched my hair.

"I'm all right. Let's just get these off him. I know Adam checked for a pulse, but he may be barely alive or something. . . ."

No one spoke as Adam, Dad, and I uncovered the body of my husband.

"He's so still," I said, half to myself, as I pulled a book from his chest. In fact, the stillness of the body gave credence to Adam's statement: Spider was dead. I averted my eyes from Spider's face as Adam uncovered it, bracing myself for what could well be a grisly sight, but to my surprise, there were no blood, no marks whatsoever.

Adam leaned down to listen at Spider's chest. He looked up and shook his head. "I'm sorry."

I didn't know what to say to that. As a rule I didn't lie, but it seemed incredibly crass to brush off Spider's demise with a curt "I'm not." So I said nothing, just looked at the empty shell that had been my husband, and wondered at what point during the past twelve years Spider had changed from a man I loved to someone whose passing left me feeling nothing inside.

"Was he crushed to death, do you think?" I asked, hesitant to check Spider's arms, legs, and rib cage for apparent broken bones. "Shouldn't he have some sort of marks on him? That bookcase looks heavy."

"It is, and he should." Adam evidently didn't share my qualms. He gave Spider's remains a quick examination. "There are markings on his throat and face."

I wasn't the only one who watched with a morbid curiosity as he went over Spider's arms and legs before returning his attention to Spider's head. "His head isn't bashed in, is it?" Pixie asked.

He frowned, glancing over his shoulder to where she hovered with bright, interested eyes. "Stay back."

I leaned forward to look at what had caught his attention. Nothing caught my eye.

"Heart attack, do you think?" my father asked.

"No. There's no way this scene could be created

by him simply falling down. We won't know what killed him until the autopsy, although the marks on his neck could indicate he was strangled." Adam's eyes were filled with glacial fury. "I do know this: whoever killed him used *my* basement to do the job!"

"Whoever . . ." Unbidden, my gaze slid over to where Meredith was having his head bandaged by Savannah.

Adam's jaw tightened as he stood up. "I'm going to have to call the office."

"Can I see? Is it gory?" Pixie asked, standing on tiptoe, as if that would enable her to see Spider. "It will be traumatic for me if you don't let me see."

"It will be more traumatic if I bend you over my knee and paddle your butt for not doing as I say," Adam answered.

Her mouth dropped open. "That's child abuse!"

"Which office are you calling?" I asked, trying to rid myself of the image of Spider's body.

Adam thought for a moment, then shrugged. "I suppose both. The watch won't be so bad, but I hate to have to explain to my mortal boss why a U.S. marshal has a murdered man in his basement."

"Then don't."

We both turned in surprise to look at my father. "You can't be serious, Dad."

"Sure, I'm serious. No one is going to miss Spider. Why do you have to report his death? We can just bury him somewhere isolated, and Karma can report him missing. After a while, the cops will stop looking for him."

"Ignore him," I told Adam. "He was raised by hyenas. How on earth are you going to explain to the marshal people about the sealing?"

He ran his hand through his hair. Despite the bizarre situation, I couldn't help feeling sorry for him. Spider had been nothing but trouble to him while he was alive, and now he was even more so dead.

"I don't know. I'll have to think on it. We have more than ten hours before the seal is up. Right now, there are more important things to take care of." He pulled a tattered green blanket out of a small wooden chest and laid it over Spider. "It's cooler down here than anywhere else in the house. Unless you have strong objections, I'd like to leave him where he is."

I allowed him to pull me to my feet. "No, that's fine. I imagine the police won't be happy if we disturb the scene any more than it has been."

"No, they won't."

"I think you're making a mistake," my father said. "Leave sleeping dogs lie; that's my policy. Or in this case, let dead insects lay."

"Not funny, and not helping," I told him.

He gave me a feeble smile.

"You guys are all mean," Pixie said, her lower lip mutinous as I pushed her toward Savannah and Meredith. Adam moved to a corner and pulled out a cell phone.

"Yes, we are. Deal with it." I assumed Adam was calling the captain of the watch. I stopped in front of Meredith, looking at him with dispassionate eyes. "What exactly happened down here?"

"I didn't kill Spider, if that's what you're about to accuse me of doing," he snapped, pushing his wife away, the better to glare at me. "That's not to say I wouldn't have earlier, but I didn't kill him."

"So you admit you wanted to kill him?" Dad asked.

"No!" Meredith said quickly, confusion tingeing his belligerence. "You're twisting my words! I just meant that he could be obstinate about some things. Sure, I wanted to punch him in the face sometimes, but I want to punch a lot of people, and you don't see me doing it, do you?"

"You were down here alone with him," I pointed out. "He was killed. It seems entirely possible to me that he struggled with you, and the bookcase was pulled over, knocking you out cold and finishing the job on Spider."

"I don't care what seems possible to you! I didn't kill anyone, let alone my partner!"

"You don't have to yell; we're right in front of you," Dad said.

I shushed him.

"I'll tell you what I was doing. I'll tell you once, because you're his wife . . . widow. But that's it, do you understand? I'm not saying anything else until I can talk to my lawyer." Meredith took a deep breath and ignored Savannah, who was plucking at his arm. "Jesus, stop looking at me like that! Spider and I came down here to find a way out of this godforsaken house. There wasn't room for us both to try to break down the door, so I stood back while Spider used the crowbar on it. While I was watching, someone sneaked up behind me and belted me on the head. That's the last thing I remember until Savannah started crying on me."

"Sounds fishy to me," Dad said.

Pixie nodded. "Totally."

I looked back toward the far wall. There were books everywhere, and a couple of boxes containing

Christmas lights had been spilled, but I didn't see anything else. "What crowbar?"

"What crowbar? What do you mean 'what crowbar'? The crowbar Spider was using!"

"Meredith, you must calm down! Your blood pressure is probably sky-high by now," Savannah said, a pleading note in her voice.

"There's no crowbar here," I said, waving toward the door.

"What the hell . . . ? It was right there! Spider had it!"

"Maybe it's under his body," my father suggested. "I'll be happy to have a peek. . . ."

"Don't touch anything!" Adam called from the other side of the room. "My captain is going to be screaming at me as is."

"Then a little more won't hurt, will it?" Before anyone could stop him, Dad pushed Spider up on his side. "Nope, no crowbar."

"It must be there!" Meredith raged. "I saw him with it! He was using it to pry open the damned door!"

"Well, it's gone now," I said slowly.

"Someone must have taken it!"

"Yes," I said. He looked ready to explode, his face red and slightly sweating. I wondered if he had a bad heart.

Adam, finished with his call, came over to us just in time to catch the flash of anger in Meredith's eyes. "We need to preserve what's left of the crime scene. We'll go upstairs, where we can talk about this quietly."

"I'd just like to know what sort of game you people are playing with me!" Meredith snarled before marching resolutely up the stairs, Savannah hot on his heels. Dad took Pixie's arm and followed them. I stood over Spider's body for a moment. So many deaths, so much sadness and sorrow. With each death, the world changed a little bit, and those of us who were left to deal with the consequences could only stand by and wonder what the future held. I sent a little prayer before slowly walking toward the stairs.

Adam was waiting for me. "The captain said we need to clear this up before we call in the mundane police."

"*We?*" I asked, not surprised that the Otherworld police force would want things straightened out before the mortal world became involved. The "we," however, took me by surprise.

"Yes. I told them who you were. The captain said that as long as you weren't a suspect, I could deputize you to help investigate the murder. Consider yourself as having the official blessing."

"We have a little more than ten hours to make things perfectly clear."

"Yes." His gaze was as somber as mine probably was. "Think we can do it?"

I bit my lower lip as I looked at him. He seemed to me to be a competent man, and a fair one. I believed that he really did want to see justice done. But there was so much at stake, and so little time to put things right. . . . "There's a murderer to bring to justice. I don't think we have a choice but to do it."

He nodded, stopping me as I was about to go up the stairs. "I have to ask this: where were you for the last hour?"

10

I will admit that my response to Adam's surprising question was to gape at him openmouthed. "Didn't you just say I *wasn't* a suspect?"

"This is to satisfy me. You're an officer of the Akashic League, and I'm fully willing to deputize you, but first I need to hear where you were, and what you were doing."

"I suppose that's fair. Let's see . . . I went upstairs earlier with a bad headache. Spider came with me, just to argue, as it turned out. I was feeling sick, and after I started vomiting, he left. I went to the bathroom to clean up, tried to relax on the bed, and finally gave up. Do you really think I would murder Spider?"

"Not really," he answered, shaking his head. "You're a smart woman. I assume if you wanted to knock off your husband, you'd do so in a much more elegant manner."

I smiled at that. "That's a backhanded compliment if I've ever heard one, but sadly, it's true. If I were planning Spider's murder, I would use an untraceable poison, and have a roomful of people to give me an alibi, not be throwing up by myself. Do you believe Meredith?"

"Do you?" He gestured for me to continue up the stairs.

"I don't know." I gave a half shrug. "He seems earnest, but there was no one else down here with Spider. If not Meredith, then who?"

"That's what I intend to find out. We'll talk to everyone separately, and hopefully come to a conclusion before I have to call in the local police."

Just as we reached the top of the stairs, a small rustling noise behind us had me freezing. Horror skittered up my spine.

"What the . . . Did you hear that?" Adam asked in a whisper.

I turned to look back at the basement. "Yes. Are there rodents down here?"

"No."

The age-old fear of the unknown kept my feet planted firmly on the stairs as Adam ran down them and stalked across the length of the basement to stop next to a hulking, antiquated oil furnace.

"All right, you can come out. We know you're hiding back there."

For a moment silence greeted his command, then the hairs on my arm stood on end as a shadowy form separated itself from the depths behind the furnace. My breath came out in a gush as the figure stepped into the dim light.

"For god's sake, you just about gave me a heart attack," Adam growled.

The woman who stood before him turned frightened eyes on me. "Are you going to let her destroy us the way that other spirit was destroyed?" Amanita asked in a breathy voice.

Poor thing. She looked scared half to death. I held my hands wide, to show I meant no harm. "Of course he's not. I wouldn't have destroyed you even if I had gone ahead with the cleaning; I'd just have moved you to somewhere safe. Sergei's death was . . ." I avoided looking at the blanket-covered mound. "It was not my doing."

"What the hell are you doing hiding down here?" Adam asked, his voice rough, but with an undertone of concern that warmed my still-numb heart.

"I didn't want the exterminator to find me. Tony said we had to hide really well so she wouldn't take us like the man who took the domovoi. So I hid down here, behind the furnace."

Adam's gaze touched mine before turning back to her. "Did you see or hear anything while you were hiding?"

I had heard that unicorns, by nature, were rather skittish. And who could blame them? Their entire history was filled with persecution by mortals who believed they held the key to immortality. Amanita seemed typical of her people, shy and easily startled. Her face was white, her large gray eyes resembling those of a startled fawn. But it was her voice—a whisper filled with unspoken horror—that had me putting an arm around her in sympathy. To my relief, she didn't pull away from me.

"There were voices. The man named Spider came. And the other one. I hid."

"Did you see anything?" Adam repeated.

She shook her head, leaning into me, shivers rack-ing her body. I wondered if she was suffering from shock. "No. But it was frightening. The two men were talking about leaving, then there was a funny noise, like a struggle, and Spider said something about things being all his when the other one was gone. Then nothing. I was too afraid to come out."

"He said *what*?" Adam asked.

Amanita looked even more frightened. "I don't remember!"

"You do too. Think, Nita. This is important. What exactly did Spider say before it went quiet?"

She wrung her hands together, her face so pale I thought she would pass out.

"Maybe we should do this another time," I murmured.

"No," Adam said, shaking his head. He spoke calmly, his eyes intense but his voice soft as he took Amanita's hands in his. "She can do this. Think back to that moment, Nita. What did the two men say?"

She swallowed a couple of times, clearly trying to focus. "The one said he didn't think they could get out. Spider said, 'I'll be damned if I stay here any longer.' Then there were the struggling sounds, and Spider said . . . I think he said, 'It'll all be mine when you're gone.' Or something like that."

"Who was he talking to, did he say?" Adam asked.

"No. No one said anything else, I swear!"

Adam made her go over the brief conversation a couple more times, but she insisted that was all she had heard. She was becoming more and more distraught with each passing moment, however.

Adam opened his mouth to say something else, caught my eye, and simply told Amanita to go upstairs to the kitchen to wait for the other spirits. "We'll talk to you again a little later."

She nodded and hurried off.

"All right, she's gone. Now, why did you give me a look that practically yelled an objection?" Adam asked.

"She was about ready to have a nervous breakdown. Even you must have seen she was nearly frightened out of her wits. It would have been cruel to press her further."

"She's always frightened about something. She's a unicorn! Haven't you ever been around them?"

"Not really, no."

"They've been hunted for centuries, with the end result being that they stay mainly to themselves. They don't like strangers, loud noises, or crowds," Adam said.

"That's understandable, but this wasn't normal fear. I think she needs some time to pull herself together."

He gave me a gentle push up the stairs. "Did it occur to you at all that you might have had me send a murderer off on her own?"

"A murderer!" I stopped at the top of the stairs and looked down on him. He shooed me forward, clicked off the light, and locked the basement door. "Amanita? You can't be serious! She's your own ward!"

"I am very serious, and I know who she is. She was down there with him—what's to stop her from bashing Meredith on the head, and killing Spider?"

I shook my head. "I can't believe you'd think that about someone who looks to you for protection. She's not at all the type to kill someone. Even if she could—and I don't think a woman would have the strength to strangle Spider—there's no earthly reason why she should want him dead. She hadn't even met him!"

"They all knew Spider destroyed your domovoi."

I remembered the horrible pain that had seemed to radiate from the hellish machine Spider had used. "I imagine every spirit in a five-mile radius knew one of their own kind had been destroyed. But she didn't know Spider."

"No. But she must have known that what he did once, he could do again—to any of them." Adam's voice was grim. I knew it must be causing him no little amount of pain to have to consider his own charges as suspects.

"I just don't think it's likely. She's shy and not at all aggressive." I gave a little smile. "This is very strange—me defending your own people to you. When it comes right down to it, Pixie is more of a suspect than Amanita. She didn't like Spider, is demonstrably volatile, and has polter strength, but you don't see me trying to suggest her as the murderer."

Adam paused at the door, giving me an odd look. "I haven't forgotten your moody teen."

I gawked in surprise for a moment before regaining my composure. "What do you think about what Amanita said?"

"I think I'm going to have to talk to Meredith."

"Agreed."

"But first . . ." Adam entered the living room. Savannah strode about, waving her arms and declaring that she would never make contact with the other side if so much negative energy was continuously trapped in the house. "I can't believe someone would murder Mr. Marx just when we're poised to explore the unknown. Don't they know how harmful a violent crime like this can be to one's psychic receptors? And then there's the circumambulation. How is that going to be performed if we're all trapped here?"

"It *is* extremely inconsiderate of someone," I agreed before I fully realized what she'd said.

"What the hell is circumwhatever?" her husband asked as he slammed down a drink he'd poured himself from the sideboard. He glared at everyone from his armchair, as if daring someone to object.

Savannah blushed under the attention of everyone in the room and made pretty little flustered gestures with her hands. "Oh, I . . . it's something I read about. It has to do with people dying, doesn't it? It's a ceremony or something?"

"Something like that." I watched her for a moment, then raised my eyebrows slightly at my father. He looked suspicious.

Meredith belched after taking a swig of what appeared to be whiskey. "A man's dead, Vanna. I think that's more important than some flaky ceremony you want to do."

"It's not just a ceremony, and it's not flaky," she answered, turning to me, her hands spread wide in entreaty. "You're the expert on poltergeists. You'll explain it much better than I could."

Yes, I was the expert. . . . But why did Savannah, who was apparently so badly informed about polters, know about one of their more obscure ceremonies? "Circumambulation simply means to walk a circle around something—an object, or even a person. It's an act performed in some religions, but it also refers to a special ceremony that poltergeists perform when someone has died within their domain."

"Thrillsville." Meredith yawned, his eyes hostile as they moved from person to person.

"It has to do with them being guardians, doesn't it, Karma? People who die where poltergeists live can't move on to the next plane of existence until the poltergeists release them?"

Adam stood silently in the doorway, watching everyone. Pixie was slumped on the couch, her iPod in her hands. Dad was moving around the room in his usual restless manner. Evidently I'd been nominated official polter spokesperson. "It's a bit more complicated than that. Without going into the whys and hows of polter caretaking, it means that the soul of the deceased person is bound to its body until a circumambulation ceremony has been performed by a shaman."

"Good god, you're all a bunch of crackpots, aren't you?" Meredith lurched to his feet and headed toward the sideboard.

"I think that's enough for one night," Adam said, moving to intercept him.

"Back off, freak boy. It's not your liquor; it's Spider's." He paused for a second, awkwardly pointing toward me with his glass. "I guess it's hers now. Either way, I'm going to drink to Spider, and no one can stop me."

"Drunkenness isn't going to help the situation," his wife chastised as he slumped back down into his chair, spilling a bit of whiskey on himself.

"Oh, shut up."

"Meredith!"

"I think we'd better get on with it before he's too sloshed to talk," I said to Adam.

The imps, evidently awake, heard my voice, burst forth from their box, and came running for me with arms outswept.

"All right, who opened the box?" Adam asked as they ran over his feet to get to me. I shuffled past him, my feet being used as transportation devices by the six imps. "If those little devils have harmed any of the furniture . . ."

"They're fully housebroken," I assured him, giving in to the inevitable and sitting in the nearest chair to de-imp my feet. "They don't start fires or potty outside their litter pan, and they pick up their toys without being asked. Most of the time."

"I don't want them running around my house, getting into trouble!"

I sighed and accepted the box he brought me. "Easier said than done."

"Oh, leave me alone, woman! I'm not drunk. Yet." Meredith suddenly stirred in his chair and shouted at Savannah. She gave him a haughty look and strode dramatically to the middle of the room.

"These negative emanations are so damaging. It's too much for someone as sensitive as myself to endure!" She shuddered delicately. "A man has been murdered. Murdered! Right here in this house, and now his soul is bound here, and other spirits are trapped with him, and who knows what sorts of negative entities are going to be attracted by all that! It's so upsetting. So harmful to the psyche. I don't know how long it will take me to recover from this terrible experience. . . . Karma, do you think I could have one of those imps as a little pet?"

11

"I think there's something wrong with me," I told Adam in a low voice.

His eyebrows rose as he looked me over. "I don't see anything obvious. You have only two arms. You don't apport. You don't even exhibit the restlessness unusual with our kind. Do you speak Poltern?"

"Yes, but not easily. The clicking I can do well enough, but the raps give me a bit of trouble. My toe joints aren't very limber, and I hate making my finger and toe knuckles pop. That wasn't what I meant, anyway. I was referring to the fact that my husband is dead and I'm not crying. I'm not overwhelmed by the tragedy of his death. I'm not feeling much of anything, to be honest."

"That's normal," he said, giving my shoulder a little squeeze. "It's shock. You feel kind of numb, right?"

I struggled for a moment to put into words the odd state of my emotions and finally decided his description was as close as possible. "Numb would be a good way to put it, yes. Worried, as well."

"Worried we won't figure out who the murderer is?" he asked, glancing around the room.

I bit my lip again. "I'm praying that won't be so. It's just that we have this one chance, and after the seal is lifted and it's in the hands of the watch . . . well, that kind of changes everything."

"More people involved, you mean?" He nodded. "It would be far easier for everyone if we have the murderer ready to hand over when the seal lifts. If we don't . . . I'm afraid my captain will tell me that we'll have to call in the mundane police, and that's not going to be good for anyone. I can set your mind at ease about one thing, at least. I've seen your sort of reaction to death before, and I can assure you that it's common with family of murder victims. As for not being overwhelmed by the tragedy of Spider's death . . ." His lips thinned. "You'll have to talk to someone else about that. I don't particularly view his death as a tragedy."

I looked him in the eye. "But that's my problem. I don't, either."

"I don't think anyone would blame you for that." His cell phone rang. He glanced at the number displayed before moving to a quiet corner. "It's my captain again. I'd better take this."

My father, correctly interpreting my eyebrow movements, flitted over to where I stood. "I assume you have something to say to me?"

"Quite a few things, actually, but most of them can wait. Adam has deputized me."

"So?"

I expected at least a bit of surprise. "He wants me to help him talk to everyone here about Spider's death. He doesn't think it was an accident."

"Accident . . . miracle . . . they're the same thing in this case."

"That's not the point." I fretted. "I'm worried Adam won't have enough time to figure things out before the seal is up."

He stopped fidgeting and gave me a long look. "Why does it have to be before then? So long as the murderer is caught, what does it matter if they figure it out today or tomorrow, or even a couple of days from now?"

"Don't you watch any of those crime reality shows?" I asked, aiming for a light tone. "The first few hours of an investigation are always critical."

"Hmmph." Dad snorted. "If that's what's got your panties in a bunch . . ."

"It's not just that." I glanced at where Adam was standing with his back to the room, and dropped my voice lower. "Think of it from the point of view of an outsider: if Spider's death wasn't an accident, doesn't it strike you that the person here who benefits the most from his death is Adam?"

Dad recoiled as if in horror. "Karma Phoenix Marx! How can you say something like that about one of your own kind?"

I shushed him before anyone could overhear us. "I'm one of Spider's kind, too, remember? Besides, that's neither here nor there. I'm not saying that Adam killed Spider; I'm just saying that someone in the watch might remove him from the case because he could concievably have a good motive for killing Spider. There are polters who are just as capable of murder for their own gain as mortals are. Adam must surely know that I will inherit Spider's possessions, and that I'm not likely to hold on to a house I rightly consider his."

"That doesn't mean he killed him."

"No, it doesn't. I'm just worried that whatever investigation he does will later be tossed away because of the circumstances." I struggled to put into words one of the worries that had been swirling around in my brain. "There's another thing. If Adam was very smart—and he seems intelligent to me—he could use being in charge of the investigation to set up someone innocent by manipulating the facts, evidence, et cetera."

"Do you think that Adam is that sort of man?" Dad asked, one eyebrow cocked.

"I don't know. I suppose not," I sighed, glancing over at the subject of conversation. "It's possible. I just don't know how I'm going to catch him if he's manipulating the investigation."

"I don't see that he can do much of that," my father answered. "If Spider was murdered, there aren't very many people who could have done it. The house is sealed, which means only those of us here now could get to Spider. You and I didn't do it. Savannah was here with me most of the time. Her husband was bashed on the head and knocked out."

"Adam thinks Pixie might have done it."

"She's a kid."

"I don't like it any more than you do, but you have to admit, from the watch's point of view, he may have a point. She's a child, yes, but she's a polter—one who apparently has a history of emotional troubles, not to mention possesses the strength necessary to throttle a grown man. What if Spider sneaked up on her and attacked? She might have defended herself and accidentally killed him. And we both know how the League deals with children who unintentionally kill."

My father gave me a jaded look. "That's stretching."

"I know. I don't really believe Pixie did it, but she could still be considered a suspect. There's something about her. . . . Dad, does she strike you in any way odd?"

"Odd?" He frowned for a moment. "Odd how?"

"It's hard to define. Kind of . . . clueless."

"She's a teenager, Karma. They tend to be that way."

"I don't mean in a normal way. It's as if she's new to everything polter, but that can't be. Unless . . ."

"Unless what?" The conversation was losing interest for my father. He had moved a few steps to the sideboard and was rearranging the bottles and glasses.

I decided to let it go. My brain was too confused to try to pick out subtle nuances. "It doesn't matter. I'll just have to make Adam see that she's not really a viable suspect. Which brings me to another subject."

"Savannah knowing more than she lets on? I agree with you on that. She's definitely a ringer. Although she puts on a good act. Look at her now, all gaga over Adam's spirits."

I didn't even look at where Savannah had been emoting like crazy after Adam had had his house spirits appear. "I wasn't referring to her, but thanks for reminding me. I want to mention that to Adam. I was, in fact, talking about you."

Dad spun around to look at me. "What about me?"

"You disliked Spider a lot," I said slowly, watching his face. "You hated his attitude toward polters."

He grinned. "Casting me in the role of first murderer, eh? I'm afraid it won't work, Karma. I was here with Savannah. She was grilling Pixie and me about the life of a polter."

"Hmm." He looked innocent. He wasn't wired or apporting, either or both of which I'd expect if he'd been up to no good. But there was the incident of the apports earlier, when I had come downstairs from being sick. . . .

"Sorry, honey. Other than Adam, there isn't anyone else."

"On the contrary, there are several others who *might* have done it," I said, going over a mental list of the house's inmates. "Adam's spirits might have felt threatened by Spider's having the power to destroy them. Amanita was hiding behind the heater in the basement. She might have felt threatened enough to kill him. It's not likely, but it is within the realm of physical possibility."

Dad patted me on the arm. "Honey, I think you're just going to have to face the facts."

"What facts?" Adam asked from behind me.

"That sooner or later, just about everyone who ever met Spider wanted him dead."

"I have no doubt of that." Adam glanced at his watch. "My captain is not happy about the events of the evening. We'd better get started with the interviews. The sooner we get this sorted out, the better for everyone."

"Will you be in trouble for not calling the mundane police right away?" I asked, pulling a notepad and pen from my purse. Dad sent me a warning glance as I followed Adam over to the far side of the room.

He shrugged. "Assuming we find the murderer before the seal is up, no. The watch will take care of everything, including fixing it with the mundane police. Karma . . ."

"Uh-oh. That look doesn't bode well. What's wrong now?"

"It's the captain . . . he looked you up."

I nodded and stared at the carpet. I'd known that eventually the captain of the watch would find out about me. "I take it I'm no longer a deputy?"

The expressions on Adam's face were almost comical. "It's my fault, really. When I first talked to him, I told him you were a TAE. Your position in the League made it natural that you would work with me."

"But then he went and looked me up and now I'm suspect number one?" I asked lightly, wrapping my arms around myself. For some reason, the air surrounding me felt chilled.

"I told him you didn't kill your husband."

I looked up to meet his pale blue eyes. They reminded me of a photo of a glacier I'd seen as a child. "Thank you for your faith."

"Unfortunately"—his Adam's apple bobbed up and down as he swallowed—"the captain feels that someone whose association with the League is due to wergeld does not have the loyalty wished for in a deputy."

"I understand. So would you like to interview me now, or should I just go sit over there with the rest of the suspects?"

"I want you to sit down here and take notes for

me." He gave me a long, level look. "I deputized you; that stands."

"But your captain—"

"Isn't here, and I am. Sit."

I found a smile and shared it with Adam. In an evening of emotional upheaval and horror, he turned out to be a small beacon of pleasure.

"Everyone!" Adam clapped his hands for attention. "Savannah, please, enough with the pictures. I'm sure Tony and Jules will be happy to model for you another time."

The faint buzzing noise that had been on the fringe of my awareness gave a little jump. I frowned, looking around for an air ionizer or some other electrical device that might have been capable of making the almost inaudible white noise, but there was nothing evident.

I moved an ancient stained glass Tiffany-like lamp from the center to the far edge of the table Adam had decided would do as our interview area. I carefully flexed the frayed cord, but it didn't make any noise. I tucked it out of the way so no one would step on it and get shocked. Adam wanted to keep everyone under his eye while we conducted interviews, a prospect I found a bit daunting. The room was filled—not only with my own gang of imps, Pixie, and my father, but also with Adam's ménage à trois. Savannah was in seventh heaven at the sight of honest-to-god spirits. It took her a good fifteen minutes to get past the fact that the spirits were real, at which point she began taking picture after picture.

She fussed for a moment about Adam's order. "Oh, I wish I'd thought to bring the digital camcorder in with me. Couldn't I please run out to the car and get it? I swear I'll be right back, and won't talk to anyone."

Adam shook his head. "The seal can't be broken for another ten hours. No one goes in or out until I'm satisfied."

"But this is a highly important historic moment!" she said, waving her hand toward Jules and Tony, who were serving coffee and almond cake. My father sat next to Amanita, while Pixie was curled up in a window seat with her iPod, clearly distancing herself from everyone else in the room. "Two, *two* genuine spirits are present, along with you poltergeists, and a . . ."

She stopped, her face screwed up.

I watched her carefully before smiling. "Finding it overwhelming?"

"Well, yes! I mean, who wouldn't!"

Who indeed? I wondered if she really was hiding knowledge of the Otherworld from us, or if she'd just happened to make a couple of lucky guesses. The best way to find out would be to give her enough rope, I decided. If she wanted an audience, I'd play along, so I continued to nod as she went on.

"I'm still not sure. . . . That woman there, she's a *unicorn*? How is that possible? Shouldn't she look like a white horse with a horn or something similar?"

"Unicorns have the ability to shape-shift. They prefer the human form because it's much easier in today's world to be human than it would be to be a four-footed, supposedly legendary beast. I've never met one before to really discuss the issue, but it makes sense to me."

"I suppose so." She cast a doubtful glance at Amanita, took a quick picture of her, then tucked the camera back into her bag.

Adam cleared his throat. "As you all know, I am a member of the watch of the Akashic League. I have been asked to investigate the death of Spider Marx before turning it over to the mundane police."

"Mundane?" Savannah turned to my father.

Dad shot me a quick glance before answering. "He means non-Otherworldian. Mortal-world police, in other words."

"Oh." Savannah nodded for Adam to continue.

He stood silent, his pale blue gaze moving quickly from person to person. "Karma is also a member of the League and, as such, has been deputized to assist me with investigating. We will interview you all, one at a time."

"I'm not a part of your underworld," Meredith drawled from the room's most comfortable chair. I noted he had managed to possess himself of yet another glass of whiskey. "I don't have to answer any of your questions. You have no right to interfere with Savannah or me, not to mention it's illegal to interview us without our lawyer present."

"It's 'Otherworld,' not 'underworld,'" Dad corrected, not looking at Meredith, "which you very well know."

Meredith shot Dad a look that I found impossible to interpret. I made a mental note to have another talk with my father at the first opportunity.

"If this murder had taken place with only mortal people, in a mortal household, then yes, I would have to abide by mundane laws." Adam leaned down over Meredith, forcing the latter back in his chair. "But you are in *my* house, and there are no lawyers in the Otherworld. We're going to do things my way. Got it?"

I looked at the clock on the table. Ten hours to go. Time was slipping by.

12

"I don't care about your Otherworld laws. We don't have to say anything to you without our lawyer present," Meredith muttered stubbornly, his eyes narrow and hard.

"I don't mind talking to you," Savannah said quickly. "So long as you agree to answer a few of my own questions about poltergeists, and this Otherworld place that keeps being mentioned."

"You will not talk to him without a lawyer," Meredith snapped, glaring at his wife.

"Please don't use that tone with me," she said, to my surprise. The Savannah who had been so flustered by everything hadn't struck me as a particularly self-confident sort of woman. "I don't like it, and it's not necessary. If I want to talk to Adam and Karma, I will."

"You will not! Dammit, woman, I forbid you to speak to them!"

Adam held up a hand to stop the bickering, addressing Meredith with a stern eye. "As I said, I am invoking the right of the watch to interrogate any possible suspects by whatever means is necessary. And I stress by *whatever* means. End of discussion."

Savannah gasped at the threat in his voice. Meredith scowled, his eyes shifty. I knew he was planning something, but whether it was just a response to Adam's admittedly high-handed manner of dealing with the situation or it was driven by guilt was not clear to me. For the first time in my life, I wished I was a full-blooded polter. I would have given anything to be able to go into unbridled scary poltergeist mode and frighten the truth out of him. I looked with speculation at my father.

He raised an eyebrow at me, evidently aware of what it was I was thinking. "It wouldn't do any good to have me fly at him," he said in Poltern. "He's not afraid of me. You could do it, though."

Savannah leaped off the couch and gawked at my father in a very fine impression of someone nearly startled out of her skin. "What on earth was that noise? Merciful goddess, are there more entities here?"

"Oh, that. That's just poltergeist-speak," Tony said as he whisked out from the kitchen with a tray. "It's how they talk to one another, although honestly, how anyone is supposed to understand a bunch of raps and clicks is beyond me. Who's for fresh-baked cinnamon-almond croissants? Jules has coffee, as well."

"That implies that Meredith is frightened of me," I said slowly in Poltern, my toe cracking barely audible. "Adam, yes. Adam is a figure of authority. But I certainly don't represent anything that would worry Meredith."

Adam said nothing, but his eyes were full of questions as he watched Meredith select two croissants from the plate Tony offered.

Savannah spread a look amongst us, rubbing her arms. Her body language read true. Maybe I was imagining my sense that she was hiding something. . . . The evening had certainly been disquieting enough to skew my ability to evaluate people.

"Can't you smell the fear on him?" Dad sniffed the air. "Every time he looks at you, it grows stronger."

I did the same. "No. The only thing I can smell is croissant."

"If only I'd not fallen in love with your mother . . . you would have been a full-blooded polter, and would be able to sense the things we can." He shook his head sadly, his face clearing when Tony offered him a powdered-sugar-dusted almond croissant.

"This is so . . . strange. Different. Indefinable," Savannah said, gesturing vaguely. "I had no idea that a language could consist of clicks and knocks. Might I ask what it is you're saying to each other?"

Adam shook his head when Tony offered him a plate, and clamped a hand on Meredith's shoulder instead. "Nothing important. Since you object the most to being interviewed, why don't we get it over with?"

Meredith muttered some pretty rude things under his breath, but he evidently decided that resistance wasn't going to do him any good against Adam. I thanked Tony as I took a still-warm croissant and a cup of coffee, following the two men to our little interview cubbyhole.

"Well! While Adam and Karma are busy with the interviews, why don't the rest of us do our part to discover the truth of what happened to Spider?" Savannah said in a bright, cheerful voice that clashed severely with the darkness outside, the late hour, and the dead man in the basement.

I stopped, slowly turning to face her.

My father made a wry face. "The truth is your husband killed him."

"He did not!" She glared at him for a moment before her naturally perky nature took over. "I realize things look bad for Meredith, but you have to trust me when I say that he would never do anything so heinous. And I can prove he didn't do it!"

"How?" I asked, my suspicions fired up again.

She flashed a smile. "It's simple. We'll ask Spider himself."

"Oh, for god's sake, you're not going to have one of your idiotic séances now, are you?" Meredith called from the other side of the room.

"Séance?" Pixie asked, pulling out her iPod's earbuds. "We're going to have a séance? Since I can't have a ghoul, can I summon a demon?"

Adam gave her a curious look before turning back to Meredith. I was going to say something, but figured I'd wait until I was alone with Pixie. Instead, I addressed Savannah. "I appreciate your desire to clear your husband's name, but I'm not sure a séance is the best thing to do right now."

"Really?" She tipped her head to the side. "I don't see why not. If anyone can tell us what happened to him, it's Spider."

I hesitated, weighing my need to have Meredith pay for his crime and my reluctance to get involved in something so potentially volatile as a séance. It was impossible to judge whether Savannah possessed the mediumistic powers needed to summon a deceased person, let alone control him or her. "Have you ever conducted a séance before?"

"Oh yes, several times."

"Have you . . ." I was tired, so I stopped to think about how best to ask the question without offending her. "Have you ever successfully contacted a spirit?"

"Well . . . not per se. But at one of my séances, the temperature in the room dropped a full seven degrees, and everyone there said they felt the presence of something unseen in the room."

I relaxed a smidgen despite being the subject of everyone's close observation, which left me feeling slightly itchy and uncomfortable. "I'm sure it was very exciting, but you know, Savannah, just because Spider's soul has not been released yet doesn't mean his spirit will be willing or even able to talk to you."

"But with him so recently deceased . . . wouldn't it be more likely that he will talk to us than if we waited until after the circumambulation?"

My father snorted and muttered something about the path to hell being a quick one.

"Not necessarily. Just because his soul is bound to his body doesn't mean he will talk to you."

"It behooves us to try to contact him," Savannah said firmly.

"You certainly can try, but you should be aware that even if you did manage to contact him, he may not yet realize that he's really dead. Or he may be confused by the transition from living to dead. Or he could be . . ." I stopped for a minute, not wanting to speak ill of the dead any more than I had.

"Or he could be just as big a liar dead as he was alive," my father finished for me.

I cleared my throat, unwilling to say any more.

"Well, we won't know until we talk to him, will we?" Savannah said, taking a seat at the large round table. "Everyone, please sit down and join hands."

My gaze met my father's. He pursed his lips as he eyed Savannah for a moment, clearly trying to judge her abilities. He shook his head slightly before taking a seat at the table.

Reluctantly, I returned to the cubbyhole, where Adam was sitting with Meredith. Adam frowned at the food in my hand.

"Sorry, I haven't eaten all day. My headache made sure of that. And speaking of my headaches . . ." I set down my coffee and plate, dusted the powdered sugar from my fingers, and picked up my notebook, fixing Meredith with a stern eye. "Would you mind telling me a little bit about that machine you gave Spider? Ever since Adam broke it, my head has been remarkably pain free."

"You can't seriously believe I will tell you anything about a machine that will make me millions," he said, his lips curling with derision.

"I *seriously* believe you will answer any and all questions put to you," Adam growled.

"You think you can get away with bullying me here, but there is going to be hell to pay once the real police come," Meredith snarled.

Adam smiled. It wasn't a pleasant smile, but it fulfilled its purpose. Meredith's eyes dilated slightly as Adam leaned forward and said in a soft voice, "I can arrange it so that you never see the mortal police, you know. The watch would be quite happy to deal with a man who has created a machine to destroy members of the Otherworld."

"That's . . . He can't do that, can he?" Meredith asked me.

"Sure, he can."

"But . . . I'm human! Your laws don't apply to me."

I smiled. "They do when they affect members of the League. Adam is quite within his rights to detain you for the watch if he believes there's enough evidence to justify such an act. If they find you guilty, you'll be duly punished, and I can assure you, the League takes a dim view of anyone who harms one of their members."

Meredith's eyes narrowed on me. "I should have known better than to ask you. You're probably screwing him every chance you get."

"Insulting Karma isn't going to help," Adam said calmly. "Answer the question."

Meredith made a big production about it, but finally he settled down and started giving us some answers. "Spider wanted a way to get rid of ghosts and such without having to rely on you," he said, giving me a nasty glare. "He said it was getting harder and harder to make you do your job, and he knew the end was coming. Once we made plans for the Fun House, he had me put together the anomaly diffuser. It did your job without any of the hassle you were sure to give us."

"Fun House?" It was difficult to reconcile the images of Spider and an amusement park.

"Every ride a guaranteed ballbuster," he said, leering in response. "Spider wanted to try the diffuser out on this house. He said that you'd been defying him and not destroying the spirits like you'd been ordered to do, and he wanted to make sure the job was done properly."

A little stab of pain pierced my heart at the thought of Sergei being destroyed so callously.

"What does the diffuser do, exactly? Does it send the target to the Akashic Plain?"

"I don't have those weirdo powers you have," he said, waving away the question. "It disrupts the pattern of the anomaly. Permanently. One blast and it's bye-bye ghost."

I wanted to ask more about how the machine worked. If such a horrible thing were made freely available, it could have terrible ramifications for the Otherworld.

Adam, however, decided we'd strayed from the point long enough. "Tell me what happened after you left this room with Spider."

"I already told you! We went down to find a door, someone hit me on the back of the head, and when I woke up, you guys were there and Spider was dead."

"Let's go through it step by step."

Meredith sighed and went over the events with reluctance. I listened with half an ear, my attention divided between him and the group at the table in the center of the room. Savannah had evidently proceeded to the trance stage, for she rocked from side to side, her head tipped back, her eyes closed, her long hair sweeping a pendulum's path across the back of the chair.

"We went downstairs. Spider remembered seeing a door in the basement. He found a crowbar, and started to pry open the door."

"Spirits who surround us, we humbly implore you to make yourselves known to us," Savannah said in a singsong voice. "Come forth and tell us your names. Share your wisdom. Guide us in the darkness."

"What happened then?" Adam's voice was a deep counterpoint to Savannah's.

"I stepped back to give him room to use the crowbar. I said something about us not being able to get out of the house, and Spider said he'd be damned if he stayed there any longer. I thought I heard a noise behind me, but before I could turn, something coshed me on the head and I was out."

"We seek enlightenment, spirits of Walsh House. Come before us and teach your humble pupils. Tell us of your lives, so that we might be better for your experiences."

"What sort of noise did you hear?" Adam asked.

Meredith made a vague gesture. "Just a noise. Something moving. Could have been anything—a person, a rat, one of those damned spirits of yours."

"Spirits of Walsh House, we call upon you now! Speak to us! We feel your presence. We welcome you with love. Speak to us now!"

"Did you see any—"

Before Adam could finish, Savannah gave a small shriek. Evidently she'd been peeking despite her "trance," for she sat now pointing at the center of the table, where the air had grown misty, as if it was gathering itself up into a tangible form.

"I . . . I summoned a ghost!" Savannah said in outright astonishment, her eyes huge.

"Mother Mary and all the saints, what is it ye want from me, woman?"

"I summoned a ghost who talks!"

"Too bad it's not someone cute," Pixie said, eyeing the materializing spirit. "And younger."

Adam froze, staring in surprise at the center table. I was just as surprised as he: with the house sealed, it shouldn't be possible to summon any being into the house. But on the middle of the table, the figure of a man was solidifying—a ghostly white, gauzy figure, but a man nonetheless. One who looked familiar.

"Grandpa?" Adam asked, a comical mix of surprise and embarrassment on his face.

The ghost turned toward us. "Adam, me boy! Ye grandam'll be delighted to know it was ye who woke me up. House looks nice. Dropped that third arm, have ye?"

"Do you . . . do you know this . . . er . . . gentleman?" Savannah asked, her voice hushed with awe.

Meredith rolled his eyes. "Oh, for god's sake. This is all we need—more freaks."

"Who're yer friends, then?" the ghost asked, turning a not-so-friendly eye on Meredith.

Adam sighed and rose to his feet. "This is my grandfather for whom I'm named: Adam Tennyson Trent. He died sixty years ago. He's supposed to be elsewhere. I had no idea he was in the house, but I'd appreciate it if you could put him back."

13

"Now, Adam, don't be takin' on like that. If'n yer havin' a party, I'd be happy to have a wee chat with yer friends. I've been sleepin'. . . . What year is this?"

"It's 2008. Go back to sleep," Adam ordered, storming over to where Savannah sat with an astonished, if joyful, expression. "And next time, pick someone else's house to take a nap in."

"Fine welcome that is from me own flesh and blood." The elder Adam had quite an Irish accent. I couldn't help feeling sorry for the younger version. The old man had a roguish twinkle in his eye that was apparent despite the wispy nature of his materialization. "It's been years, lad. How is your work comin' along? The last yer grandam and I heard, ye was workin' for the government."

"I still am," Adam said, his shoulders slumping in resignation.

"How come she can summon a ghost?" Pixie asked me in a whisper, her eyes narrowed on Savannah. "I thought the house was sealed."

"It is. I suspect the gentleman there was dormant." She gave me a blank look.

"It's another word for sleeping. Polters and spirits can lay dormant for decades so long as they're not disturbed. But you should know that."

She rolled her eyes.

"This is your grandfather?" Savannah asked, beaming with happiness at the spirit. "How do you do, sir? I am Savannah Bane, president of the Psychical Mysteries Society. We're delighted you decided to grace us with your presence. Would you mind if I took a few pictures of you?"

"Not at all, dearie. Me left is me best side." Adam senior turned and struck a dramatic pose.

Savannah muttered something about hoping she had enough film left as she dug her camera out of her purse, then quickly took a few shots.

"All right, you've said hello and had your picture taken. Now go back to sleep," Adam ordered.

"He always was an impatient lad," the old man confided to Savannah, much to her delight. "Now then, me boy, ye're not even goin' to tell me about how yer grandam is gettin' on?"

Adam raised his eyes heavenward for a moment. "She's fine. She is very busy."

"Raisin' hell, as always, I'll wager," the ghost cackled, slapping his leg. "Raisin' hell, ye get it? Ah, boy, it's good to see ye."

"I want to sleep for decades," Pixie announced. "I don't want to wake up until all the teachers at school are long gone."

"Eh?" The spirit spun around to look at her. "Who be ye, then?"

"Morbent Vixen," she answered.

"I thought it was Obsidian Angel," my father said. The look she gave him was one of pure scorn.

"That's *so* half an hour ago. I changed it to something better."

The old spirit eyed her for a few seconds before turning back to his grandson. "This be yer woman, boy? She's a bit on the young side."

Adam bore the air of one well persecuted. "She's not my woman. She's fifteen, and the ward of Karma."

"Karma?" The ghost squinted as he looked at the rest of us, his gaze finally settling on me. "Ah. Now, there's a pretty lass. Much better choice. Not a pureblood, though."

"We're not together," I said quickly. "Not in a relationship way, that is. We're just working together for a bit."

"She's an exterminator," Adam added.

The old man whistled and took a few steps backward. "I'd best be on me way. Feeling a mite sleepy, I am. Give yer grandam a kiss for me, Adam, and tell her to wake me up as soon as she's done runnin' things in the Court."

"I will if you promise to go back to sleep," Adam warned.

The ghost's eyes flicked in my direction for a second; then he faded.

"Oh, but wait! I have questions—" Savannah stopped as the elder Adam disappeared entirely. "Dammit! There was so much I wanted to do with him!"

"Please don't bring back any more of my family," Adam told her.

Her brow furrowed. "Are there more dormant here?"

"Not that I know of, but I could be wrong."

"Well, I'll try not to if you insist, although I thought your grandfather was delightful. But why did he only have two arms?"

"He used to be mortal," Adam said, abruptly turning and marching back to where Meredith was eating the last of my croissant.

"Court?" I asked, following him.

"Court of Divine Blood."

"Your grandmother lives in *heaven*?"

"It's not heaven, it's the Court, and yes, she lives there. She's the polter ambassador to the Court. Grandpa doesn't get along well with Court life, so he sleeps a few decades at a time, then wakes up to see how things are going."

"You people just get freakier and freakier," Meredith said with a shudder. "It's a good thing I had more than one diffuser made. Sooner or later, I'll be rid of all of you that aren't turning a profit for me."

Adam's gaze met mine. It was pregnant with meaning.

"Let's go over the events of the evening again," he said to Meredith.

"I just told you what happened!"

"I want to hear it again."

My coffee was more lukewarm than hot, but I sipped it as Adam forced Meredith to go over the evening's activities yet another time. Savannah went into another summoning trance but produced only one other spirit, a process server, who served Tony for breach of contract.

"But that was a century ago," Tony said nervously, glancing at his partner. "It was before I met you, honey, I swear! Angelique meant nothing to me, nothing! She completely misinterpreted my offer to go in together on a scheme to farm kobolds."

"Indeed!" Jules said with injured dignity.

"Thank you for waking me up," the process server said with a bow to Savannah. She sat with open-mouthed surprise. "I lost track of time. I remember stopping here and thinking I'd take a little nap until someone summoned me forth, but I guess I was more tired than I thought. Still am, for that matter. Think I'll take another little nap. . . ."

He disappeared before she could say anything. Adam's two spirits went off to the kitchen, no doubt to work out their relationship woes. Savannah blinked a couple of times, shook her head as if to clear it, and then announced they would continue trying to contact Spider.

"Tell me again what you said to him, and what he said to you."

A sulky look slid over Meredith's face as he repeated what he'd told us earlier.

"Is that all he said?" Adam asked.

"That's all I heard before I was knocked out," Meredith answered with obvious exasperation. "If you're done with this third degree, I'm going to get a drink."

Adam's gaze met mine. I shook my head.

"Go ahead," Adam told him, then waited until Meredith was out of hearing before asking, "What do you think?"

"I don't know. It didn't seem to me like he was lying. You must be able to read people better than me; what do you think?"

Adam looked thoughtful for a moment. "I'd just

about swear that he wasn't lying. But if Spider wasn't talking to Meredith, then who else was there?"

I nibbled on the end of my pen. "Good question."

Adam called Amanita over.

"I hope you're not frightened by me being here," I told her with an encouraging smile as she settled into the chair next to me. "I'm not going to clean this house, so you really don't have anything to fear from me."

"I know. Adam said he would keep us safe." She didn't look me in the eye when she spoke, her fingers working the material in her gauze peasant top.

Despite her statement, I could feel her fear. I sat back, nodding at Adam. It was clear she would respond much better to him than me.

"Nita, this is important. I want you to tell us again everything that happened after Karma came into the house."

Her voice was low and hesitant, but it gained both a little volume and confidence as Adam guided her through the happenings of the last few hours. While she was recounting her actions, a cold chill brushed the back of my neck, making the hairs on my arms stand on end. I looked around, but there was no one behind me.

"And was anyone in the basement when you went to hide there?"

"No, it was empty then. But a little later, there were voices, so I hid even farther behind the furnace."

Kaaaarma. The wind seemed to speak my name, another chill wisping past my back.

"What were they . . . Are you all right?"

I looked up as Adam interrupted himself. "Yes,

sorry. I'm just tired, and there's some sort of draft that's hitting me the wrong way."

He frowned for a second before turning back to Amanita. "What were the men saying, do you remember?"

She repeated the conversation she'd told us about earlier.

"Kaaarmaaaa." The skin on my arms and back crawled at the voice. I wasn't imagining it.

"Oh, goddess! It's Spider!" Savannah cried.

"Karma, darling wife—"

I jumped up at the voice, too vague to be identifiable, but eerie enough to cause me to knock my coffee over. There were a horrible burning smell and a bright blue flash, then the house was thrown into darkness.

"Dear goddess, he's come!" Savannah shrieked, her voice high and frightened.

Mass pandemonium followed. Amanita squeaked, a rush of air passing me indicating she was running for a hiding spot. Dad and Pixie both shouted as Adam pushed the table back slightly. Meredith demanded to know what was going on. Adam's spirits were calling for each other from the dining room and the kitchen. The imps, which had been sleeping at my feet, woke up and started *ee*king in a confused manner.

"Everyone stay put!" Adam bellowed over the cacophony of confusion. "It's probably just the fuses."

"It's my fault," I said loudly, feeling my way along the walls to follow Adam. "I knocked my coffee over onto a frayed lamp cord. It's nothing to get excited about."

The imps clung to my feet as I shuffled toward the hallway.

"Watch where you're going," Meredith snapped as I inadvertently bumped into him.

"Sorry. I'm just going to help Adam with the fuse box."

I felt my way blindly down the hall, then froze when someone whizzed past me. There were only three people in the house who had the combination of excellent night vision and speed needed to zip around in the darkness, and one of them had already gone ahead. "Dad?" I whispered. "Pixie?"

There was no answer. I cursed the fact that I didn't inherit the polter ability to see in the dark. My cursing became more pronounced as my shins took a beating running into various pieces of furniture. I finally gave up and limped painfully back toward the living room. A whisper of air that passed me indicated that someone had beaten me back. The lights came on just as I entered the room, its occupants providing a tableau of startled faces.

Pixie and my father were both seated at the table. "What were you just up to?" I asked Dad in Poltern.

His eyebrows rose. "What do you mean, what was I up to? I'm just sitting here."

"Uh-huh." I turned to Pixie. She had her iPod fired up again, her head nodding in time to the music. One of them had taken a quick trip out of the room, but I had no idea which. I shrugged it off, telling myself I was making too much of nothing.

"It was the fuse, nothing more," Adam said as he entered the room. "The wiring needs badly to be updated. It's on my list of things to do this summer. Nita? You can come out now. We're almost done."

"I've lost contact with Spider," Savannah said, her

voice reflecting the frustrated expression on her face. She sat back down at her seat, frowning at the table. "I'm not sure I can get him again."

"I think that someone here doesn't want Spider to talk," Meredith said. His eyes narrowed as he looked at Adam.

Amanita shot Meredith a nasty look as she walked over to us.

"You're not going to start that again, I hope," I said, too tired to temper my words.

"You're sitting there so high-and-mighty, like you're above it all," he snapped back at me. "You're just protecting your boyfriend there. Everyone knows how much Adam wanted to get his house back. He threatened to sue the bank, for god's sake! And Spider told me that Adam made all sorts of wild threats to him on the phone. So it's no use, you trying to cover it up; we all know who the real murderer is here."

"Yes, and his name is Meredith Bane," my father said, sallying. I smiled at him.

"You freaks all band together, don't you?" Meredith answered. "I wouldn't be surprised if *you* were the one who killed Spider. He's hated you long enough; I'm sure the feeling was mutual."

"Please, Meredith, this isn't doing any good," Savannah said with a hand to her head.

"You stay out of it. This is between me and the freak cop over there." He pointed at Adam. "He's trying to railroad me into a murder charge, but it won't work. I have no reason for wanting Spider dead! He was my partner!"

"Don't partners often make legal arrangements so

any business assets are given directly to the surviving partner in case of death?" I asked. "One that guaranteed if he died, you'd get it all . . . and vice versa?"

The sneer on Meredith's face was not a pleasant thing to behold. "You'd like that, wouldn't you? Sorry, Karma, Spider owned his assets outright. We didn't have any sort of a survivor clause in our agreement." He paused for a moment, a speculative look in his eye. "Something I'm willing to bet you knew. Which gives you, Miss High and Mighty, the perfect motive for killing your husband."

I frowned at him. "What on earth are you talking about?"

"You're sooo innocent, aren't you? You pretended you didn't know anything about the Fun House, but I'm not buying that innocent act. Spider was more excited about the brothel than anything else we'd worked on. He must have told you how much money we were going to make on it, and you decided you wanted it all for yourself, didn't you?"

"Brothel?" Savannah gasped, half rising from her chair.

"Oh, sit down," her husband snarled. "Like you give a damn where I get the money you're always demanding for your crackpot hobbies."

She threw a startled look at him, an outraged "Crackpot! Oh!" quickly following.

"Are you saying that this Fun House place you mentioned is a brothel?" I asked, unwilling to believe Spider would have anything to do with a project like that, but knowing it was entirely too possible.

"Don't act like you don't know what it was. Spider told you."

So that was why this house meant so much to Spider, why he wanted so badly for it to be cleaned, and why it was important enough to agree to not fight a divorce. "No, wait, that doesn't make sense," I said, shaking my head at the confused thoughts chasing themselves around and around. "Why *this* place? What's so special about Adam's house? I believe your statement that Spider was excited about a brothel—he had no morals that I knew of, so it doesn't surprise me that he'd happily take on the role of pimp—but it doesn't explain why he wanted *this* house so bad."

"Oh, for god's sake, are you so stupid you think this innocent act is fooling anyone?" Meredith said, a disgusted look on his face.

"Stop speaking to her that way!" To my surprise, Savannah jumped up and stood behind me, glaring at her husband.

"I'll speak any way I want. Shut your mouth and sit down!" he yelled back at her.

Savannah wasn't having any of it. She reminded me of an angry Chihuahua taking on a mastiff. "That's it! I have had it with you! You are being rude and unfeeling, and downright insulting to these good people!"

"They aren't people," he answered with yet another sneer. "They're not human."

"Hmm." Adam ignored the argument between the husband and the wife, his gaze blank as he clearly tried to work out the puzzle of the house.

"They are so! Just look at them! Well, all right, I admit the extra arms are a bit . . . different . . . but they are human in every other respect! And Karma and Adam look one hundred percent human!"

"You should have seen Adam before he finally lost

that third arm," Jules said as he drifted past us, carrying a coffeepot. "He went through hell trying to hide it. I thought he would rot his brain with all the glamours he used to look mortal. That was before he got a job in the mundane world, of course. Anyone want a refresh?"

Savannah turned distraught eyes to me. "Tell him you're human."

"I'm half human," I said slowly, not wanting to upset her any more than she already was. The situation was volatile enough without anyone else freaking out. "Polters aren't really the same as mortal humans. It's more than just the extra arms; they have several other traits inherent to the species, one of which is a life span about four times that of a mortal."

"Four times . . ." Her eyebrows rose. "How old are you?"

"Late thirties," I said with a little smile.

"I'm eighty-one," my father said with pride. "I'm told I don't look a day older than fifty."

I patted Savannah's hand as she slumped back into her chair. "Adam is over a hundred. Polters age much slower than mortals, so it really doesn't do to pay too much attention to the number of years lived."

"They're freaks, Savannah," her husband yelled. "Freaks! And if you hang around with them, you'll be a freak, too."

"There's only one freak here, and he's not a polter," Pixie said in a soft voice.

Meredith snarled something rude at her, leaped up from the table, and stomped over to the fireplace. I glanced back at Adam, who was still apparently deep in thought.

"Your family hasn't harmed Spider in some way, have they?" I asked him. "You know, something someone did a while ago that would make him seek revenge on you now?"

"No. I'm sure—" Enlightenment dawned in his eyes. "My family . . ."

A chill skittered down my back. My father gasped as the thought struck him, as well.

"What is it?" Savannah asked, looking from Adam to me.

Pixie pursed her lips. I didn't want to go into too much detail in front of her. She might be more worldly than was expected in one only fifteen, but there was no need to expose her to the dark side of human nature any more than was necessary.

"Polters don't live in just any house." Even to my ears, my voice sounded weary. "There has to be a bond with a mortal family in order for them to move in, and once they do that, it's exceedingly hard to get them to leave. In the old days, they used to act as stewards, taking care of property for owners who had large estates. In the last hundred or so years, many polter families were forcibly displaced when their mortal hosts downsized. Some took over the property when the mortal line died out. But a house that has been in the care of a polter is forever changed."

"Changed? Changed how?" Savannah asked, looking around the room as if the answer would make itself apparent.

I smiled at Adam as he tried to explain. "It becomes kind of sacred land. There's a Poltern word for it, but it's untranslatable. The closest I can come is 'sanctuary.' The house in effect becomes a safe haven for Otherworld beings."

"Oh." Her eyes went to Amanita.

"Exactly." Adam nodded. "Nita and the boys were attracted to my house because of its history with my family. I became their guardian, dedicated to preserving the house so it will continue to provide them sanctuary from the mundane world."

Savannah's brow furrowed. "But what does this have to do with Meredith's plans for a . . . for a . . ."

"Brothel?" Adam growled.

"Yes, that. I don't see the connection."

Everyone was silent. Pixie looked down at her hands, fussing with the fingerless black lace gloves she'd pulled from her bag. My father was suddenly fascinated with a book sitting on a table next to him. Adam watched me for a moment, one eyebrow cocked in expectation.

I sighed. Why did these things always fall on my shoulders? "It means that Spider and Meredith weren't planning just any sort of brothel. They needed a house that could offer sanctuary, one that would be comfortable to spirits and other beings, who would become the entertainment, assumedly in exchange for room and board."

"Dear goddess above," Savannah gasped, her face reflecting the horror in her voice. "They'd use ghosts as whores?"

"And polters, and sprites and sylphs, and whatever other freaks we can get, so long as they turn a profit," Meredith said. "Don't make that face at me! You don't have any idea the amount of money we were sitting on! Otherworld brothels are a gold mine waiting to be tapped! Spider knew that with his connection to the polter world, he'd be able to bring in the best sort of hookers. We'd have every freak for a hundred miles around knocking at our door, hoping to get a chance at one of the—"

"Thank you for that confirmation," I interrupted, sending Pixie a warning look as she was about to make a comment.

She scowled at me but sat back, her lips tight.

"So you see, dear wife," Meredith said, strolling over to Savannah's chair, "there's every reason for your new friend here to have wanted her husband dead. She must have planned all along to knock off Spider, and set me up as the prime murder suspect in order to take over the plans for our brothel."

Adam looked at me with speculation in his eyes. I could see he was wondering if "It'll all be mine when you're gone" meant I had murdered Spider for his share of the venture.

"No," I told him softly in Poltern. "I swear I had no idea about any of this."

He nodded, murmuring that he believed me.

Savannah looked as if she was going to burst into tears, but once again, she surprised me. She took a deep breath, pushed back her chair, and stood to confront her husband. "You sicken me, Meredith. It's as if I've never really known who you were, and now I see you for your true self. You are evil, truly evil, and unless you repent, I don't see that we have a future together."

"You stupid bitch!" I thought he was going to hit Savannah, and stood up at the same time Adam did. Meredith snarled obscenities at us as he snatched the whiskey bottle and backed up a couple of steps. "Fine! If you'd rather stay with the freaks, you're welcome to them. I'm going to bed. I'll deal with all of you as soon as I can get out of this madhouse."

"Happy nightmares," Pixie called after him.

"Hope the bedbugs bite," my father added.

"I told you we should get ourselves a nice domovoi like that Sergei to be a housekeeper," Jules said to Antony in a loud whisper from the corner of the room. "They know about the bugs!"

14

"I believe I'm fading fast," Savannah said in the silence that followed her husband's dramatic exit. "If you wouldn't mind, I'd like to rest, as well."

"Everyone is tired, but I'd like to get a statement from you before you retire for the night."

She passed a languid hand over her forehead. "Oh, I don't think I'm up to that, Adam. I will be happy to answer your questions in the morning, but right now . . . The séance was so draining. . . . And all the negative energy in the house due to the killing . . ."

I slid Adam a look as I put an arm around her. "Of course, we understand. It's been a trying night for everyone."

"I should be the one comforting you in your newly widowed state," she said as we walked toward the stairs. Adam, correctly reading my glance, followed. "You must be beside yourself with grief."

"I'm still numb with shock, to be honest."

"Shock!" She shuddered. "I know how you feel. I'm in absolute shock that Meredith could be involved in something so heinous, so reprehensible!

Imagine wasting poltergeists and spirits on a brothel, when there are so many other uses for them."

I paused for a second. "Other uses?"

"Of course!" She stopped at the bottom of the stairs and turned to face us, her hands spread wide. "There is so much we have to learn from them! From you . . . You know what I mean. From beings of the Otherworld! To use them to satiate carnal desires . . . well, that's just a waste of a good resource. And so I will point out to Meredith in the morning!"

Adam raised his eyebrows and covertly made a note in his notebook.

"Good luck with that. Meredith doesn't seem to be the sort of man who would be overly welcoming to suggestions," I said.

"He's not, but sometimes you can get through to him," she replied, slowly ascending the stairs.

"How long have you been married?"

"Nearly six months now." She must have sensed my surprise, because she tossed her head and laughed. "I know, we argue like an old married couple, don't we? That's Meredith's stubbornness for you."

"Men can be that way. He seemed awfully tight with Spider, though. Spider's mentioned him to me a few times, but I had no idea that they had such grandiose plans. I wonder if Meredith felt threatened by Spider in any way."

"Threatened?" She paused at the top of the stairs. "Which room might I have, Adam?"

"You can rest in mine. It's down the hall, last door on the right."

"Meredith wasn't threatened by anyone," she continued, not looking left or right as she marched down the hallway. "He got along very well with your husband. I admit there was difficulty in Meredith getting funding from him for the electronic devices; Spider seemed to think they were a waste of money until Meredith showed him a prototype of the diffuser. He gave Meredith the money quick enough after that."

We stopped in front of the door to Adam's bedroom. "Do you mean that you knew your husband had a machine that would destroy spirits? And you did nothing about it?"

Her laughter spilled out into the hallway. "Oh, Karma! I did everything but threaten to throttle the man to get him to stop working on them, but it did no good. To be perfectly honest, I never thought it would actually work! I would have destroyed the horrible machine if I thought it would do what it was intended to do, but even if I did know for a fact it was truly dangerous, destroying it would have been difficult. Meredith always kept them locked away at the bank."

"*Them?*" Adam asked, opening the door.

"I beg your pardon? Oh, what a lovely room. I imagine it has a glorious view during the day. Is that furniture original to the house?"

"Er . . ." Adam looked slightly discombobulated as he glanced around the bedroom. "Some of it. You mentioned your husband was working on electronic devices? Plural?"

She patted a large chest that sat at the end of the four-poster bed. "This is lovely, just lovely. Such a beautiful chest. Is it mahogany?"

Adam frowned. "Yes. Can you answer my question?"

"I'm sorry; I'm just overwhelmed by this lovely

room. Did I say 'them?' I'm so tired, I'm not really thinking straight. Meredith only made the one diffuser, but there were several versions of it before he got it right, so I always think of it as more than one device."

"He said he had another one," I said slowly, watching as she flitted around the room admiring the Victorian furniture. "Do you think that might have been the cause for an argument between Spider and him?"

"You'd have to ask Meredith, but I doubt it. From what I saw, they were on very good terms. Certainly nothing that would indicate Meredith would kill Spider."

"You didn't see either of them after they left the living room?" Adam asked when she opened a window and breathed in the night air with exaggerated movements.

"I so love the smell of the sea. No, I didn't see them. I stayed in the living room until everyone returned, and we decided to have the séance."

"Everyone?" I asked, confused. "Who left the room while I was upstairs?"

"Oh, goodness . . . let me see. . . ." She sat on the bed to take off her shoes. "Spider and Meredith went downstairs to look for a door, as you know. Obsidian Angel said she had to use the bathroom. Matthew said he was going to check on you, but he didn't come back until just before you came downstairs. And Adam went off to . . ." She paused, turning to him. "Why *did* you leave?"

"I had to check on Nita and the boys. Did you see anyone go down to the basement?"

"I'm afraid I wasn't looking," she said, scooting

back on the bed. "I took a few moments to do some communing with the house. Would you mind if I rested now? I feel drained, absolutely drained, by the murder and Meredith and everything."

"Of course. Rest well," Adam said, holding the door open for me.

"Oh . . . Karma, do you have a few seconds?" she asked.

"Sure. I'll just be a minute, Adam."

He inclined his head, gave Savannah a quick, curious look, and left.

"I'm sorry to disturb you after everything that's happened, but I thought it would be best to do it now," Savannah said, twisting a bit of her dress between her hands.

"Do what now?" Why was she suddenly so uncomfortable?

She got off the bed and took a hesitant step toward me. "I was wondering . . . I thought you might not like . . . Oh, this is so very awkward."

"I don't know what's awkward, but you needn't feel concerned about discussing something unpleasant with me. I'm stronger than I look. Is it something about Spider?"

"Yes. No. That is, I was wondering what your plans are for this house." The words tumbled over one another as she sat on the end of the bed, one hand touching her amulet bag. "I know it's too soon after your husband's death to have any specific plans, but I thought I would mention that I am very, very interested in the house, and if the unpleasant circumstances of Spider's death have tainted the house in any way, I would be only too happy to buy it from you."

"Stop," I said, holding up a hand to interrupt her.

"It's Meredith, isn't it?" she asked, shaking her head. "You needn't worry: I have no intentions of allowing him to destroy this lovely old home by turning it into a brothel. If you sell me the house, I can protect it from him. I will continue to allow it to be a sanctuary to homeless entities and beings. It will become the apex of paranormal study in the Pacific Northwest. I will conduct—"

"No, seriously, you must stop," I interrupted again. "You misunderstand my objections. Legally this house may have been Spider's, and thus will probably pass to me, but I don't consider it morally his or mine. This is Adam's home."

"But surely . . ." She frowned. "Surely I am remembering correctly what I read about poltergeists: they are guardians of the home, not actual owners?"

"That's been the traditional role throughout history, yes. But times have changed in the last century. Many polters now own the properties that were tended by the generations of their families. At some point, the original family who owned this house must have sold it to Adam."

She was silent for a minute. "With all due respect to Adam, don't you think that perhaps he's best suited for the former role, rather than the latter? The house is in a terrible state of disrepair; it desperately needs an owner who will care for it."

"He does have two jobs," I said, feeling rather defensive on his behalf. "And his wards seem to be very happy and comfortable. I don't think there're any signs of neglect on his part. Is that all you wanted to talk to me about?"

"Er . . . yes." She didn't look happy at my abrupt dismissal of her attempt to buy the house, but I was not at all comfortable discussing it with her. The house wasn't really mine, and I had no intention of doing anything with it but giving the deed back to Adam.

"Get some rest. I think we can all use it."

Adam was waiting for me downstairs. "What was all that about, or am I prying?"

I looked up into his pale blue eyes and wondered what lengths he'd go to in order to protect his home and wards. "She wanted to buy your house."

"*What?*"

I nodded. "I told her I didn't consider it mine to sell."

"Ah. I see. Er . . . thank you." Two faint spots of color touched his cheeks. "I meant to talk to you about that, but thought I'd wait until after we're through with this mess."

"There's nothing to talk about," I told him, smiling to myself over his obvious embarrassment. Adam was clearly one of those men who felt awkward being beholden to someone. "The house is yours. Just as soon as the probate is worked out, I'll return the deed to you."

"That's very generous of you." He looked downright uncomfortable. I decided to end his misery.

"What do you think about what she said?"

"She's nuts if she thinks she's going to get this house—"

"No, not that. Earlier."

"Ah. Hmm. Interesting, that."

I worried my lower lip as I ran over again the brief interview with her. "She's not telling us everything."

"Agreed. That bit about the devices, for instance.

What are you willing to bet that Meredith made something else that she doesn't want us to know about?"

"Another ghost-killing machine?"

"Perhaps. Or maybe something worse."

"I can't imagine what could be worse than that horrible diffuser," I answered, anger a bitter taste in my mouth.

"I can."

"Adam . . ." I stopped him before he could enter the living room. "This is incredibly awkward. There's no way I can say this without ruffling your feathers, so I'm just going to say it. Amanita didn't mention you checking on her."

His pale blue eyes held mine with apparent frankness. "That's correct."

"You're really not making this easy for me, are you? If you weren't checking on the spirits and Amanita, then what were you doing?"

"I'd rather not say." He started to walk away.

"Adam!"

"What?" He continued to walk with infuriating indifference.

"You know what! Is that it? That's all the explanation you're giving me?"

He spun around and marched over to me until our toes touched, his gaze boring into my head. "Do you believe I murdered your husband?"

"I think people who don't know you might find the facts rather damning. You certainly had a reason to want Spider dead. You had the ability, as well, with your polter swiftness and strength-enhancing law-enforcement training. And now you admit you were off doing something on your own when Spider was killed."

He leaned closer to me, until I could see little flecks of silver in his pale blue eyes. "Do you think I murdered your husband?"

I shook my head, my shoulders slumping with weariness and capitulation. "You're too . . ." I struggled to find a word to describe him, and finally settled on "honorable." "You're just too honorable to do something so reprehensible."

"Then it doesn't matter what I was doing, does it?"

As he strode away, I followed slowly, wishing I had a better grasp on the way polter minds worked.

"What the hell is going on here?" Adam bellowed as I entered the room.

"Imp races," my father answered from where he squatted on the floor. Several imps, prompted by my father as he held out bits of croissant, ran around what appeared to be a makeshift racetrack. "Can you believe Murdered Vortex hasn't seen an imp race? I've got five bucks on the one wearing the pink."

"It's *not* Murdered Vortex. It was *never* Murdered Vortex. I decided Morbent Vixen was too boring, so my name is now Misericordia." Pixie eyed us all as if daring us to challenge her latest choice of name.

"You've never seen an imp race?" Now, that was curious. Imp races were standard fare in most polter kids' lives.

"There will be no imp racing in my house!" Adam yelled, glaring at me. "Those are your pests; you take care of them!"

"I told you they were housebroken."

"I don't care. I don't want them running around, getting into trouble."

"Yeah, you wouldn't want anyone doing something unauthorized, like murdering someone," Pixie said in a dry voice.

Adam bent a frown upon her. "I could do with less lip from you."

"Whatever." She stood up and stretched. "Since you ruined all the fun, I gotta go to the can."

"They're really not harmful imps," I told Adam. "They're Australian. Very domesticated, not at all like the common European variety."

"If you don't take care of them, I will," he warned.

"Imp Nazi," my father muttered as he helped me round up the imps and replace them into their box.

"I imagine he's just as tired as the rest of us."

Pixie had donated her scarf for the imps to curl up on. I tucked them away with her scarf before returning to my spot at the table and flipping open my notebook. I raised my eyebrows at Adam. "Who's next?"

"Your father and the girl are the only ones left. We'll take her as soon as she comes back from the bathroom."

I chewed on the end of my pen. It wasn't surprising that he had excluded his wards from the list of possible suspects. I had a feeling the only reason we had talked to Amanita was that we'd caught her in the basement. "What about Jules and Tony?"

"What about them?"

"Don't we interview them, as well? We did Amanita."

Adam sat down across from me, and for a moment, weariness showed in his face. I knew he was tired—I certainly was, given the events of the evening and the lateness of the hour—but polters had deep reserves of strength that should have bolstered him. "Jules and Tony aren't suspects."

I hesitated, knowing I had to tread carefully. "They aren't to you, but can you say without a shred of doubt that someone at the watch might not wonder if there wasn't some nepotism displayed on your part if everyone isn't treated to the same interview process?"

That brought him up short. He snorted but seemed to consider it.

"The truth has to be faced. They can interact in our world, they were alone at the time of the murder, and they had good cause to fear Spider and the diffuser after Sergei was killed, I'm sorry, Adam. That's means, opportunity, and motive."

"That means nothing. You and I had all three as well, and we both agree we didn't do it."

"I think it would be wise if we formally eliminated everyone."

Adam sighed. "Fine, but if you upset them, there'll be hell to pay. You have no idea what horrible sorts of meals they can produce when they're not happy."

"I'll use kid gloves, I promise," I said, looking through the door at the empty hallway and staircase. "What on earth can she be doing?"

"If she's anything like my daughter was, she'll be in there for hours."

I sat back, intrigued by this unexpected glimpse into Adam's private life. "I didn't realize you had a daughter. The League files didn't say you'd been married."

"I haven't, and the League doesn't always know

everything about people. Take, for instance, the incident concerning you. There's remarkably little detail about it—just a note that you were charged with the extirpation of a six-year-old child, for which the penalty was wergeld."

"You're trying to distract me from the subject of your daughter," I said with a little smile.

"And you're trying to avoid talking about your past. It seems we both have things we'd like to keep private."

My smile faded. "True enough. I have an admittedly annoying curiosity about people. I'm sorry if I stepped on your toes. I was just surprised to hear you had a daughter."

"She's in college. I don't see her often." He was silent for a moment, then leaned forward, his breath brushing my face as he asked, "Why did you kill a six-year-old girl?"

I glanced at my father. He was chatting with Jules and Tony, who had come into the room to pick up coffee cups and empty plates. I didn't want to talk about what had happened so many years before, but somehow, I felt that Adam might understand what I'd gone through.

The familiar sensations of guilt and loathing rose at the memory. My hands cramped as I twisted the lace tablecloth tight between my fingers. I made a point of flattening my palms against my thighs. "It was an accident. I was only six myself, which is why the League gave me a punishment of wergeld rather than banishment. They said I wasn't cognizant enough to know what I was doing."

Adam nodded, saying nothing. I couldn't stand sitting still, so I grabbed a couple of tissues and started

dusting a knickknack shelf that sat behind Adam.
"They were right about one thing: I didn't know
what I was doing. Tami was my friend. She had a
cruel streak, but I was a bit of a loner, being only
half polter in a polter society. I didn't know I had
the power to banish anyone to the Akasha, let alone
destroy them. My parents didn't suspect anything.
No one did, least of all me."

My voice dribbled to a stop. I took a deep breath.
"One day we were playing around with Tami's father's scrying bowl. She thought it would be fun to
use it to light a fire, only she wanted a live target,
and decided her mother's cat was suitable for the
experiment. I was horrified. I loved animals, and I
wanted no part of the torture of a cat. I tried to get
her to stop, but she caught the cat and hauled it and
the bowl outside."

The tissues were dirty. I tossed them into a waste-
basket, moving it a few feet to the side. Strong emotions always made me feel antsy, as if my skin was
itching, leaving me with the need to be doing something physical to work off the excess energy. Adam
must have known well those feelings, for he said
nothing as I flitted back and forth tidying things up,
rearranging the various bottles on the sideboard.

"I tried to take the bowl away from her, but she
just teased me that I wasn't quick enough or strong
enough to keep up with her. She ran off with the cat
and bowl, with me in hot pursuit. I fell at one point,
skinning both knees badly, but even that didn't stop
me. When I reached her, she had the cat tied down
and was trying to position the bowl to catch the
sunlight."

The emotions I had felt thirty-odd years before

were still as fresh in my mind as when I had originally felt them. "Anger, pain, horror . . . they mingled together into one terrible moment that erupted when I managed to snatch the scrying bowl away from Tami, my emotions focused into the bowl until they exploded outward, knocking me back. When I shook the stars from my head and sat up, it was to find myself alone with the cat, Tami's terrified howl still echoing in my ears."

Slowly I turned to Adam. His face was blank. I knew he was trying to encourage me to talk, much as if I was a suspect he was interviewing. I moved a few inches to the side of the now burnt lamp. "At first, everyone thought my inadvertent eruption of power had banished her. Her parents got permission from the League to search the Akasha. They looked for her for three days before they gave up."

If I closed my eyes, I could still see the scene in my head: my father, newly separated from my mother, drawn home by the tragedy. The two of them sitting side by side on our old green couch. Me hiding in the coat closet, eavesdropping as Tami's parents tearfully told mine that there had been no sign she had ever been to the Akasha. The look of horror on my mother's face as she realized that her daughter had destroyed another living being . . . I turned away from Adam, the pain and shame of that moment still too much to share with anyone.

"Everyone was very nice to me. They said I wasn't at fault; I was too young to know what I was doing, too young to know how to harness my powers. But they worried that what could happen once, could happen again, that I'd get angry and out of control, and another innocent person would suffer. So the wergeld was bound to me, and I spent the next thirteen years being tutored in the art of transmortis anomaly extermination."

"That's harsh for a child," he said softly, his gaze holding mine. "Thank you for telling me, Karma. The experience you went through was traumatic, but it's clear that it tempered you into a champion for those weaker than you, be it a cat or a spirit. It also validates my impression that you are incapable of truly harming anyone."

I thought of the beings I'd cleaned and said nothing.

15

"Houston, we have a problem."

The living room was empty of everyone but Adam when I returned to it. He looked up from making notes. "We do?"

"Pixie is missing. She wasn't in the bathroom, and wasn't in any of the unoccupied rooms. Where's my father?"

"In the kitchen, helping the boys make more coffee. He said you looked worse than roadkill that had sat in the hot sun for three days, and could use a cup or two."

"A gallon is more like it," I answered, rubbing my forehead. I was so tired it was getting difficult to think with any sort of clarity. "Have you seen Pixie?"

He shook his head. "She hasn't been downstairs. I'd have noticed her if she used the front stairs, and the back stairs only go to the kitchen. Don't worry about her, Karma. She can't get out, and she can't get into any trouble in the house."

"I can't help but worry about her. I'm responsible for her! There's a murderer in the house, and there's no telling what horrible things he could do to her. . . ."

"*He?*" Adam asked.

"Or she. The point is, there's a murderer running around, and I can't find Pixie."

He looked thoughtful. "Very well. I'll go look for her."

"I'll get the guys from the kitchen to help. She's probably just hiding somewhere, thinking it's cute to cause us worry, but I don't like her off on her own until Meredith is in custody."

"You're certain Meredith is the killer, aren't you?" Adam asked, stopping at the bottom of the stairs.

"Oh yes. He's guilty of murder. The job is going to be proving it."

"If you're so certain, then why am I busting my balls to interview everyone else?"

I couldn't help smiling at the disgruntled expression on his face. "Because you're a member of the watch, and you won't commit yourself to a suspect until you've sifted through all the evidence. I don't mind doing the interviews with you, if that's what you're implying. In fact, I think they're helpful. I'm positive there are a few secrets that need to come out."

"Spoken like someone who has bared her soul," he answered with a wry smile. "Some of us may not wish to have all our secrets out in the open."

"I don't think you have anything to worry about. I was thinking more along the lines of what other machines Meredith has up his sleeves. I'll check the kitchen and the ground floors. Shall I send the spirits up to help you?"

He nodded and went upstairs. I found my father and the two ghosts sitting in the kitchen quite cozily around a small table, the scent of brewing coffee making my mouth water.

"—and I said to her, 'Karma, don't let one little incident ruin the rest of your'—oh, hello, honey."

"I don't suppose there are any more of those croissants left?" I was too tired to muster up even the feeblest glare at my father for airing my dirty laundry to the two spirits, although I did mentally utter a couple of swear words when it was apparent they were now very wary of me.

"Yes. You're welcome to them," Jules said, nudging a plate of two croissants toward me as if he expected me to snatch it up and decapitate him with it.

I acquired both coffee and a croissant, saying nothing to them other than "Adam would like to see you two upstairs. Pixie has gone missing, and we're trying to find her. Dad, you can help me search down here."

We looked all over the ground floor of the house, but there was no sign of Pixie.

"I take it by the silence from upstairs that Adam isn't having any better luck," I said, one finger tapping on my lips as I mulled over possible hiding spots that would appeal to a teenage polter.

"There's always . . ." Dad waved a hand toward the basement door.

"She wouldn't go down there. Would she?"

He shrugged. "She's an odd one. Maybe she likes dead bodies."

"Way off the ew meter there, Dad." I sighed. "All right, let's go check."

"I'll do it, honey. You just stand on the stairs and

alert the marines if Spider's body rises up and tries to eat my brains or something."

I followed him down the stairs, thanking my stars that I hadn't inherited his warped sense of humor.

Dad flicked on the lights, moving swiftly to the junction in the room. "Body's still there. Doesn't look like it's moved."

"I'm not concerned about him becoming a zombie," I said dryly.

"It's 'revenant,' not 'zombie,' Karma. How do you expect to get ahead if you don't use the correct terminology? Was it here the unicorn was hiding?"

He slipped behind the heater, then emerged to dust cobwebs off his sleeves.

"Yes. Anything?"

"No." He stooped to pick up something. "Not unless you're interested in a handful of apports. These appear to be . . . oh."

I turned at the sound of Adam's calling my name from upstairs. "We're down here. They appear to be what, Dad?"

"Nothing important."

"There you are. We looked upstairs and couldn't find her. Anything down here? What did Matthew find that wasn't important?" Adam asked as he made his way down the basement stairs toward us.

"Apports, I gather. From the floor in front of the heater."

"Let's see."

Dad shot me an odd look as he dropped a couple of jade green stones into Adam's hand. We followed Adam up the stairs and into the better light of the hall, both of us peering over his shoulder.

"Those are apports all right," I said.

"Hmm." Adam poked at them with his finger. "Green. I've never seen these before. My apports are white."

"They must be Pixie's," Dad said, zipping into the living room to fuss with things that didn't need fussing with. "She must have been in the basement when we weren't looking."

I watched Adam, fear building steadily inside me, as he turned the apports over in his hand. "She has to be here. She can't leave. She must be hiding somewhere. Did you look in Meredith's room?"

He nodded. "Jules looked there. Tony went into Savannah's. There were only the designated occupants. No Pixie in either room."

"She has to be here," I repeated, rubbing the back of my neck wearily.

"She is. You know as well as I do that it's almost impossible to find a polter when they don't want to be seen. I'm not too worried about her; she appears to be savvy enough to take care of herself."

"I doubt if she can handle a murderer, though."

Adam squeezed my shoulder. "I set Jules to watch Meredith's room. If he leaves it, we'll know. That's the best I can do until we find Pixie, OK?"

I hated to leave the girl alone and unprotected, but I didn't see any alternative. If Meredith was being watched . . . well, that would have to do. "All right. Dad, I guess you're up."

"Interview?" His face brightened. "Excellent! Do you mind if I don't sit?"

"Not at all." Adam led the way over to our little table and took a seat opposite me.

Dad walked around us in a fast circle, one that

caused dizziness if watched too long. I raised my eyebrows at Adam, distracted by a sudden thought.

"You don't seem to have any problem sitting still."

"Decades of training. I wanted a job in the mundane world, and although I used glamours at times, I figured it was better if I learned to pass as a mortal before the third arm dropped off. Plus, I'm a quarter human."

"It does help," I agreed.

"You don't seem to have inherited much of your father's traits. They're downright quiescent," he said, giving the pair of us a questioning look.

"It's sad, isn't it?" Dad asked. "She does have my eyes, though. And my good taste, in all things but her choice of men. The rest of her comes from her mother, sadly."

I ignored my father and gave Adam a little smile. "Like you, I knew I was going to make my way in the mortal world. It just took a little work to stifle the polter traits."

"You disapproved of Karma's choice of husband?" Adam asked, shifting his attention to Dad.

"Good lord, yes. I loathed the man, and he me," Dad answered, whipping around us in his circuit of restlessness. "He hated all our kind, except those he could sexually exploit. I didn't understand at first why he wanted to marry Karma, until I figured out his perverted sexual tastes."

"Gee, thanks, Dad."

He patted me on the shoulder as he went past me. "No offense intended, honey. You know I loved your mother deeply, at least until she turned into a shrew."

"Dad!"

"Sorry. Until she decided she needed a life without me. I have nothing against mixed marriages—but Spider didn't want you for yourself, as I did your mother. He wanted you because of what you were."

"Did Spider ever threaten you?" Adam asked.

"Hell, yes. All the time!" Dad answered cheerfully. "He started by threatening to cut me out of Karma's life, but by the time he knew she wouldn't go along with that, the threats turned to permanently eliminating me."

I gawked in astonishment. "He threatened your life? You never told me that!"

He gave me an oddly meaningful look as he passed by me. "Unlike some people not a million miles away from here, I don't feel obliged to spill every secret I have."

"God damn it, you listened to my private conversation with Adam!"

"I couldn't help but listen to it. You didn't even bother to leave the room."

I muttered a curse against the excellent hearing I knew he possessed. "Next time, you are free to excuse yourself from the room."

"What, and miss all the good bits?" He grinned. "Not likely."

"Can we get this conversation back on topic?" Adam asked. "We've established your profound dislike of Spider, and vice versa. Were your feelings about him enough to make you want to kill him?"

"Every day. Every time I saw his face smirking at Karma. Every passing year, when I saw what effect he had on her, how he was draining the life out of her."

"No one has drained the life out of me! I'm just fine!"

"Honey, honey, honey." His hand clapped onto my shoulder. "You're a shadow of what you used to be. You were vibrant before you met Spider. Now you're just . . . worn out."

I twitched my shoulder out from under his hand. "I don't know if I'm going to be able to cope with all these compliments, so let's get off the subject of me, and back to Spider. Where were you when he was being killed?"

He tossed all three hands into the air. "How do I know? I don't know when he was killed."

"You left the living room before I did. What did you do after Karma and Spider went upstairs?" Adam asked.

Dad paused in his circuit for a moment as he tried to recall. "Hmm. I went up to make sure my girl was all right, but when it was clear she was holding her own against him, I had a look around the house. You've got bats in the attic."

"I know. Did you go downstairs into the basement at any time?"

"Well . . ." Dad flitted over to the far window and twitched back the curtain. "I did for a minute, just to see what was down there. I heard someone breathing, and had a look-see about that, but it was only Amanita behind the heater. I was leaving when Spider and Meredith came in. Before you ask—I hid behind a rowboat until they'd gone into the other section of the room. Then I came back upstairs."

Adam frowned in thought. "You didn't see anyone down there other than Nita?"

He looked downright innocent, which usually

meant he was anything but that. "No. There was no one there but her."

"Ah," Adam said. "Did you see anyone going into the basement?"

"Not a soul. I have a bit of a sweet tooth, so I went to the kitchen to see if there wasn't something to nosh on. Didn't see anyone there. Since the two ghosties were gone, I took a few liberties with some pecan pie I found in the fridge. By the time I was done, Karma was up from her nap, so I came back here to see what was going on."

Apporting as he entered the room . . . which meant he was under stress or in the grip of some strong emotion, neither of which would be applicable if what he told us was true. I bit the end of the pen as I thought about what he could possibly have been up to that had left him in such a state.

"Anything else you want to know?"

Adam's pale gaze met mine for a second, asking a question. I shook my head.

"OK. Think I'll go have another look for Pixie. I'm an old hand at finding little girls who like to hide, aren't I, honey?"

"I was never very good at hiding," I pointed out.

"No, but you sure tried. It was instinctive. See you later, then." He hurried off toward the kitchen, no doubt to molest the pecan pie a bit more.

"Where are Tony and Amanita?"

"Hmm? Oh. Bed. I told them we'd talk to them in the morning. Once we find Pixie, I'll tell Jules he's off sentry duty."

I gave him a silent look of disapprobation.

"I know, you still think the boys are suspects, but I'm telling you they couldn't be. They don't have the energy to do it, for one. It takes just about everything they have to manifest enough energy to cook. And tonight they served coffee, and were visible a lot longer than they're used to. They couldn't do that if they'd spent every bit of strength they had killing your husband first."

"True." I sighed, too tired to sort through my thoughts.

Adam eyed me as if I were something that had crawled out of the river. "You look like hell. There's a room on the third floor you can use if you'd like. It's nothing fancy, but at least you can get a little rest."

"I'd thank you for such a chivalrous comment, but sadly, I feel like hell. I'd better go make another attempt to find Pixie. I won't be able to sleep until I know she's all right."

"We can swap floors if you like. I'll give this floor a once-over, and you can do the upper floors."

I nodded wearily and trudged up the stairs, trying to think of where I would hide if I were an angsty teenage polter. A half hour and three sweeps of the floor later, I found her hidden in the back of a linen closet.

She gave a little startled yelp when I yanked the door open. "*Deus!* You made me apport!"

"Out," I said, jerking my thumb toward the stairs.

She scooped up the couple of shiny black stones and tucked them away before picking up the flashlight she'd been using to light her journal. "I'm busy. Go away."

"And I'm exhausted, my husband has been killed, and I think I'm getting crampy, so if I were you, I'd get moving. *Now.*"

"Move where?" she snapped, getting to her feet. "Where am I supposed to go? All the rooms are taken."

"You're going upstairs with me. Adam has given us an attic room."

I gave her a little shove in the direction of the narrow flight of stairs at the landing. Adam looked up as we passed.

"Found her, I see."

"Yes. Thank you for your help. Morbidia will apologize for causing so much trouble in the morning."

"*Deus!* It's *Misericordia!* Is it so much to ask that people remember what my *name* is? And what do you mean we're going to share a room? Do you expect me to *sleep* with you? Are you some sort of psycho-lesbian? I'm *not* sleeping with you! I refuse to sleep at all! I just want to be left alone so I can write my *poems!*"

She stomped up the small stairs with a mutinous look on her face. I summoned a feeble smile for Adam.

"Get some rest," he said.

"I will. Sleep sounds heavenly right now." I walked slowly up the stairs, pausing midway to look down on him. He stood half in shadow, his pale eyes oddly illuminated, as if lit from within. "Things will look better in the morning, right?"

He grimaced, flipping off the light, and his bodiless voice emerged from the inky darkness. "I've always found they look worse."

16

The yelling didn't wake me up a few hours later, but Pixie kindly remedied that.

"Karma, wake *up*! Meredith is *yelling*! He says he's *dying*! *Deus*, why won't you wake up?"

I opened one very sleepy eye to squint at her kneeling on the bed, shaking my shoulder in an attempt to rouse me. "I thought you said you'd sooner have hot pokers shoved under your fingernails than be on the same bed as me."

She whumped me on the arm. "This is an emergency! Someone tried to kill Meredith."

"Too bad they didn't succeed." I snuggled into the pillow and tried to go back to sleep, but I knew in my heart of hearts that it wasn't going to happen.

"You have to get out there!" She gave me one last shove, then jumped off the bed and ran out of the room. I rolled over and sat up to peer with blurry eyes at my watch. It was early morning now, the sun up, but just barely. I'd gotten all of three hours' sleep.

"Karma!"

"All right, all right, I'm coming." I grumbled to myself as I got out of bed and staggered to the stairs.

"Although I don't see why I have to get up. If Meredith is yelling, he's not actually dead, so where's the hurry?"

"Morticia, did you—Oh, there you are, honey." My father smiled when he caught sight of me.

"Misericordia!"

"You better come down. There's been some trouble with that murdering bastard Meredith."

"My name is Misericordia! It's not Morticia or Morbidia or Mephistopheles! It's Misericordia! Cheese on toast, people! Why can't you remember that?"

I clutched the banisters to keep from plunging headlong down the narrow staircase. Dad slid me a quick look. "You look like hell. Didn't you get any rest?"

"Why does *everyone* feel the need to tell me just how awful I look?" I asked, straightening my shoulders.

"We care," Dad said, giving me a little pat before hurrying down the hallway to where several people were gathered around the bathroom door.

"Aha! I knew it! You didn't think I'd find this, did you?" Meredith's voice bellowed from the bathroom, quickly followed by the man himself. He shoved a small bottle under Adam's nose. "Tell me I'm imagining it now!"

"What's going on?" I asked, peering over Adam's shoulder. He was holding the small green bottle up to the light. The label on it read SYRUP OF IPECAC.

"Someone tried to poison me, as if you don't know," Meredith snapped. I frowned at him. He was always snapping at someone, usually me.

"You have some serious anger issues," I said. "I'm thinking therapy is in order."

"Or a hammer upside the head," my father offered.

Meredith glared at both of us. He did *that* a lot, too. "Why don't you just admit you tried to poison me?"

"Me?" I hoped I looked as surprised by the accusation as I felt. "I was sleeping. What's been happening?"

"Someone tried to poison me! That stuff was in the bottle of whiskey I brought up to bed with me. I damned near barfed my guts up. I could have been killed!"

"It's an emetic. I think all it can do is make you vomit," Adam said with such calmness I couldn't help giving him a little smile. He acknowledged it with a brief nod.

"You take enough of anything, and it'll kill you," Meredith said darkly, his face flushed. "Someone here tried to kill me, dammit! I demand you do something!"

"What would you suggest?" Adam asked, pocketing the ipecac.

"You're the police! Do your job! Figure out who tried to kill me, and turn 'em over to the real cops!"

"I don't deny that someone somewhere may want to poison you, but why would you imagine one of us would want to do so now?" I asked, waving my hands around at everyone gathered in the hallway. Savannah, strangely silent, stood with her arms wrapped tightly around herself. Antony stood next to her, wearing a minuscule pair of fishnet briefs, while Jules was clad in scarlet silk pajamas that made my mouth water. Amanita peeped out every now and again from her slightly opened door. "We're trapped here for another four hours or so. It doesn't make sense that anyone would be so stupid as to attack you now."

Meredith's mouth opened and shut a couple of times while he tried to work up an answer. Finally, he sputtered, "I know what I know, and I know that someone tried to poison me!"

Some peacekeeping urge drove me to try to point out the ill reasoning of that statement. "You were fine when you went upstairs, right?"

Grudgingly, he admitted that was so.

"Have you been drinking the last few hours, or did you go to sleep?"

"Not that it's any of your damned business, but I dozed on and off a bit. I woke up a few minutes ago, puking all over myself."

"Ew!" Pixie said softly.

"Which means that the whiskey couldn't have been poisoned while it was downstairs," I said, yawning. "I think you'll find everyone was asleep for the last couple of hours. I was upstairs, in a room with Pixie all night."

"I slept on the chair! We weren't in bed together!" she said quickly, brows pulled tight in her perpetual scowl.

"My father roomed with Jules and Tony, right?"

The three of them nodded. Dad, who had the most innocent expression on his face, trailed apports.

"Oh yes, he was with us," Tony said. "He slept on the divan in our room. We wanted him to take our bed, but he wouldn't hear of it."

"No reason to put anyone out," Dad said quickly with a weak smile. I turned a look on him that had the smile melting away to nothing.

"I was alone," Savannah said slowly. "But I was sleeping. All this has been so trying. . . ." Her hands fluttered for a moment, then dropped.

"After you puke your guts up because someone has attempted to poison you, then we'll talk about what *so trying* is," her husband replied before narrowing his eyes at Adam. "And just where were you?"

"Sleeping." Adam's face gave nothing away.

"Sleeping where? Isn't that your room she came out of?" Meredith asked, pointing at Savannah.

"Yes."

Meredith swaggered over to Adam, or swaggered as best someone who'd just spent a session praying to the porcelain god could. "So just where were you?"

A click had us all turning to look at Amanita's door. Speculation was rife in everyone's eyes as we looked back at Adam.

His color was high, as if he was blushing. "My whereabouts aren't a concern, since I didn't put ipecac in your drink. In fact, I'm inclined to believe no one did. . . . No one but you, that is."

"Jesus, Mary, and Joseph! If I wanted to kill myself, I'd sure as hell have a nicer way of doing it than poisoning!"

"I agree. Which makes it clear to me that this so-called poisoning was really an attempt at gaining pity. No doubt you thought to avert suspicion on yourself by making it seem like the murderer was attacking you."

"And I say you all did this together! You've set me up as a scapegoat, and now you're trying to get rid of me before the police prove just how trumped up and ridiculous the evidence is against me! Well, no more! I'm not going to eat or drink anything else in this madhouse until the police come to rescue me!" Meredith shoved Adam aside, stomped through the bathroom to the door adjoining his room, and slammed it without a backward glance at us.

I pinned my father back with a look. "I'd like to have a word with you, Dad."

"No time now," he said, whisking past me toward the main stairs. "I promised Jules I'd make my world-famous bacon omelet. Must get started."

I grabbed his arm before he could get out of reach, spinning him around and pushing him toward the smaller flight of stairs, leading upward. "I would *like* a *word*."

"Karma! I am your father! There is no need for you to manhandle me in this fashion!"

"Oh, I think there's every need," I said, pushing him into my room. To my surprise, Pixie, Adam, and Savannah followed us.

"Oooh, pretty," Savannah said, picking up something from the floor. She held out her hand. A couple of my dad's apports lay on it next to two shiny black stones. "Is it hematite?"

"No. Those are from Pixie. Er . . . Misericordia." I raised both eyebrows at my father. I knew the signs, knew he wouldn't be able to stand my unwavering stare for long.

My room was small to begin with, and now, filled with people, the space in which he could move was nonexistent. He tried to pace, tried to avoid my persistent stare, but it was no good, and he knew it. With a small cry, he finally collapsed onto the bed, his hands covering his eyes. "All right! You win! Now let me get out of here before I go crazy!"

"Not until you answer a couple of questions." I glanced at Adam. He looked confused for a moment; then his eyes widened with comprehension. "Why did you try to poison Meredith?"

"What makes you think I'm the one who . . ." Dad took one look at me and slumped into a miserable blob of polter. "I wasn't trying to poison him. I just wanted to make him a little sick. You can't kill someone with ipecac. If I had wanted to kill him, I certainly would have used something else."

There was that. The way Meredith had been slugging back the whiskey, it would have been laughably easy for Dad to slip something a little less benign into his glass while he was napping.

"He has a point, damn him," Adam said to me.

I nodded. "All right, I'm willing to absolve you from attempted murder, but that doesn't excuse you for poisoning Meredith's drink with ipecac."

"He deserved it," Dad answered with a sullen look on his face.

"He deserves a lot more, but that's not the issue." I remembered too late that Savannah was in the room and, while apparently on the outs with her husband, probably didn't appreciate the plain speaking going on. "I'm sorry to have to say that in front of you, Savannah."

She shrugged. "I see now that it's true. The scales have fallen from my eyes with regards to Meredith. He's not the man I married. He's . . . changed. And I don't like it."

"That seems to happen a lot to people," I said,

thinking of the way Spider had changed the last few years. "Still, it was wrong of me to say that so abruptly, and wrong for my father to get his jollies at your husband's expense."

"Oh, don't give me any crap about not being judge and jury," Dad suddenly said, getting quickly to his feet. "I won't buy it, not from you. You know full well if I didn't do it, you would have."

I opened my mouth to protest, but Adam stepped in. "I think we've said everything that needs to be said. Matthew, I will have to charge you with malicious mischief for the attack against Meredith."

With lightning quickness customary to full-blooded polters, Dad's countenance changed from accusatory to mischievous. "It was worth it," he said, grinning and rubbing his hands together. "Did you hear him puking up his guts? Music to my ears."

"You are in trouble with me, too, buster," I said, pointing a finger at him.

"Shakin' in my boots, honey. Shakin' in my boots."

"I suppose it's too late to try to get any more rest," Adam said, consulting his watch. "The boys are probably starting breakfast. Shall we go downstairs?"

"She talks to you just like she does to me," Pixie said to my father as the two went out the door. "Is she always this bossy?"

"Always. Has been ever since she was a little girl. She gets that from her mother's side, you know. . . ."

Their voices faded as they tromped downstairs. Savannah murmured a desire to wash up before breakfast, quickly heading for the bathroom.

Adam and I were left alone in the room.

"I'm sorry about my father," I said after a moment of silence. "I don't blame him for what he did, but I don't condone it, and I certainly didn't encourage him to do it. It does, however, bring up an interesting point."

"That if he wanted to kill Meredith, he certainly had the opportunity, and yet he only pulled a prank instead . . . which leaves the idea of murder a little less likely?"

"Exactly." I chewed on my lower lip. "As far as my father is concerned, it would have been completely reasonable for him to pull something like that with Spider. I think the only reason he didn't was because he knew I'd live with the repercussions of such an act. But it's totally out of his character to murder someone. Pranks? Yes. Murder? No. I just don't think he could do it."

"Neither do I, as it happens."

A little knot of tension I hadn't been aware of relaxed at Adam's words. "I appreciate that. Dad isn't always the most levelheaded of people, but I admit that Meredith is particularly trying."

Adam threw me a curious look. "You really don't like him, do you?"

"Meredith, you mean?" I sat on the bed to put on my shoes. "I think he's responsible for murder, so no, I don't like him. In addition to that, he's clearly some sort of electronics genius bent on destroying as many spirits as he can. He needs to be stopped, Adam. The question is, are you going to turn him over to the watch when the seal expires?"

"Mmm." He moved over to the window and twitched back the curtain, exposing sky that was beginning to change from gray to rosy pink. "I don't have any concrete proof that he killed your husband."

"He's guilty of murder, Adam. I know that as sure as I know my name. I feel it in my bones. He's guilty, and I don't want him to get away with it."

"Unfortunately, the feeling in your bones isn't enough to get a conviction, not even with the watch. I need some real proof in order to charge him."

"I know. It's just so wrong that he should do something so cruel, so heinous, and get away with it." Frustration roiled within me. Time was running out and Adam didn't seem to be any closer to nailing Meredith. Once the seal was gone and the watch took over, my chances of convincing Adam of Meredith's guilt would be nil. I had to do something to make him see the truth. . . . But what? What more could I do?

"There're still a few hours to go before the seal lifts. We can question him again."

I sighed and nodded, following him out of the room. "Let's do that. I have a feeling I'm missing something important, something someone said that refuses to come into focus. Maybe talking with him again will help."

"After breakfast." He stopped at the bottom of the stairs, a smile slowly spreading as he sniffed a couple of times. "Smells like the boys are pulling out all the gastronomic stops. Shall we?"

The heavenly scent of bacon wafted out from the dining room, along with the pleasant chatter that accompanied people sitting down to a much-anticipated meal. I was surprised to feel a dull, hollow rumbling in my stomach. I couldn't imagine how I could be hungry, but I was. "Oh yes, please. I'm famished."

"Good. I'll take a plate up to Nita; then we can make a game plan for the interview with Meredith."

"You're very protective of her," I said, half-distracted by the sight of all the food on the sideboard that took up almost an entire wall in the dining room.

"She's shy around people she doesn't know well."

"I have one of those at home. A Roman goddess of doors. We ought to get the two of them together," I said with a smile before giving in to the temptation that lay before me. "That looks wonderful, Tony."

The spirit made a little bow as he deposited a carafe of coffee on the table. "We won't be worth dirt for the rest of the day, but we thought you all deserved a hearty breffy. The potato-and-sausage frittata is particularly . . . good god, Julie! What are you thinking—parsley on eggs? If I've told you once, I've told you a thousand times: parsley is passé. It's all about basil now!"

Jules tweaked the tablecloth and adjusted a plate. "Parsley can never be passé. So sayeth the Iron Chef."

"My dear, it's gospel according to Martha. And you know she's never wrong!"

The two spirits floated back to the kitchen, arguing over which of their cooking gurus was right.

I set my plate down at the end of the table. Dad, reading the previous day's newspaper, was happily stuffing his face with parsley-bedecked eggs. Pixie had her iPod going, but her eyes were wary as she sipped tea and nibbled on a naked piece of toast. Savannah entered just as Adam left to take a plate up to Amanita.

"Everything looks so tempting," Savannah said, pouring herself a cup of coffee. "No, thank you, Tony. I'll help myself in a few minutes."

Tony set a carafe of orange juice on the table and shrugged, then returned to the kitchen.

"Did you get any rest?" I asked her.

She smiled. "I was about to ask you all the same thing. I had a difficult time relaxing. I think it's because there's something I need to do, and haven't yet done."

"Divorce your husband?" my father asked, still reading the paper.

"Dad!"

He looked up and made an apologetic face at Savannah. "I'm sorry. That was rude of me. It kind of slipped out. . . ."

I gave him the gimlet eye, but as usual, it did little good.

"My marriage is something that I will need to reevaluate," Savannah said with placid acceptance as she sipped her coffee. "But I will meditate on that later. I communed with my spirit control, and he told me that Spider's ethereal being—his essence, if you will—was restless, and wanted to communicate with us."

"Not another séance?" Pixie asked, crumbling toast. "They're no fun if you won't summon a demon or two."

"Demons! Gracious goddess, no. I would never condone such a thing! It's bad enough to call a poltergeist, but a demon!" Savannah fingered her amulet bag and gave one of her delicate shudders. "No, indeed. I had thought to try a little automatic writing, though. I haven't always had the best luck with it, but Jebediah—he's my control—thought that we might have a better chance of reaching Spider if we used a method that taxed his essence less than a séance."

A thought clicked into place in my mind. I looked up at my father to see if he had caught the same thing I had, but he was engrossed in the newspaper. I puzzled over the point for a moment before asking Savannah, "How long have you been interested in spirits and polters and all the rest?"

"Oh, since I was a little girl. I had a poltergeist experience when I was about twelve. It was very unnerving. I dabbled in it a bit growing up, and through college, but didn't settle down to do serious research with the PMS until last year." She glanced at Pixie and my father before turning back to me, saying in a lowered voice, "Although I had no idea at all about any of this. No idea whatsoever! It seems so fantastic, and yet makes so much sense, that people like you all exist. But that you could pass for normal people . . . I just had no idea!"

I kept my expression pleasant despite the backhanded compliment. "What sort of research have you done with the PMS group?"

"We investigate hauntings, primarily. The Admiral's Mansion in Aberdeen—you've heard of it? It's supposedly one of the top twenty-five haunted houses in the U.S. Well, PMS has done extensive research there. We've spent nights in the house filming, conducting séances, and attempting to isolate and identify the hot spots of psychic activity there."

"I see." That wasn't telling me anything useful. "But with regards to polters—have you or your group done any special research on them?"

An odd look passed over her face. "Why, no. I just

told you that I had no idea that you people were as you are. No idea!"

"Indeed." I leaned forward and looked her dead in the eye, willing every ounce of my polter heritage to let me sense any variations in her body language. The strange faint buzzing noise caught the edge of my consciousness, but I dismissed it. "But you know the difference between summoning and calling, don't you?"

"I beg your pardon?"

I dropped my voice until it was a whisper, and continued to pin her back with a gaze that sought confirmation of my suspicions. "You mentioned *calling* a polter. Only someone with experience in the Otherworld would know the difference between summoning and calling."

"I . . . I don't quite see . . ." She looked confused, but I wasn't fooled. She'd slipped up, and we both knew it.

"Spirits and demons are summoned. Polters are called. If you are as naive about polters as you say, why do you know the difference?"

She sat back, a gentle smile on her face, but her fingers were white as they twisted a napkin. "Goddess, you startled me for a moment! I thought something was wrong. I have no idea when or where I learned the difference. I assume someone at PMS mentioned it. Or I might have read it; I'm very big on doing research, you know."

"How reassuring." I sat back, as well, having gotten my answer. In genetic structure I might not have inherited much from my father along the polter lines, but even I could read Savannah's body language. She was trying very hard not to appear flustered, but it was clear she was lying about something.

Why on earth would she want people to think she was clueless about polters when the opposite was true? And why was she so nervous about my knowing her secret?

17

I puzzled over Savannah's odd behavior while she chatted brightly to my father and Pixie—neither of whom made much effort to converse. Adam entered the room and served himself, then sat down across from me.

"Meredith says he's feeling better. He'd like some breakfast," he said to Savannah.

She raised an eyebrow. "He's perfectly capable of getting his own breakfast, I assure you."

"He said he'd prefer you to bring him up a plate," Adam answered, applying pepper rather heavily to his eggs.

Pixie and I both sneezed.

"Sorry. Pepper gets away from me."

"My days of waiting on that man hand and foot are over." Savannah rose with a graceful movement, collecting a plate and a small sampling of the breakfast fare.

"I believe he's expecting you to bring him something," Adam said.

She tossed her head. "He can just wait, then."

"Should I tell him that, or leave him alone?" Tony

asked, drifting through the table with a plate of what looked to be burnt toast in his hands. "I was going to take these odds and bobs from breakfast up to Karma's imps. Do they like cantaloupe?"

"They'll eat just about anything but asparagus; that makes them swell up like puffer fish. I'd leave Meredith alone, personally."

"Ew." Pixie made a face at the comment about my imps before dropping her scowl back to her plate.

"Yes, by all means, let the bastard starve."

My eyebrows rose at the vehemence in Savannah's voice.

She continued on with blithe disregard for her husband's welfare. "Adam, my spirit control suggested I try automatic writing this morning, to contact Spider before the seal is lifted. There will be time for me to do that, won't there?"

"Er . . . yes." Adam didn't look like he had much faith in her ability to get Spider to do anything, much less tell us who his murderer was.

"Excellent. I've had some luck with automatic writing in the past. Have you ever tried it?"

"No." Adam picked up a section of the paper my father had discarded. Despite it's being a day old, he propped it up in front of himself and appeared to read the news with a strange avidity.

"Oh." She looked crestfallen for a moment before turning to Pixie. "You'd like automatic writing, Misericordia."

"*Nephthys.*"

I smiled to myself. Nephthys was one of the most famous figures in polter history. Every polter child was taught about how she'd married the Egyptian god Seth, bringing the polters forth as positive beings

rather than frightening entities. Pixie had made a fit-
ting choice for her new name.

"Pardon?" Savannah asked.

"My name is *Nephthys*. Misericordia wasn't working. *No one* could remember it." The glare she sent
me should have singed off at least a hair or two, but
I gave her a bland smile in return.

"I see. That's very pretty. It's Egyptian, isn't it?"

Pixie shrugged. "I dunno. I saw it on the Web. It
has something to do with the underworld, and it
sounds dark. *People* should be *able* to *remember* it!"

I ignored yet another of her glares and glanced
with disbelief at Adam and my father. Had neither
of them heard her? Apparently they hadn't, for both
of them kept their respective noses buried in the
newspaper.

"Yes, it's very dark, and I'm sure no one will have
any trouble remembering it. You're very into that
sort of thing, aren't you? Perhaps you'd like to try
automatic writing, as well?"

Pixie frowned down at the tabletop, her face set in
a sullen expression.

"Oh! I'm so sorry. . . ." She shot me a flustered
glance. "Are you people not able to do it? Communicate with spirits, I mean?"

"Dunno, I've never tried. Although I'd prefer to
summon a demon. I've always wanted a demon of
my own," Pixie said.

All the warning bells and whistles in my head
went off at her words. I tossed down my napkin,
rising, then took a firm hold on her shirt as I walked
past her. "If you're done mauling your toast, I'd like
to have a word with you. Right now!"

Adam glanced up questioningly. I shook my head

at him and hustled a sputtering Pixie into the next room, closing the door firmly behind us.

"Stop it! You're hurting me!" she complained, jerking her arm out of my grip and smoothing over the rumpled bit of shirt. "*Deus!* This is child abuse, you know! I could complain to the League about you!"

"Oh, really? You know what they'd say? You haven't been a polter long enough to be considered a real citizen, and thus aren't eligible for protection."

She froze, her pupils dilating slightly. "What?"

"Just how long have you been a polter?" I asked, crossing my arms in an attempt to look as intimidating as possible.

"I don't know what you're talking about." The expression on her face might be stubborn, but she couldn't look me in the eye when she spoke.

I relaxed slightly as another piece of the puzzle clicked into place. "Let's go over the facts, and I'll see if I can't make myself a little clearer. First, there's the matter of your name."

"What about it?" She peeked up at me from under her dense overhang of bangs.

"Names have power. Everyone in the Otherworld knows that. People here don't change their names at the drop of a hat."

She said nothing.

"That can possibly be explained away by your youth and desire to blend into the Goth lifestyle. What can't be explained is the fact that you don't know who Nephthys is."

Her head snapped up, her eyes mutinous. "Are you calling me stupid?"

"No, I'm not. The tale of Nephthys is something

that is taught to every polter child, from a very early age. For you to be ignorant of it says you weren't raised in a polter home . . . which leads me to your wanting to summon and command a demon."

"What, is it like a crime to summon a demon?"

"No, it's not a crime," I said quietly, eyeing the stormy, troubled girl in front of me and wondering who she really was. "It is, however, quite impossible for a polter to summon a minion of a demon lord. Everyone knows that. Everyone who was raised in the Otherworld, that is."

Her gaze faltered and dropped, her shoulders slumping. She swayed for a moment, and I put a hand out to steady her, but she jerked backward, stumbling over to the window seat. "Leave me alone. Just leave me alone."

I squatted down next to her while she curled up into a ball of misery. "What happened, Pixie? Why were you made a polter?"

She mumbled something that sounded like "Stupid demon lord."

"Pixie, I'm sorry I have to ask you to tell me about something that's obviously very painful. But I need to know the truth."

"Why?" she asked sullenly.

It took me a few seconds to sort through what I wanted to say. "Protection, mostly. I'm . . . We're not going to be together much longer, but I will do everything I can to protect you until the seal is lifted. After that—well, things are going to be a bit dicey, but I will talk to the League home and make sure they understand that you have to be protected."

She raised her head enough to ask, "Protect me from what?"

"From the mundane world. And from situations in our world. What happened to you?"

"You won't understand." She wrapped both arms around herself, burrowing next to the wall and turning her face to look out the window.

"You'd be surprised what I can understand."

"Oh, that's right, you're a murderer. Maybe you *will* understand."

I didn't even flinch at the accusation. "What happened?"

"*Deus!* You're not going to leave me alone, are you? You're going to keep picking on me until I tell you!"

"Persistence, thy name is Karma," I agreed.

She heaved a martyred sigh and traced a protection-ward symbol on the glass. I wondered where she'd learned to draw wards. "I borrowed a ring from my stepsister, OK? She cursed me. Or had a demon lord do it. I don't remember much about it. All I know is I borrowed it and she had me turned into a polter."

"I see."

"No, you don't see," she suddenly snapped, turning an agonized face to me. "You were born this way. You weren't born normal, then turned into this, and kicked out of your family and school, and all your friends wouldn't have freaked if they'd seen what you really were. You don't know what it's like to be me!"

"Just because I haven't lived your life doesn't mean I can't empathize," I said, handing her a box of tissues from the table next to me. She snatched it from me and angrily scrubbed at her wet cheeks. "Although I'm puzzled why your stepsister took such an extreme action for so minor a situation."

"She was a Follower."

"Ah. Which demon lord was she bound to?"

"Bael."

I flinched. Bael was the premier prince of Abaddon, the ruler of all the demon lords. If Pixie's stepsister had sworn to serve him, it was entirely possible she wielded a lot of power through him. I'd run into only one Follower in my time, but the aura of dark power that surrounded him had given me the willies. I would have liked to question Pixie more about her past, but I'd been intrusive enough. I contented myself with patting her on the leg and saying, "I don't understand why the League felt they had to conceal your origins, but that's neither here nor there. Now that I know you're a neophyte, I can help you over possible stumbling blocks."

"I'm not a neophyte, whatever that is," she grumbled, but her dark scowl eased a little.

"You certainly won't be for long." I glanced at the closed door to the dining room, getting to my feet with a sigh. "I'd better make sure my father isn't being obnoxious to Savannah."

"Karma . . ." Pixie bit her lip and looked out the window again.

"Hmm?"

Her thin shoulders twitched in wordless emotion. "You said I can't stay with you. Is it because I'm a freak?"

Sadness tinged my smile. "You aren't a freak in any way."

"Then why can't I stay with you?" she asked, her eyes dark with pain.

"Spider . . . ," I said, and choked to a stop. "Spider's death has changed things, I'm afraid. If the situation was different, I'd be happy to have you stay with me; I truly would. But sometimes life just doesn't work out the way you would like it to, and regrettably, this is one of those times."

"That's just lame," she said, turning her face away from me.

The condemnation lay heavily on me, but there was nothing I could do to deny it. "Yeah. Life sucks sometimes, doesn't it?" I said, forcing down a painful lump in my throat as I left the room to check on my father.

"You're sure they won't break anything?"

I closed the door gently on the sound of imps cooing with happiness as they splashed around in a couple of inches of water in the bathtub, and smiled at the worried look on Adam's face. "They're not that sort of imp. They get into things and sometimes make a mess, but they aren't destructive. Besides, they love water. They'll be quite happy to play in the tub for a couple of hours, especially since Jules donated his devil ducky."

Adam gave me a long look. "You are one of the oddest people it's been my pleasure to meet."

"Thank you. I think. Shall we tackle Meredith again? Dad is Pixie-watching for me."

Adam waited for me to precede him up the stairs. "Does she need a babysitter?"

"Not in the normal sense of the word, no. But I

don't want her disappearing again." I stopped in front
of the door to Meredith's room and took a deep breath.
"Do you want to be the good cop or the bad cop?"

"Don't be ridiculous; we don't do that anymore."
Adam gave a couple of curt knocks and tried the
door handle. "Dammit, he's locked it. Meredith?
Open up. We want to talk to you."

It took a minute, but at last Meredith opened the
door a smidgen. "Where the hell's my wife with
my breakfast?"

"She's a bit busy now," I told him. "If you're absolutely starving, I suppose something could be
brought up for you."

The look he gave me could have stripped paint.
"And be poisoned again? No, thank you. Tell Savannah to get off her ass and bring me some food. Some
safe food."

"I don't think your wife is inclined to do you any
favors," Adam told him. "I believe her words were
'Let the bastard suffer,' weren't they, Karma?"

"Yup. It would seem she has washed her hands
of you."

Meredith swore with colorful, if impossible, cre-
ativity. "That stupid bitch. Parading around like her
shit don't stink, demanding money from me all the
time for her crackpot schemes, telling me how she's
going to use those damned machines to get what's
rightfully hers. You want to know what's rightfully
hers? Jack shit, that's what!" Meredith shoved his
enraged face toward us, his eyes bloodshot from lack
of sleep. The whiskey on his stale breath made my
nose wrinkle. "She'd have nothing without me, nothing! Those machines are worthless without me. And
you can tell her that!"

The door slammed in our faces before Adam and I had time to do more than blink in confusion.

"Machines?" Adam asked.

"What's rightfully hers, I wonder?" I said at the same time.

He pursed his lips for a moment. "I think we need to have another talk with Madam Savannah."

"I think you're absolutely right."

18

We arrived at the dining room, which was now bare of breakfast, to find the table covered in papers.

". . . and keep my mind a blank. I'm totally unaware of what my hand is writing. As you can see, I don't even have my eyes open," Savannah was saying to an audience that consisted of my father, Pixie, and the two spirits. "Now, dear, if you would just replace the paper . . . perfect. That way, you see, my hand can continue to write without stopping."

Pixie looked from the piece of paper she held to the others littering the table. They contained nothing but random loops and waves. "What's it mean?"

"Not every page shows actual writing. Sometimes it takes a bit to get to a communication from a spirit. We can help it by asking specific questions, but in a situation such as this, I prefer to just let whatever entity who wishes to make contact do so without pressure. So I just keep my mind blank, and let my hand move as it will."

"I thought with the house sealed, no spirits could get through to anyone here," Pixie said, pulling another sheet of gibberish from Savannah as she reached the end of the page.

I picked up a couple of the topmost sheets of paper. As I'd suspected, there was no communication on those, either, only random waves and swoops.

"That's true, but as we found out with the séance, there are dormant spirits in the house. Who knows what else may be residing here? And I have high hopes that we'll make contact again with Spider."

"If you wake my grandfather up again . . . ," Adam said warningly.

"I can't control who uses me at all," Savannah murmured, her eyes closed as she swayed ever so slightly with the movement of her hand over the sheet of paper. "I'm a blank manuscript, waiting to be written."

"Sounds stupid," Pixie muttered.

Tony suddenly sat up straight. "Oh, my dear, no! It works, it really does! One of Adam's old girlfriends tried it with us that time we went underground— When was that, Julie?"

"The 1950s," Jules answered with a shudder. Both ghosts were barely visible, in what I thought of as a low-watt mode.

"Those shoulder pads!" Tony answered with a similar shudder before pulling himself to the present. "That was such a grim time, Julie and I thought we'd take a little rest, only somehow, we forgot to tell Adam. So his girlfriend, a really lovely woman once you got past the fact that she was a Moravian, did some automatic writing to contact us."

Jules cackled to himself. "She was ever so startled when she woke up Tony and he started dictating the most risqué limericks. What was it, now?"

"There was a young man from Perth, whose cods were the finest on Earth—," Tony started to recite.

"I think that's enough of a trip down memory lane," Adam interrupted with a glance toward Pixie. "Karma and I would like to have a word with Savannah, if you don't mind. Alone."

"We want to see who comes through," Tony protested. "This is the most excitement we've had for years!"

"I don't care. Go rest up. We may need you later," Adam said, making shooing motions with his hands.

I turned to my father and cocked an eyebrow.

He heaved a martyred sigh and pushed himself up from the table, holding out a hand for Pixie. "Looks like we're de trop, my girl. Shall we go check on the imps?"

"I am not a *child*! I don't *have* to be gotten out of the way!" she said with an indignant look tossed in my direction.

"Of course you're not. But there are times when three is company, and seven is a crowd."

"Lame excuse. What's a Moravian?"

"Another word for vampire." Dad gently pushed her through the door, pausing to say in Poltern before he left, "I want to hear the full details when you're done."

"What's all this about?" Savannah asked in a dreamy voice, cracking one eye open briefly to shove aside a filled paper and start on a new one. "Karma, would you mind taking over page duty? It's distracting for me to have to keep track of it, and the more distracted I am, the less entities can use me to write for them."

"We had a little chat with your husband," Adam

said, standing in what I'd mentally termed his confrontational pose: arms crossed over his chest, weight balanced on the balls of his feet, eyes glittering with icy blue intent.

"I can't be distracted with such negative thoughts as that man spawns," she answered without opening her eyes. "Page, Karma."

"Oh, sorry." I obediently whipped away yet another page, giving Adam a meaningful look.

"I regret having to distract you, but we need to talk. This is important."

Savannah was silent for a few seconds before heaving an exaggerated sigh. She set down her pen, laced her fingers together, and opened her eyes. "I only hope that when you're done I'll be able to attain the state of mental awareness I just had. What is it you wished to discuss with me?"

I took a seat at the end of the table, trying unobtrusively to pull out my notebook. Adam, evidently feeling a less authoritative air would be conducive to confidences, also sat down, absently tidying up the mass of scribbled-on papers. "During the course of our brief conversation with your husband, he said you'd told him that you were going to use the machines to get back what was rightfully yours. Would you care to explain that?"

Her face was placid, but her fingers tightened. Her laugh wasn't its usual water-tinkling-in-a-brook variety, either. "Goddess above, how am I to explain anything that man says? I'm sorry to have to say this about someone in whom I had placed so much trust, but I see now that Meredith is not in full control of his faculties."

Well, that was a new one. "Are you saying he's insane?" I asked.

"Not insane per se," she answered, unlocking her fingers to make an airy gesture of dismissal. "Not institutionally insane, just . . . not very grounded in reality."

"So, if we were to ask him to explain what he meant by the accusation, you don't think he could tell us anything?" Adam's hands lay relaxed on the table. I took a moment to admire his self-control. I knew how hard it was for me to sit still when I was excited; it must have been much more difficult for him, with his almost pure polter ancestry.

"On the contrary, I'm sure he'll have lots to say." Savannah looked just as relaxed as Adam, but I got the feeling we were seeing only what she wanted us to see, as if she, too, were enacting the strictest control over her emotions. "It's just that none of it will be the truth. I can assure you I have no ulterior motive for anything I do, save the intellectual pursuit of knowledge."

Adam's expression was unreadable. I wondered if he was as suspicious of Savannah as I was. "Hmm. And the machines Meredith mentioned you using? What would those be?"

"Machines? I told you before: I'm the most technophobic person on the planet. I don't even try to work the TV remote. Electronics and I do *not* get along."

I might not have the polter ability to accurately read emotions, but I could generally recognize a lie when I heard it, and Savannah had just told a whopper. I took a peek over the top of my notebook. Adam met my gaze, acknowledging my suspicion.

Almost imperceptibly, his body language changed to that of an interrogator. "Indeed. How long have you lived in this area?"

"In Washington, you mean? Oh . . . about four years. My family is from a small town in northern California."

Lie, I wrote down in the notebook.

"And what did you do before you met your husband and became involved in the psychic group?"

"I was an insurance actuator for a national company."

Lie.

"You had no knowledge of the plans your husband was participating in to turn this house into an Otherworld brothel?"

"None whatsoever. I would have thought my statements before made it quite clear that I'd never condone such a heinous act."

That, at least, was the truth. Whatever else she might have going on, she didn't appear to have known about the plans for the house. Which left me to wonder exactly what Meredith was talking about. What did she hope to regain? What had been lost? Money? Prestige? An heirloom? And did any of that have something to do with Adam's house? She'd been poking around the house earlier in the day; was there something there that she wanted?

Adam continued grilling Savannah while my thoughts ran along grim lines. At one point I was struck with the chilling idea that perhaps it was Adam's spirits that she had in her sights. I'd heard about supposed scientific groups that trapped spirits and used them to generate income, much like Spider and Meredith had planned, but without the sex. Could she be pretending innocence to capture Tony and Jules?

"Why on earth do you want to know what my

maiden name is?" Savannah's voice, tinged with exasperation, pierced my dark musings. "What does that have to do with anything?"

Adam shot me an inquiring glance.

"Honestly, I'm happy to answer questions so long as they are pertinent, but I am getting the feeling that you're fishing for something you can use to accuse me. I have explained repeatedly that I did not kill Spider, and I do not have some deep, dark ulterior motive for anything."

Ding, ding, ding! Lie!

I made a little face at Adam. He rightly interpreted it to mean I had nothing to add.

"I'm sorry if my questions or manner have been offensive or overly taxing. If you could run through your actions of last night one more time, I'd appreciate it."

She sighed and rolled her eyes heavenward, apparently looking for patience, recounting yet again her movements of the night before. Adam, having heard it a couple of times, absently shuffled through the papers before him, nodding and making encouraging noises as Savannah spoke.

I listened with half my attention, still puzzling over what it was she was hiding, and why. She wanted the house; that I knew. But did that have anything to do with whatever secret she was keeping from us? Or was it a coincidence? I had a feeling that the answer was right before me, but I couldn't bring it into focus. It was a maddening sensation, the source of which seemed to become more elusive the harder I tried to pin it down.

". . . and then I said I'd find Meredith, and we all went down to the basement. You know what happened after that."

"Mmmhmm," Adam murmured, glancing down at a page. "Who's Bethany?"

I shot out of my chair, snatching the paper from him before he could so much as blink. "What?"

"Bethany. That's the name on the paper. At least I think it is. What's wrong with you?"

I stared at the sheet of paper clutched in my hands, my world narrowing to it and the name it contained. It couldn't be. It just couldn't be. How could Savannah know about the death of my little cousin? She couldn't. Bethany's death hadn't reached the mortal media, and coverage in Otherworld circles had been kept to a minimum out of respect for my aunt and uncle. There was no way Savannah could have heard about Bethany . . . unless it was Bethany herself who had made contact.

"Karma? Is something wrong? You look as white as snow."

Grabbing the rest of the papers and quickly searching them, I shook away the feeling of horror that crawled up my arms. The random scribbled loops filled page after page, but at the bottom of one page, the word "release" was discernable.

"You're scaring me, Karma. Did I make contact?"

Two faces came into focus, one worried, one puzzled. I gave myself a mental shake and summoned up a smile I knew was feeble at best. "Sorry. I didn't mean to scare you, Savannah. I was just taken by surprise."

"Then I did make contact!" She leaned over to look at the sheets I held. " 'Release.' What did you say the name was, Adam? Beth?"

"Bethany," I answered, quickly scanning the rest of the sheets. There was nothing else, just her name

and the word "release." My throat ached with the
swell of emotions brought on by the sight of my
cousin's name scribbled on a sheet of paper. Had she
really made contact, or was this just some sort of a
cruel trick?

"Do you think it's she who wants release?" Savannah asked, going through the other papers. "I assume
you know who she is, Karma. Do you see anything
else? Just the two words?"

Adam's intent gaze was on me. It took an effort,
but I put the papers back onto the table, just as if
they were nothing more exciting than sheets with
scribbles on them. "Yes, I know her. She was my
cousin. She died three weeks ago."

"Oh, my dear," Savannah murmured, moving over
to put an arm around my shoulders. "I'm so sorry.
How traumatic for you. But you must set your mind
at ease; if I contacted her once, I can do it again. You
just sit there and handle the paper changing, and I'll
reestablish contact."

"No!"

The shout echoed, starkly abrupt in the sleepy,
sunny dining room.

Savannah pulled her arm away from me. I took a
deep breath, pushing down all the confusion and
pain that roiled inside me. "Thank you for the offer,
Savannah, but I really think it would be best to . . .
to not go forward with this."

"It would be no trouble to make contact again, I
assure you."

Adam's eyes were rich with speculation. I avoided
looking at him, pushing myself back from the table.
"I appreciate that. I know you must both think I'm
crazy, but my cousin is much mourned. I do not

think anyone in the family would want her to be . . . disturbed."

"Of course," Savannah said with silky reassurance.

There was a faint questioning note that I ignored. If she was pulling a cruel joke on me, I wouldn't give her the pleasure of getting any further reaction. If she wasn't . . . well, the least said there was the best.

"Your cousin?" Adam asked. "What's she doing in my house?"

I shook my head. "I don't know. She can't be here; there's no reason for her to be here. Unless . . ." The words trailed off as a sobering thought struck me.

"Unless you are grieving her loss so much that her spirit is bound to you and unable to find the peace she seeks," Savannah said in a voice brimming with sympathy.

"Perhaps," was all I said.

Savannah handed me the sheets of paper. "Well, it would seem that my spirit guide, Jebediah, was right again. There *was* something I needed to do this morning. I shall write up my experience here for the PMS journal—without including names, naturally. I'll just go take a few notes now, while it's all fresh in my mind."

She bustled off, leaving me alone in the room with Adam. For some reason, I felt a bit nervy, my hands smoothing the paper over and over again. "I expect you'll want to hear about Bethany," I said finally, disturbing the thick silence of the room.

"I can get the facts from my watch captain, if you'd rather not talk about it." His tone was sympathetic but matter-of-fact.

"There's no need. I can tell you the details quickly

enough. My cousin's body was found in the rubble of an apartment complex that was being razed in order to be rebuilt. The coroner determined that she'd been raped, and dumped there. She was fifteen."

Adam frowned, his fingers twiddling with a pen. "I don't remember hearing about a murder of a fifteen-year-old girl. You said this was three weeks ago? I was out of the state then on marshal business, but I should have heard about it from my watch captain."

I walked to the window, closing my eyes for a moment at the sensation of sunshine bathing me in its warm embrace. Sunny mornings always reminded me of my childhood, when I'd wake up to a day filled with exciting possibilities. "She wasn't exactly murdered. The coroner said she killed herself, but I know it was a direct result of the rape. My cousin wasn't a tramp. She was bright, and loving, and . . ." My throat closed up.

Adam moved behind me, his hand warm on my shoulder as he offered awkward comfort.

"I know it won't mean much, but I'll do everything I can to help find the person who did that to your cousin," Adam said.

I gave him a small smile. "Thanks. I'll be counting on you."

19

Adam was right, I mused sourly to myself a half hour later as I emerged from the kitchen.

"Well?" he asked, following me as I stopped at the dining room table, now clear of paper but bearing a suede glasses case that belonged to Savannah. I picked it up and clicked the lid open and closed a couple of times.

"You're going to make me say it, aren't you?"

"Yep. Was I right, or was I right?"

I sighed, turning to face him. "You were right, and I was wrong. Happy now?"

He grinned.

"Smugness ill becomes you." I made an annoyed noise and mentally ran over the interview we'd just conducted. "I will admit that I didn't really think that Tony and Jules had the motive, let alone the ability, to kill Spider, but dammit . . . if they didn't do it, and you say Meredith didn't, who did? We've talked to everyone, and only Meredith stands out, as the one who was on the scene at the time. Other than Amanita, and I agree with you that she's not at all the type of person to commit a cold-blooded murder."

His grin faded as he pinched his lower lip and thought. "I haven't ruled out Meredith completely. I just don't see any solid evidence he did do it. He might have been physically on the spot, but he has no real motive."

"There's got to be something." I turned the glasses case over, a faint chinking sound causing me to pop open the lid and pour the contents out into my hand. They were the apports Savannah had been collecting.

"If there is, Meredith isn't likely to tell us." Adam looked at the stones. "What are you doing with those?"

"Hmm? Oh, Savannah was saving them." I showed him the stones. "Goodness knows why. Probably a memento or something. She must have put them in here for safekeeping. I'll give the case back to her as soon as we see her. What about hypnosis?"

"For Meredith, you mean? I doubt he'd consent to it, and even if he did, we only have slightly over two hours before the seal dissolves. There wouldn't be enough time to thoroughly interview him, assuming we got him to that point. Where did she get these?" he asked, poking a long finger through the apports.

"She picked them up from all over. I don't suppose you have any truth serum or anything like that lying around the house?"

Adam raised one eyebrow.

I sighed. "I didn't think so. If we could only get Meredith to spill his guts, I'm sure there would be enough evidence to convince even you."

"I'm not going to torture a confession out of him,

if that's what you're going to suggest next." Adam held up one of the jade green apports, rubbing his thumb on it.

"Rats. And here I was hoping."

"Where did Savannah find these apports, do you know?" he asked, showing me the stone.

"The green ones?" I frowned, sorting through my memories until I got to the one of the discovery of Spider's body. Adam's eyes were icy bright as I met his gaze solidly. "I'm pretty sure she found them in the basement. Is it important?"

His face was an unmoving mask as he gave the apport back. "I'm not sure."

"We'll have to ask her, then. And speaking of asking . . . Adam, I hate to do this, but . . ." I tried to think of a way to phrase the question that wouldn't offend him. I opted for the straightforward approach. "This is probably none of my business, but how did you end up with this house?"

"No, it's not any of your business. Nor is it pertinent."

If the closed look on his face was anything to go by, I'd clearly stepped on his toes. But I had a feeling that the house was important in some manner. "I'm sorry for prying, but I've been wondering about it ever since Savannah spoke up. I thought perhaps there was something in the history of the house that would indicate why she would want it so badly as to try to get me to sell it to her a few hours after Spider's death."

His eyes turned positively glacial. "Why wouldn't she want it? It's a wonderful house. It's very much in demand; I'm always receiving offers from people who want it."

"I'm not saying it isn't wonderful. I just wondered what happened to the family who owned it. Did their line just die off? Or did they ask you to take over ownership?"

"There's nothing in the history of the house to interest anyone." His tone was final, but I wasn't one to let a little thing like that stop me.

"Then there will be no harm in you telling me how you got it."

"You're damned persistent, aren't you?" His jaw worked a few times before he spoke again. "The Walsh family used to own the house, as you might have guessed from its name. It was passed down via a Walsh daughter to the McConnaughts around the 1920s. All of that family but a son died in a car accident. The son was an obnoxious, self-centered little prick who deluded himself into thinking he had a great career as an actor waiting. I offered to buy the house from him, but he . . . well, as I said, he was a prick. He and I didn't get along, and he was determined to sell the house to someone outside of the family who wanted to raze it and subdivide. I saw to it that he sold the house to me instead."

" 'Saw to it' being a euphemism for what? You roughed him up? Bribed him? Something worse?" I had no problem seeing Adam as a staunch defender of the house but couldn't quite picture him doing anything truly reprehensible. He was just too honorable for that.

He cleared his throat, a look of agonizing discomfort clearly evident on his face. "I used . . . er . . . a little Otherworld pressure. Unfortunately, his mental state wasn't quite what I had guessed it was, and he went insane for a little bit."

My jaw dropped. "You drove the man insane to get the house?"

"Just for a little bit!" Righteous indignation shined in his eyes. "It's not as if he was the most mentally stable person in the world to begin with! I just didn't know that at the time, or I wouldn't have put quite so much pressure on him. Regardless, he got the money he wanted, and after a few years in an asylum, he went back to Hollywood."

"What happened to him?" I couldn't help asking.

Adam looked away. "I don't know."

"Uh-huh. Look, I may not have inherited my father's ability to read emotions, but I can read basic body language, and you're looking guilty as hell right now. What happened to the guy?"

"I'm beginning to regret ever saying anything," he answered, tight-lipped with exasperation. "He died a few years later of a drug or alcohol overdose. I don't remember which. The point that you seem to be missing is that there was nothing untoward about my taking over the house, and there was nothing in its past to work up any suspicion."

"No, I admit, there doesn't seem to be anything there," I agreed.

He picked up my notebook. "If you're done poking your nose into trivial matters, we need to—"

"There you two are! Come quick. Something's happened to Meredith," my father said, racing into the room, then zipping past us and out the other side before I could so much as blink.

"Oh lord, what now?" Adam groaned, running after Dad. I dumped the apports back into the case and tossed it onto the table before hurrying into the hall and up the stairs. Adam and Dad had used the back staircase and were already in Meredith's room by the time I got there.

Pixie and Amanita stood outside the room.

"What's going on?" I asked.

"It's not my fault!" Pixie said quickly, her frown firmly in place. "All I did was peek in to see what the noise was all about. I *found* him like that! I didn't do *anything*!"

It was with no little sense of foreboding that I stepped around her and Amanita to look into Meredith's room. Adam and my father were blocking the view, but both moved aside as I entered. My father had one arm around Savannah, who had a hand over her mouth, her eyes huge with horror as she looked at her husband.

At first glance, there didn't appear to be anything awry with Meredith. He stood in the middle of the room with no wounds, nothing apparently amiss. But as I took another step into the room, a glimmer of green shined briefly in the air before shimmering away to nothing. Meredith glared at us all, strangely silent and unmoving.

I pursed my lips and looked at Adam. "OK, who drew the wards on him?"

"That is the question, isn't it?"

We both looked at my father.

"Don't look at me; I was with the boys, having a little chat about the good old days."

"The boys?" I didn't see either Jules or Tony present. "Where are they?"

"We're here, just a little low on energy." Tony's disembodied voice came from the direction of the closet.

"Do you want us to materialize?" Jules asked.

"No, that's fine." I raised an eyebrow at Adam. "I take it the binding ward is solid?"

"So far as I can tell, yes. Which means it was drawn by someone who knew what they were doing."

"It wasn't me!" Pixie declared from the doorway. "I don't even know how to draw a binding ward."

"Hmm," I said, walking around Meredith, as if that would give me an answer.

Adam looked at Pixie curiously. "You don't know how to draw a binding ward?"

She cast a distraught glance at me.

"It's a long story. I'll tell you later," I said to Adam in Poltern. "Just drop it for now, if you don't mind."

"I'm not sure . . . a *ward*? I don't think I've ever heard . . ." Savannah's voice trailed off as her hands gestured helpless confusion.

"A ward is a sort of spell that is drawn by the practitioner. Most are benevolent, like luck, but there are also a number of protection wards that can be used to bind someone to a place, or silence them, or keep them from going through a door or window, that sort of thing."

"All I know is a protection one," Pixie said, her posture still defensive.

"No one is accusing you of doing it," I said smoothly, leaning in to Meredith to get a closer look at the wards. Like most of the others of their kind, these two looked like intricate Celtic knots, doubling over in a complicated confusion of twisted lines. "I'm no expert on wards, but these two appear to be very efficient. I don't suppose anyone admits to having drawn them?"

Five pairs of eyes looked at me. No one spoke.

I sighed and turned back to Adam. "I guess we're going to have to do this the hard way."

"Looks like it. Tony and Jules are out. They can't draw wards."

I nodded.

"Why is that?" Savannah asked.

"They're spirits. Spirits can't draw wards. Nor can demons or anyone bound to a demon lord, but since we're assuming no one here is the servant of a demon lord, a Follower, or a demon, those points are moot." I rubbed the back of my neck and glanced at Pixie. "You want to tell us why you decided to peek in on Meredith?"

Her shoulders twitched. "I was going up to the room you kept me in earlier to get my bag, and I heard some thumping noises. I thought maybe he might have found a way out of the house, or was having a fit, or maybe was hanging himself, so I opened the door to see."

I looked around the room. There were a bureau, the bed, a small bench at the foot of the bed, a nightstand, and nothing else other than the door leading to the bathroom.

"Bathroom," Adam said.

We all crammed into the doorway to peer inside the bathroom. The door to the hallway was slightly ajar, but the bathroom was empty. Which came as no surprise, since everyone in the house was in Meredith's room.

Adam closed the door, turning to Pixie. "Was that the sound you heard?"

She scrunched up her face. "Maybe. I don't really remember what it sounded like. Just that there was an odd noise."

Adam's frosty blue gaze touched me for a moment. "Someone here is lying."

I stood up a bit straighter and lifted my chin at him.

"Oooh, this is so exciting." Jules' whisper came from directly behind me. "Just like one of those murder mysteries on BBC America. Who killed the evil Realtor? Who poisoned the chief suspect? Who warded the same suspect so he couldn't move . . . or talk?"

Who indeed? So many secrets had been uncovered that evening: my past, which wasn't really a secret, at least not to people in the Akashic League; the plans Spider had had for the house, which he'd kept from all but Meredith; Pixie's origins, which left her especially vulnerable; Meredith's "poisoning" by my father; the truth of how Adam had acquired the house; and whatever it was Savannah was hiding.

"That's it," Adam said, giving everyone a piercing look. "I've had it. It's slightly less than two hours before the seal expires. We're going to get to the bottom of this before then if it kills me. And I'm a very hard man to kill. Everyone downstairs to the living room."

I nibbled my lower lip, indulging in a bit of speculation about Adam. Were my instincts about him wrong?

"What do we do about him?" I asked, nodding at Meredith as Amanita and Pixie headed out the door.

Adam marched over to the still man. "We'll take him with us. Matthew, get his feet."

"This is *so* Agatha Christie," Tony said as Adam and my father carried Meredith out of the room. "Gathering all the suspects together for the final denouement. Throwing suspicion on everyone present until, finally, the real murderer is unmasked. Followed by a brief, but in the end futile, attempt at escape by the same. So thrilling. It's giving me goose bumps!"

"Should we serve coffee, do you think?" Jules asked as the two of them wisped past me. "Or tea? What's appropriate at a denouement? WWHPD?"

"WWHPD?"

"What would Hercule Poirot do?"

Their voices drifted out of the room. I stood for a minute by myself, trying to put the last few pieces of the puzzle together. One thing stood out: someone here was a whole lot more powerful than they were letting on.

20

"Oh dear, Meredith's tipped over again. Can someone . . . Thank you."

When I entered the living room, my father and Adam were propping Meredith up against the wall. The only things on him that moved were his eyes, which resembled those of an indignant elderly pug as they glared in turn at everyone in the room.

The imps, which had followed me when I had released them from their confinement in the downstairs bathroom, were a bit pruny from playing in the tub so long, but fortunately also sleepy. I herded them to their box, where they settled down for a nap on Pixie's scarf.

"I don't want that back, you know," she told me, peering over my shoulder as I closed the lid of the box. "It'll have imp juice all over it."

"Imps don't make juice unless you use a blender," my father said.

"Ew!" Pixie squealed, making a face. I made one at my father—one that told him to knock off the smart-ass comments. He rolled his eyes in response, wandering around behind the couch where Savannah sat.

"Everyone sit down, please," Adam ordered, picking up the small round table we'd used during our interviews, and placing it in the center of the room.

Tony and Jules were just barely visible as Tony sat in an overstuffed chair with Jules seated on the arm. Pixie claimed the window seat, wrapping all four arms around her knees. Amanita pulled a footstool over to a corner and perched unhappily on it. I sat next to Savannah.

Adam placed on the table the glasses case containing the apports Savannah had picked up, the mangled remains of the box Spider had used to destroy Sergei, and the ipecac bottle.

"What's all that stuff?" Pixie asked.

"Exhibits."

Tony gave a happy little sigh. "Exhibits! This is so Perry Mason!"

"I thought it was all very Agatha Christie," Jules said to him.

"That too. Although Perry Mason was so very . . . mmm . . . rugged and manly!"

"Hercule Poirot didn't need to be rugged or manly. He was sophisticated. He had the little gray cells."

"I'll take Perry's savvy legal sense over Hercule's sophisticated gray cells any day of the week."

"Shhh, he's starting."

"Matthew?" Adam cocked an inquisitive eyebrow at my father.

"I prefer to just . . ." Dad waved his hands in a vague manner and continued to drift around the room.

Adam nodded at my father and took a moment to

eye us all before saying, "Someone here is a murderer. Someone is lying. Someone has deceived us all from the beginning. And I for one am getting a little tired of having my house used as the backdrop of this little drama. In exactly one hour and thirty-seven minutes, the seal will dissolve, at which point the watch will arrive, and I will have to deliver into their possession one bona fide murderer. The question is, who will that person be?"

"He's ever so intimidating, isn't he?" Tony whispered to Jules. "Quite gives me the chills!"

Adam's head snapped around to look at them.

"So sorry. I'll stop, shall I?"

Jules whapped his partner on the shoulder as the former made a locking gesture over his mouth.

"I don't see that the watch need to be brought in at all," my father said as he flitted past us in a never-ending circuit of the room. "It's not like anyone is going to miss Spider. The world is a better place for his leaving."

I sighed to myself. There were times when the urge to slap a big piece of duct tape over my father's mouth was almost impossible to resist.

"We're well aware of your opinion, thank you," Adam said, giving my father a chastising look that completely missed its mark. "The fact remains that Spider was killed, here, in my house, and he had strong business and personal ties to the Otherworld. The watch will demand that his murderer face justice. What we must determine in the next hour and a half is who will face that justice."

"Justice," I said softly, my eyes moving from Meredith to Pixie. Would justice be done that day? "So, what now?"

"We're going to do this logically, step by step. After due consideration of the facts, I've come to the conclusion that there are two solutions to the problem that we have to think about: one likely, and one very unlikely. We'll take the likely solution first, by beginning with a brief examination of the motive for killing Spider. First of all, there's his widow."

"Me?" I asked, somewhat surprised.

Adam nodded. "You told me the payment you were charging Spider for cleaning the house was a divorce. From that statement and other comments you've made, I believe it's safe to say there was no love lost between the two of you."

"There's no love lost between several people and myself, but I don't go around murdering them," I answered with what I hoped looked like a sincere smile.

His expression remained grim. "We're not addressing the issue of your relationship with other people. However, given that Spider was going to agree to a divorce, you don't seem to have had a reason to want him dead. Unless he had a fortune that you will inherit?" Adam's eyebrows rose questioningly.

I made a wry face. "Our house is mortgaged to the hilt so he could use the money on real estate speculations. I'm sure I won't even get back the money Spider paid for your house, so no, there is no hidden fortune, no assets tucked away. Just a bunch of debt."

"I'll talk to you later about the situation with my house. For now, I think it's safe to say that you didn't have a motive to kill Spider. And since you haven't exhibited any homicidal tendencies, I think we can move on."

"Wait just a minute," Savannah interrupted. She sent me an apologetic glance. "I'm sorry, Karma. I like you, I really do, but what Adam said just isn't true."

I blinked at her in surprise. "What isn't true?"

"That you're not homicidal."

Everyone gawked at her, although I doubted that anyone was as stupefied by her statement as I was. "What?"

"That wergeld that you were charged with. You killed someone, didn't you?"

"How did you find out . . ." My gaze narrowed on my father as he whisked into view.

"I didn't say a word," he answered, holding up all three hands in innocence before I could accuse him.

"Neither did I," Adam said quickly.

"Who told you about the wergeld?" I asked Savannah.

She fretted, looking at her amulet bag. "Oh, I wouldn't be comfortable saying. The sanctity of sources and all that, you know."

My hair spun out as I whipped around to glare at Pixie. She had curled up into a little ball of teenage polter, one that peered at me with miserably guilt-riddled eyes. "I didn't exactly tell her. I just asked how long she thought wergeld would last. . . ."

"We're going to have a little talk later about the responsibility that goes along with keeping some-one's secret," I told her sternly before turning back to Savannah. "It's true that I did destroy someone when I was very young and not in control of my abilities. My father and Adam both know the details."

"That was an isolated situation," my father said, continuing his endless patrol around the room. "Karma wouldn't kill anyone unless it was life or death."

"But how do we know it wasn't?" Savannah asked. I shot her a look.

"I'm just playing devil's advocate," she said with a particularly insincere pat on my hand. "I don't for a moment believe you did it, but just to make absolutely certain, shouldn't we go over every possible reason before dismissing them?"

"I won't be accused of not being thorough," Adam said with a nod at her. "If you can think of a reason Karma wanted her husband dead, I'd be happy to hear it."

"Well . . ." She toyed with the gauze scarf draped around her neck. "I can't think of any reason. I thought perhaps someone else might be able to. What about her alibi? Where was she when Spider was killed?"

Adam frowned. "We saw her go upstairs with Spider. He came back down and went to the basement with Meredith."

I nodded.

"Yes, but what about after that? She could have gone down the back stairs to the basement," Savannah said.

"You're missing your calling as a prosecuting attorney," I told her.

"We'd have seen her if she had," Tony answered quickly.

Jules nodded vigorously. "Yes, we were hiding in

the kitchen. Adam had told us to go to our room to be safe, but we wanted to see what was going on, so we stayed in the kitchen and peeped out every now and again. No one came down the back stairs. We'd have seen them if they had."

"Besides, I saw her upstairs later," Pixie said, scooting forward on the window seat. "After she'd ralphed all over the floor. I saw her coming out of the bathroom when she was cleaning up."

"And that, I believe, is an alibi," Adam said dryly.

Savannah leaned back, an odd expression on her face. "I just think it's smart to be sure."

"Agreed. Why don't we go over your possible motives and alibi next?" I resisted the urge to smile a catlike smile.

"Me? I have no motive whatsoever, and my alibi is that I was with Matthew and Morbid . . . oh, whatever her name is."

"It's . . . er . . ." Pixie stopped, looking nonplussed. "I'll get back to you on that."

"I hardly knew Spider. I had no conceivable reason to want him dead, but even if I had, I couldn't have killed him. I was with people the whole time."

"Not the whole time," my father said, pausing for a moment to strike a dramatic pose. "Dischordia went upstairs for a few minutes, which is when she saw Karma. And I had to use the downstairs john. Adam was off smooching up his girlfriend, which means, my dear, you were alone for a short time."

"Oh!" Savannah gasped, outraged. "How cruel of you to imply that I used the one or two minutes I was alone to creep downstairs and kill someone! Even if I wanted to, I couldn't! Unlike your daughter, I am not a violent person."

"Hey, now," I protested. "That is thirty-odd years in the past."

"Just playing devil's advocate," my father told Savannah before resuming his parade around the room.

I smiled and forgave the lesser of his sins.

"Well, in this case, it's not necessary. I did not have the time, know-how, or desire to kill Spider."

My eyes narrowed at her. I could feel the sudden interest in the air as both my father and Adam picked up on the lie Savannah had just told. "What was that? You said you didn't have the time to murder him?"

"Of course not. I was only alone for a few minutes." The look she shot me was scathing, but I didn't get a sense that she was lying.

"Then you meant you didn't have a motive to murder him?" my father asked, stopping in front of her.

"I just said that, didn't I?"

I glanced at Adam. He nodded slightly. For some reason, Savannah was lying about not having the ability to kill Spider. Why on earth would she hide that fact when it was the least damning?

"But you could have killed him, if you'd really wanted to," Adam said slowly, taking a step toward her.

Her eyes widened slightly, as if she scented danger. "No, of course not!"

Lie.

"We don't even know what killed him!"

"True, but that doesn't mean you couldn't have killed him, either by poison or some other method that wouldn't leave obvious marks on the body," I said, leaning forward toward her. The faint buzzing noise that ebbed and flowed rose briefly.

One hand fidgeted with the amulet bag; the other crumpled her skirt. "I didn't kill him. I've told you that over and over again. And since you have no proof to the contrary, I will thank you to just move the hell on!"

I narrowed my gaze on the amulet bag, which hung from a silken cord. "What sort of an amulet do you carry?"

"What on earth does that have to do with anything?"

"I like amulets. What one do you use?"

She shot an indignant look at Adam. "This really is going well over the line of what's reasonable, and into persecution. I am not guilty of the murder, and no matter how much—"

"Would you answer Karma's question, please?" Adam interrupted.

"I . . . You people . . . Goddess! Very well, since you're all clearly bent on finding me guilty of something. . . ." She opened the bag and took out a pretty purple heart-shaped stone. "It's an amethyst. A very old one, charged by a local Wiccan. Are you happy now?"

Her tone still spoke of a lie.

"It's very pretty. May I?" I held out my hand.

"If you think I won't remember this treatment when this whole thing is over, you're quite wrong," she answered, sharing a glare with Adam, my father, and me as she dropped the amethyst onto my outstretched palm.

The second the stone hit my hand, I felt as if I

were holding on to a live wire. It was so strong a sensation, it knocked me backward off the couch. I yelped, getting to my knees to examine my hand before turning my attention to Savannah. "Good god, what was that?"

"Honey, are you all right?" Adam squatted next to the fallen stone, reaching out as if to pick it up.

"No!" I yelled at the same time that Tony and Jules demanded that Adam leave it be.

"You don't know where it's been," Jules added.

"That is the most insulting thing I've ever heard!" Savannah declared.

"You haven't been here long yet," Tony told her.

"What is it?" Adam asked me, ignoring the byplay behind him.

I shook my head and allowed my father and Pixie to help me to my feet. My arm still tingled from the sensation of the stone. "I don't know, but whatever it is, it's very powerful."

We all turned to look at Savannah.

"What is the amulet you carry?" Adam asked.

"I told you! It's an amethyst, charged by a Wiccan."

"Charged with what?"

"Hope. Strength. Clarity of mind. Nothing negative, I assure you."

I pursed my lips, eyeing her, and rubbed my palm. She wasn't lying, but the stone contained a massive amount of *something*.

"Karma?"

I couldn't answer Adam's unasked question. I shook my head. "I don't know. It didn't seem evil. It was just very, very strong. . . ." An idea occurred to me, something I felt like whacking myself on the head about. "What else do you have in the amulet bag?"

"Oh, this is too much!" she snapped, leaping off the couch and backing away, her hands held out before her. "I have been as tolerant as I know how due to the circumstances. I have answered your endless and very personal questions. I have tried time and time again to contact Spider in order to find the killer. I have given and given and given, and not said a single word about the abuse that's been heaped upon my head."

"She's good," Tony said sotto voce to Jules. "I particularly like the little throb in her voice."

"Must have taken her weeks to get it just right."

"Oh!" she shrieked, grabbing a small ceramic statue of a dog and throwing it at the ghosts. Since they were in ephemeral mode, it went straight through them and bounced off the chair cushion to land harmlessly on the carpet. "You horribly rude spirits! If I was Karma, I'd banish you so quickly your ectoplasm would spin!"

She'd been backing up as she'd spoken. Adam and Dad and I looked at one another.

"Grab her?" Dad asked.

"Grab her," Adam answered, and before Savannah could do more than turn around to race out of the room, the two men had her, Adam reaching for the amulet bag hanging around her neck.

"No!" she screamed at the same time that he touched it. His yell joined hers as he was knocked backward, the amulet bag flying out of his hand onto the floor a few feet away. The blow knocked a small white object out of the bag, but that wasn't what caught the attention of everyone in the room.

"What the . . . what is she?" Pixie asked, rubbing her arms as she backed away.

The air tingled with power.

"She's a Guardian," I answered. "One of the most powerful people in the Otherworld, someone who thinks nothing of dealing with demons and demon lords."

Savannah raised her head slowly, her face not giving away anything, but her eyes—oh, how her eyes glittered with fury.

21

"OK, I'm going to sound totally noob here, but what exactly is a Guardian? It sounds familiar, but . . . meh."

Pixie's whisper was soft enough that only I could hear it. I answered her in a similar volume, not wanting to have to explain to everyone why it was that she didn't know. "Guardians are basically glorified demon wranglers. They usually guard portals to Abaddon, and are responsible for taking care of any problems with beings of a dark nature—the latter having their origins in Abaddon."

"Abaddon being hell, right?"

"It's what the mortal world thinks of as hell, although it's not technically the same."

"So if Guardians are the good guys, why are all of you looking at Savannah like she's got herpes or something?"

That was a good question. I glanced over at where my father and Adam stood together, identical expressions of astonishment on their respective faces. Beyond them, Meredith leaned drunkenly against the wall, his eyes mirroring the surprise that everyone else seemed to feel. Evidently the fact that his wife was a Guardian came as news to him, too.

"What exactly is that machine?" Adam asked, nudging the small white square with the toe of his shoe.

"None of your business!" Savannah snatched it up and tucked it back into the silk and velvet amulet bag. The instant she touched it, the electricity that filled the air ebbed away to nothing. Or almost nothing. By leaning forward, I could catch the faintest buzz, almost imperceptible.

"Well, at least I'm not going crazy," I said with no little relief.

"Eh?" my father asked.

"You can't hear the noise?" I asked him.

"What noise?"

I turned to Adam. "How about you?"

"From Savannah's machine?" He shook his head. "It's silent."

"Why am I the only one who can hear it?" I asked Savannah.

She shrugged. "You're a TAE. Your perception differs from the others'. I'll have to adjust it in the future so as to take that into account."

"So, that machine of hers has some sort of a masking effect?" Dad asked.

"It's a dampener, yes," she answered with a toss of her head, glaring at Adam. "And it doesn't mean I killed that wretched man, if that's what you're about to suggest."

"You're a Guardian. You have incredible power at your disposal," he replied.

"Against demons and their ilk, yes. But apparently

it's escaped your notice that Spider wasn't a demon, and I have little to no power over mortals."

That wasn't strictly true, but I wasn't about to argue the finer points with her.

"You lied to us, in word and in deed, by hiding the fact that you're a Guardian. You certainly can't deny that you did that to Meredith," I said, waving at the ward-bound man.

His eyes bugged out in agreement.

She looked at him, her head tipped to one side. "No, I don't deny it, although I think it's a tremendous improvement."

"I second that," my dad said.

"Why?" Adam asked, taking a step forward. "Why did you hide the truth from us? Why wouldn't you want us to know you're a Guardian? Why pretend that you're ignorant of the Otherworld?"

Her lips tightened, one hand absently stroking the amulet bag.

"I knew she was evil from the start," Pixie said, curling back up on the window seat. "No one who looks *that much* like a hippie can be anything but evil."

"You'll get a bonus point for your insight later. Right now, I'd like to know just what it is Savannah wants."

"What she wants?" my dad asked as I walked in front of Savannah, peering deeply into her eyes. She met my gaze without wavering, a hint of smug obstinacy visible in her eyes.

"Yes. No one goes through the trouble it must have taken to have her husband create a dampening machine—"

Her eyes flicked over to my shoulder for a second.

"—to create a dampening machine herself without having a very good reason," I corrected myself. A flash of startled surprise was visible, then her face resumed its normal placid mien. "You created those machines, didn't you? The monstrosity that killed Sergei and this one. That's what Meredith meant about you and your machines."

Adam stepped forward. "And that's why you shut him up, so he couldn't tell us about your ulterior motive."

"That little ignoramus doesn't know anything about my reason for being here," she snapped.

"And that would be . . . ?" Dad asked.

She toyed with the amulet bag for a moment, then shoved me aside and sauntered over to the couch. "You all think you're so clever; you figure it out."

"Oh, it's not as difficult as you think," I said, slowly walking around the couch to face her. "We know you want this house."

"Eh?" Dad looked confused.

"Why else would you spin such a song and dance about wanting to buy it from me?"

"You're not going to sell, are you?" Tony asked, leaping to his nearly invisible feet.

I waved him and Jules back into their seats. "The house isn't mine to sell; it's Adam's, but even if it wasn't, I wouldn't sell. It's sanctuary . . . but you knew that long before you got here, didn't you, Savannah?"

"Of course she did," Adam answered for her. He strode into the middle of the room. "Every member of the mortal family who lived here knew what the house was. And you're part of that family, aren't you?"

Her eyes all but spat fire. She leaped to her feet and accosted him, shoving her face into his. "I'm part of the family from whom you stole this house, yes. And I intend to have it back! Don't think I don't know what you did; you tricked my great-grandfather into handing the house over to you. You drove him insane in order to get your hands on the house, but I'm not as weak as he is, and I intend to get back what's mine!"

"Oh, really?" I cocked an eyebrow at her. "If you're so determined, why has it taken you so long to confront Adam? Could that be because you know you don't have a foot to stand on legally?"

She opened and closed her mouth a couple of times. "I have every legal right to this house, and I will be petitioning the Akashic League to recognize my true ownership."

"She's bluffing," my father said. "Take it from one who knows how to bluff. Karma's right: if she had any true claim on the house, she would have acted on it long ago."

"You people don't know anything," she snarled, and stomped back to the couch.

"I wonder," Adam mused, stroking his chin. "It's true that she can't get the house from me by conventional means. But does she want it badly enough to commit murder for it?"

Her head snapped around to glare at him.

"You mean that she might have killed Spider to force the League to give the house to her?" I shook my head. "I don't see that the one would ensure the other."

"She might have a case for claiming the house if I was charged with the murder," he said in the same slow, thoughtful voice.

"But you didn't kill him," Dad said. "And there's no reason to think you did."

"No, but she might have thought that if I was discredited enough, it might be easier to petition for ownership of the house. The League takes sanctuaries very seriously; they wouldn't want one in the control of someone who demonstrates blatant irresponsibility."

Pixie lifted her chin from on her hand, where it had rested. "Weak."

I nodded. "I agree; it's weak."

"True, but it does give her a motive, which we were missing. However, I think we can clear her from the possible charge of murder."

"I'm grateful for such kindness," she said in a snarky tone.

Adam ignored it. "She wasn't alone long enough to have killed Spider. There was only a very small window of opportunity for the murderer to get downstairs and do the job. Nita, how long was it from the time you heard Spider and Meredith enter the basement, to the sounds of a struggle?"

I'd almost forgotten that Amanita was in the room, so silent and still was she. She hadn't moved from her perch on the footstool in the corner, and somehow, without appearing to slouch, gave the impression that she was curled up in a defensive posture. She jumped slightly when Adam turned to address her. "Oh, me? How long? About half a minute. Maybe less. Not very long at all. I heard the men talking, and then the sounds of breathing and grunting, and then nothing."

"As I thought." Adam turned back to us. "There wasn't time for anyone mortal to get downstairs that quickly. Which basically eliminates everyone who isn't a polter."

I leaned heavily against the nearest chair. "You're saying a polter killed Spider?" I looked from him to my father to Pixie. I shook my head. "I don't believe it. None of you had a reason to want him dead."

"Oh, I wouldn't have minded bashing his brains in," my father piped up cheerfully. "But as it happens, I didn't. I knew Karma would never forgive me if I did."

"We're going to have a *very* long talk later," I told him with a stern look.

"I didn't kill him, either, although I kinda wanted to after he hit on me," Pixie announced.

"He what?" Dad spun around to look at her.

"He hit on me." She gave a little shrug and tried hard to be insouciant, but failed. "It's not a big deal. Nothing for you to go all eyes bugging out like you are."

"My eyes do not bug out," Dad protested. "And you don't realize the seriousness of what you're saying."

She tipped her head to one side. "I'm not stupid, you know. I know more than you think. But it wasn't a big deal. Karma was there."

All eyes turned to me.

"Is that true?" Adam asked, his face unreadable.

"Not exactly," I said, my gaze dropping. "I was sick in the bathroom a couple of times. The first time I came out, Spider was standing next to Pixie, but she shoved him aside and ran off. I didn't see him hit on her . . . although I had no doubt that was in his mind."

Adam's voice was rich with anger. "Why didn't you tell me that earlier?"

I lifted my eyes to his. "I honestly didn't think it was important. I could see that Pixie wasn't harmed, or even overly upset."

"Yeah," she said with complacency. "Guys hit on me all the time. It's no big deal."

"Regardless, you should have told me," Adam said, his stare continuing to bore into mine.

"I'm sorry. I just didn't want to involve Pixie in it any more than she was. If it makes you feel any better, I've been angsting about it all morning."

His jaw tightened. "It doesn't. Is there anything else you want to tell me?"

I shook my head, feeling about as low as a snake's belly button.

"Well, I have something to say!" my father said, his voice loud. "His killer should be given a medal for bravery! Spider deserved to die! He was having sex with minors!"

"He what?" Adam asked, looking more than a little startled.

"He was molesting children," Dad said, waving toward me. "Karma said earlier he bragged as much to her."

I nodded wearily as Adam turned his gaze on me. "He admitted upstairs that he was having physical relationships with teenage polters."

Adam frowned, mouthing silently, "Bethany?"

I nodded again, my eyes flickering to Pixie.

"He wasn't the only one," Savannah murmured, smiling acidly at her husband.

Adam looked between the two of them. "Are you saying your husband sexually abused children, as well?"

"Not human children, no. Like Spider, Meredith had a taste for polters."

I held my father back as he tried to leap forward.

"Are you willing to swear to that in court?" Adam asked, his voice flinty.

She brushed an invisible speck of dirt off her skirt. "I suppose so. His peccadillos can have no bearing on my situation."

"So we've got two child molesters!" Dad said, glaring at Meredith as he shrugged off my restraining hand. "I hope they hang him. But . . . wait. Correct me if I'm wrong, but doesn't that eliminate everyone? If Pixie didn't do it, and I certainly didn't do it, and Adam didn't do it . . . that's all the polters present."

"Who says Adam didn't do it?" Savannah demanded.

"I say I didn't," he answered, glowering at her.

"That's fine and well, but just where were you while he was being killed?" she asked.

"I went upstairs to check on Nita and the boys."

Her smile was one of profound smugness. "But they weren't there. They said themselves that they were in the kitchen, eavesdropping."

"It wasn't so much eavesdropping as overhearing. . . . Sorry. Lock and key." Tony's voice subsided into silence.

"And you just said that your girlfriend was in the basement, with the two men. What was to stop her from having killed Spider? She wouldn't have needed polter quickness to get to him, since she was right there."

Amanita gasped. "I didn't!" she said, her voice breathy with fear.

"So you say, but what proof do we have that you

didn't? For that matter, what proof do we have that Adam didn't polter his way downstairs and do it? For all we know, you two might have been in it together."

"But . . . we weren't! I didn't!" Amanita looked truly frightened. For a moment I considered her as a possible suspect, but dismissed the idea.

"Stop scaring Nita," Adam said, moving over to put a supportive hand on her shoulder. "She couldn't have killed Spider, for the simple fact that she's a unicorn—and they can't harm mortals."

She nodded vehemently. "I can't! Not even if I wanted to!"

"Oh, that's an old wives' tale," Savannah said, dismissing it with an airy wave of her hands.

Adam's eyebrows pulled together. "No more so than the one that says all Guardians are tainted by the dark power they supposedly repress."

"Ooh, nice one, Adam," my father said, licking his finger and drawing a tally mark in the air. "That's one for our team."

"Very well, I'm willing to concede the unicorn, but that still leaves you," Savannah said.

Adam dropped his hand from Amanita's shoulder. "No, it doesn't. I didn't murder Spider."

Savannah crossed her legs and arched one delicately shaped eyebrow. "You had a reason to want him dead, the ability to get to him in time without anyone seeing you, the strength to kill him, and you refuse to say where you were during that oh-so-important few minutes when Spider was killed. That says 'guilty' to me."

"I don't care what it says to you; I'm not guilty."

Dad looked troubled. The two spirits looked

equally troubled, their heads together as they whispered. Pixie watched everything with bright eyes.

I said slowly, "I have to admit, Adam, it doesn't look too good. What exactly were you doing during the time Spider was being killed?"

"Blast it all to hell and back again!" His jaw worked a couple of times, indicating the amount of control he was commanding. "I couldn't have killed him because I wasn't in the damned house, all right?"

Of all the excuses I was expecting him to make, this wasn't one. Judging by the exclamations of surprise and astonishment from the others, they were just as taken aback.

"I thought the house was sealed," Pixie said.

"I thought so, too." I looked questioningly at Adam.

He shoved his hands into his pockets, scowling something fierce. "The house *is* sealed. I . . . er . . . called in a few favors and had a friend summon me out of the house to the League offices. The same friend shoved me back through a rift."

"What's a rift?" Pixie leaned forward to ask in a whisper.

"Sort of a rip in the fabric of reality. Kind of like a portal to wherever you're going."

"Cool. Can we make those?"

"No."

"You left the house? You said no one could leave the house!" Savannah said, her voice rising on the last few words.

"No one can . . . without expert help." Adam was still scowling, but embarrassment tinged his dark expression.

"Spill," I said, propping myself up on the arm of the couch.

"I wanted to see if it was possible to get the League involved in the matter of the house. Once I sealed it, I knew Spider couldn't go anywhere, so I called a mage friend and had him summon me to the League office. I explained the situation, and they promised to send a mediator just as soon as the seal was lifted." He glanced at his watch. "Which should be in less than an hour now."

"Why didn't you just tell us that's where you'd gone?" I asked.

His gaze slid toward Savannah. "I figured if you all knew there was a way to leave, you'd be after me to get you out of here, and I wanted Spider to stay put until the mediator arrived."

"You could have told us that afterwards," I gently pointed out.

He gave me a hard look. "I'm the watch representative here. I couldn't risk having my authority undermined."

"If you got sent back through this portal-rift thing, why didn't you have the mediator come with you?" Pixie asked.

"Rifts don't work like that," I murmured absently. "They are temporary tears in the fabric of being, and shouldn't be used more than once at any one location until the fabric has repaired itself. Adam was risking seriously damaging the fabric by traveling back, but I assume it's all right."

"That means a polter couldn't have killed Spider," my father said triumphantly.

Savannah looked more than a little put out.

Tony leaned forward, tugging on Adam's sleeve. "If it wasn't a polter, and wasn't Savannah, Karma, or Nita, who did kill him?"

Adam's frown cleared as he lifted his head and looked across the room. I followed his gaze, a slow smile creeping across my face.

Dad laughed outright. "I knew it! I just knew it!"

Meredith, the subject of all our attention, rolled his eyes around in a distressed fashion, as if to protest the accusation.

"We're back to who would benefit most from Spider's death. Savannah, what do you know about the partnership between Meredith and Spider?"

She shrugged. "Very little. I had my own concerns. Beyond shutting up Meredith's yammering about making him a dissipater, I didn't pay much attention to what he was doing."

"Why on earth did you marry the man if you disliked him so much?" I asked her, my curiosity getting the better of me. "I may have had no love left for Spider at the end, but I did love him when I married him. Why bind yourself to a man for whom you had so much contempt?"

"What better cover could a person have than being the wife of an apparently respectable bank manager?" Her smile was positively sinister.

"Plus there's the fact that it was his bank that held the mortgage to Adam's house," I said thoughtfully.

Her smile dimmed as she shot a nasty glance at her husband. "Fat lot of good that did me. The second I started talking about getting the house, he had to run to Spider and blab about it. You just never could keep a secret, could you? Not even when you tried. I always found them out, didn't I, Meredith?"

Meredith's eyes blinked rapidly.

Savannah laughed a low, sinister laugh. "You needn't look so startled; I know about more than just your predilection for underage polters. I know about the bank account you think is so untraceable in the Cayman Islands, and that little arrangement you have to buy certain medications without prescription. Oh, and I know about your fetish for wearing women's thongs, too. In short, there's nothing about you that I don't know, husband of mine."

"Indeed. I'm sure the watch and mundane police will be interested in statements from you," Adam said. "They will want proof, though."

"Proof? Oh, I have proof. He's really quite disgusting," Savannah said absently, reaching for her purse. "He took videos of his sessions with the polters. They're all on his laptop. I'll be happy to turn them over to the police."

Adam looked thoughtful, his gaze touching me before moving away. I rubbed my hands against the goose bumps that suddenly appeared on my arms, my stomach turning over at the thought of the perverse videos.

"I'm confused," Jules said, holding up a hand. "Meredith killed Spider? Who hit him on the head, then?"

"No one," Adam said, turning to the spirits. "Or rather, Meredith did it himself. He probably banged his head on the door frame a couple of times to raise a welt and give himself a little cut. The bookcase was no doubt pulled down by Spider as he was being attacked, probably in a last-ditch attempt at self-defense. All Meredith had to do once he was dead was give himself the appearance of an injury, and artistically arrange the scene. Would that fit what you heard, Nita?"

The unicorn sat with her arms around herself. She

looked startled to be addressed, but after thinking for a moment, quickly nodded. "There wasn't much noise, just a few grunts, Spider saying it would all be his when he was gone, and the crash of the bookcase. That was it."

"But why did he kill Spider?" Tony asked.

"Money," Savannah said, pulling a nail file out of her purse. She glanced up at the startled silence that followed. "He was always bitching at me whenever I asked for the minutest amount of money. He said more than once that we'd end up on the street if I didn't stop spending, which was ridiculous. I told him the machines I created didn't come from nothing."

"Money would do it," Adam said. "The sad truth is that this damned scheme they had to turn the house into an Otherworld brothel, desecrating its sanctuary, was financially sound. There would be no small supply of people, both Otherworldly and mundane, who wouldn't hesitate to fork over exorbitant fees to indulge their darkest desires. They were set to make money hand over fist . . . but clearly, that wasn't enough for Meredith. I wouldn't be surprised at all if an inquiry into the bank and his own personal finances showed he was in dire straits."

"So by killing Spider, he stood to save himself from financial ruin, and in fact would have become quite wealthy if their plans had gone through," I said, nodding. "It's plausible."

"Exactly. Being the savvy businessman he is, he probably wrote into their partnership agreement a survivor option. If one of them died, the other would inherit all their business holdings."

"But we asked him about that," I said, remembering a conversation from the prior evening. "And he said he hadn't."

"So he lied," Pixie said, standing up. She sat back down quickly when everyone turned to look at her. "Didn't Meredith also say something about you trying to add another nail to his coffin, but that it wouldn't work because Spider owned his assets outright? He accused you of knowing that, and said that's why you wanted Spider dead."

"Classic case of misdirection," Jules told Tony. "Very Hercule."

Tony rolled his eyes.

I dredged around in my memory of the conversation. "That's right, he did. I'd forgotten that, because it didn't make any sense to me; I had no idea of what Spider was up to."

Dad marched over to Meredith's still-stiff body, which leaned against the fireplace. He peered closely into Meredith's eyes, which rolled over to look back at him. "You're going to rot in the Akasha. Although I think you should get a few years off for bumping off Spider. Still, you deserve to rot."

"Why did you put binding and silence wards on him?" I asked Savannah.

The look she shot her husband was nearly lethal. "He started telling you things. He mentioned my connection to the machines. The little rat was going to set me up and let me take the rap for Spider's murder while *he* got my house."

"A woman scorned," Dad said, nodding sagely.

"So, what now?" I asked Adam.

"Now we wait until the watch comes and takes him away. I don't believe my captain will want to bring in the mundane police, since both the murder and the charge of child molestation concern the Otherworld."

I glanced at Pixie. "How likely is it that your captain will do otherwise? I don't see anything but trouble if we bring in the mundane police. There's Pixie and the spirits and Amanita to explain, and I hesitate to expose any of them to what would follow should the mundane world find out about them."

"Oh, absolutely," Jules said, nodding. "They'd want to take us away, and we're quite comfortable here."

"Quite comfortable," Tony agreed. "Nita wouldn't like it either, would you, dear?"

She seemed to shrink into her chair, her voice a faint whisper. "No."

"I don't think it's likely, although there's a chance if he feels Spider's murder charge won't stick."

"It'll stick," I said firmly, lifting my chin. "I have no doubt of that."

"Savannah could, I suppose, make a case for it to be turned over to the mundane police," Adam said, glancing at her.

She looked up from her nails with an acid smile. "Much as I would love to see all this dragged out into the open, I have my own career to think of. The Guardians' Guild frowns on its members becoming the focus of too much attention, so there really is no choice to be made. I won't fight Meredith being charged by the watch."

"That's all there is, I think," Adam said, his hands behind his back as he surveyed the room. Meredith rolled his eyes with great vigor.

"Quiet, you," Adam told him before facing us again. "We'll turn Meredith over to the watch, and

let them handle the details of what is to be said to
the mundane police."

"Justice," I said on a happy sigh, and sank into
the nearest chair with a profound sense of relief.

22

Forty-five minutes later, a slight popping noise heralded the dissolving of the seal. A half hour after that, the watch—who had shown up just before the house was unsealed—took Meredith away. I felt no pity for him, no sympathy, nothing but a sense of relief that it was all over. The man was a murderer, pure and simple, and he reaped what he had sown.

The watch captain, a somber man by the name of Muir, had stood quietly while Adam had made his report on the happenings of the last day. Savannah had tried to get him to arrest Adam, my father, and me in turn, but the captain listened implacably to her demands, then said simply, "The situation with the house is out of my domain, madam. I suggest you take it up with the proper officials."

Savannah was so annoyed by that response that she outright refused to lift the binding ward on her husband.

"If you want it lifted, you can call a Charmer. Otherwise, he can stay that way until it wears off," she said, marching off to collect her things.

Three members of the watch circled the now vertical, but still frozen, Meredith, scratching their heads. "Those are a hell of a couple wards," one of the men said. "No way that's going to fade away quickly."

"We'll have to take him out as he is," Muir told them, and so it was that they carried Meredith out to their car, one man at his head, the other at his feet.

Savannah sailed past us, trailing gauzy scarves, then tossed her head as she paused at the door. "Don't think for one minute that you can get away with keeping what's rightfully mine. I will present my case to the League. You might not have murdered Spider, but they will see that only the true owner of the house is best suited to care for it."

"I think you'll find people aren't quite so gullible as you believe," Adam told her before moving over to hold a quiet conversation with his boss.

"She's really pissed," Pixie said, peering through the window to watch the car drive away with Meredith. Savannah followed shortly in her SUV. "You think she's going to get the house?"

"No. She may be a Guardian, but the house is legally Adam's. His family were the resident polters, and he bought it legally from the mortal owners. No court in the Otherworld or mundane world would think about taking it away from him."

"Well, that's a relief," Tony's disembodied voice said from behind my shoulder. "You lot look famished. Shall we whip up a crab salad?"

"What on earth are you thinking? Crab salad after a denouement? Were you raised by sloths? Everyone knows the proper luncheon to be served after such an event is quiche. Seafood, yes, but in quiche, not a salad." Jules' voice was just as disembodied as his partner's, dropping in volume as the two spirits argued their way out to the kitchen.

Adam glanced toward the hallway, then nodded to my father.

"Honey, why don't you and the girl go into the kitchen and ask the boys to make a fresh pot of coffee?" Dad asked, his hands moving restlessly.

I frowned. "Caffeine is the last thing you need."

"Yes, but"—Dad shot a quick look toward the hall—"I think you and Pixie should go into the kitchen, anyway."

I guessed what it was he and Adam were up to. "No, I won't, but Pixie will."

The teen absolutely refused to go. "This is my last chance to see him," she argued as the sound of feet thumping on the hard wooden stairs leading to the basement became audible.

"I'm just trying to save you from potential trauma," I told her, attempting to shove her toward the kitchen. She dug in her heels and wouldn't budge.

"Trauma? Are you kidding? This is wonderful! Can you imagine the sort of poems I'm going to be able to write now about death? I can't wait to get started!"

I stopped trying to push her, shaking my head with puzzlement. "You are the oddest child I've ever met."

"I'm *not* a child. What do you think of Tertia?" she asked with her trademark change of topic.

"As a name? It could be worse. I have a suggestion: why don't you just stick with your own name?"

"Do I *look* like a Pixie?" she asked, waving her arms around.

I had to admit she had a point. I was about to suggest she find one name and stick to it when the amused glint in her eyes rapidly changed to profound interest as the men carried Spider's body, still covered by the old blanket, out the door to a waiting watch ambulance.

"Weird kid," my father mused as she hurried off to watch the ambulance. He turned an impish grin upon me. "Reminds me of someone I know. Think I'll go help the lads with that quiche. Their food is good, but not as good as what my Karma makes," he added, poking Adam with his elbow and waggling his eyebrows.

"Dad, wait, I . . ." I bit my lip as I glanced around. The three of us were alone. "Can you take Pixie for a couple of days? She can't stay with me, and I doubt if the League can find her a new home so quickly."

His eyes met mine and held them in a gaze that seemed to see all. "You don't have to do this."

I looked at him in surprise. "You know?"

"Of course I know. I'm not stupid. Or blind."

"But how . . . ?"

He shook his head, looking at Adam, who was watching us both with a speculative look in his bright blue eyes. "You think I don't recognize apports when I see them? Things are fine as they are, honey. Let it go. You don't have to do anything," he repeated.

"Yeah, I do," I said with a little smile. "Doing nothing was never an option."

"So much like your mother," he said, shaking his head again. "Don't worry about Pixie. I'll see to her."

"Thanks."

Dad went off muttering things about foolish pride and obstinacy.

"You want to tell me what that was about?" Adam asked. "Wait—before you tell me, what's up with Pixie?"

I gave him a brief rundown of the pertinent points. I'd just finished when the captain came back into the house, followed by Pixie and my father.

"I believe I'll speak to the young lady first," he told us. "We will do our best to not upset her, but we understand you may wish to protect her delicate sensibilities. We will allow you to be present during the interview if you like, Mrs. Marx."

Adam choked slightly at the phrase "delicate sensibilities."

I managed to keep a straight face as I raised an eyebrow at Pixie. "I'll be happy to be there with you."

"Oh, puh-leeze!" She rolled her eyes and grabbed Muir's sleeve, pulling him toward the small sitting room he'd commandeered as his work space. "Did you get pictures of the body, by any chance? Karma wouldn't let me get a close look at him, so I'd really like to see exactly what death looks like. . . ."

I fought a little giggle at the horrified expression on the captain's face as he allowed himself be hauled away. "Poor man has no idea."

"I have a feeling Pixie is going to be the one doing the interviewing," Adam said with a grin that faded as he looked at me. "Do you want to tell me what you were talking about to your father? Or should I tell you?"

I blinked in surprise. "You tell me? Er . . ."

Pulling out of his pocket a slim green glasses case, he waved me over to a corner of the room, where we could talk without being disturbed. Without saying anything, he popped open the lid and poured the apports onto my hand.

They were all green. My fingers closed around them as I looked up into his eyes.

Glacial blue, they gazed back at me with understanding. "You look so human, sometimes I forget that you're half polter. Which means that in addition to having inherited the abilities to meld into shadows, move with increased quickness, and generate strength abnormal in mortals, you manifest apports in times of stress or great physical output. Those are yours, aren't they?"

"Yes," I said, suddenly breathless.

"I figure it's this way: when Spider left you upstairs, you were retching as the result of a headache. But you didn't stay upstairs the entire time being sick. You followed Spider down the stairs, sticking to the shadows, keeping yourself unseen as he met with Meredith, and sneaked down to the basement. It wouldn't have taken much effort for you to silently sneak up behind the men, knocking Meredith out, and killing Spider before he had the time to turn around."

The apports grew hot in my hand. I unclenched my fingers, placing the stones on the table.

"Then you pulled the bookcase down on Spider's body, arranged the scene with Meredith, and sneaked back upstairs to the bathroom without anyone seeing you. With your quickness, the whole thing probably took . . . what, a minute? Two at the most?"

I cleared my throat, unable to say anything.

"You know," he said, giving me a considering look, "if it wasn't for the apports, I would never have known the truth."

"That's not quite what happened, although it's close," I said, my emotions a tangled knot that sat heavily in my stomach. "I followed him downstairs after he tried to grab Pixie. He knew I'd seen him. All I wanted to do was warn him to stay away from her, but he must have figured I'd tell you about his connection to Bethany."

"Your cousin?" Adam asked. "What was his . . . Wait a second. You said Spider was having sex with her. Are you saying now that Meredith also had something to do with her death?"

I nodded, bile burning my throat. "They both raped her."

"Why, for the love of all that is good, didn't you tell someone?" he asked, his voice rough.

"I didn't know until we got here. It's like I said: upstairs, in the room I went to lie down in, Spider gloated about Meredith and him having had sex with Bethany. He said something that I didn't pay attention to at first: he said she had cut her own throat. That fact was never made public, so it meant he must have been there when she killed herself. He and Meredith killed her just as surely as if they'd cut her throat themselves."

"You should have told me," he insisted.

"And what would you have done? It was his word against mine. I had no proof, no tangible proof, that he or Meredith had anything to do with her!"

"So you killed him in revenge."

There was a coldness in his voice, a coldness that stung. "No, I didn't. As soon as I saw him with Pixie,

I knew what he would do: he'd use and destroy her just as he did my cousin. I followed him to the basement to warn him away from her. I kept to the shadows, and heard the two of them talking about Pixie as they went downstairs to the basement. I admit that I coshed Meredith on the head; I wanted him out of the way so I could warn off Spider, but I guess Spider thought I was going to attack him, too, because I didn't have time to say a word to him before he grabbed me and threw me up against the bookcase."

The memory of that moment assailed me: pain exploding in my head as Spider grabbed my hair and banged it against the bookcase, his eyes lit with an unholy pleasure, his mouth twisted and snarling.

I wrapped my arms around myself and sank to the floor.

"What was it you had that he said he'd have when you were dead?" Adam asked, squatting next to me.

I couldn't look at him, speaking to my knees instead. "Amanita didn't hear exactly what he said. It was actually 'I'll have her when you're gone.'"

"Meaning Pixie."

I nodded. "Until that moment, I wasn't fighting back. Death seemed like such a pleasant escape from the sorrow of knowing my husband killed my little cousin. But he swore he'd have Pixie, and the next thing I knew, he was lying at my feet, dead."

"You . . . er . . . exploded on him? Like you did as a child?"

"It was in self-defense this time, but yes. Just as unintentional, though . . . and just as deadly." A sob rose in my throat.

"Let me see your head," Adam said, his face expressionless.

I leaned forward so he could run his fingers along the back of my head. I winced as he found the sensitive spots.

"You probably have a concussion," he said, tipping my head back to look deep into my eyes. "You have three good-sized lumps back there."

"Polters are strong," I said miserably, overwhelmed with sorrow—both for what had been and for what might have been.

"So strong that they can kill easily in self-defense," he said, nodding. "And so rather than tell me all this, you decided to frame Meredith for the murder."

I looked up at him, blinking away tears. "No, that was never my intention. I knew that as soon as the seal was lifted, I'd have to tell the watch what happened. I killed my husband. It was an accident, and done in self-defense, but I killed him. I am prepared to face the consequences of that. But I figured I had twelve hours to make you see the truth about Meredith."

He was silent for a few minutes. "Earlier, when you were talking about how sure you were that Meredith was a murderer, you weren't referring to the death of your husband, were you?"

"No. But there was nothing I could tell you that you'd believe, especially if you knew I just killed my husband. I thought . . . I hoped that if the truth about Meredith was revealed, his connection with Bethany would come out. I had no idea that Savannah held the key to all that until she turned out to be a Guardian."

"I told you I would do whatever I could to see that your cousin's rapist was caught," Adam said gently, putting an arm around me. "The watch would never have let them get away with it."

I made a frustrated gesture. "Thus far the watch hadn't connected the two of them to her, and I had no proof, nothing to convince them. And before you say that wouldn't matter, please remember that I *did* tell you Meredith was a murderer—but you demanded proof, and that was the one thing I didn't have." I ran my hands through my hair, my throat tight with unshed tears. "I had no choice, Adam. I just had no choice. I had to take the chance that I could prove the truth about Meredith before the seal was up."

"We'll let that point go," he said.

I moved out of his supporting embrace and gave him a weak smile. "Thank you. For . . . everything."

"I'm not the monster you seem to think I am," he said, getting to his feet and holding out his hand. I took it, his fingers warm as they wrapped around mine. "I won't say that if I had been in your shoes I would have done exactly the same thing, but I do see your point. I think you need to learn to trust people more, however. Especially me."

"Have you seen this?" I let him pull me to my feet, then held up my hands. On the outer edge of each hand there was a faint crescent-shaped scar.

Adam frowned at them. "Did you injure your hands?"

"Not exactly. I was born with six fingers on each hand. My mother had the doctors take the extras off when I was a baby. She wanted me to fit in, you see."

His pale eyes watched me with consideration.

"She's never understood that no matter how

human I look, I will never fit in with either world. I'll always be on the fringes of both the mortal and polter worlds."

"The Otherworld is more forgiving of those who don't conform than the mortal world is," he pointed out.

"But even it has limits. A wergeld-bound exterminator who killed her husband . . . I don't know, Adam. I think even the Otherworld is going to have issues with me."

He squeezed my hand, his fingers reassuringly solid. "You'll handle that, too."

The sun was shining brightly two weeks later. The sky was blue, the birds sang happily, people on the streets outside the building that was the local headquarters of the Akashic League paraded up and down the streets, enjoying the warmth of a sunny summer day.

"Stupid bright sun," I muttered to myself as I jogged down the steps to the sidewalk. "Stupid singing birds. Stupid happy people."

"Man, she's really cranky. Is she going to be like that all day? If she is, someone had better book another appointment with my therapist, because it's sure to traumatize me."

I gritted my teeth at Pixie's cheerful voice and stomped my way down the sidewalk to the parking lot, trying desperately to ignore the voices of the three people following me.

"Pixie, my dear, you're just going to have to get used to Karma's little ways. It won't be easy, but I'm confident you can do it."

"Tortured," I heard Pixie say.

"Eh?" my father asked.

"It's *Tortured* Pixie. I told that you before the trial. *Deus*, do you have Alzheimer's or something?"

"No, but I do have an itchy sweet tooth, and I see an ice cream place. Want some?" Dad asked in unusually good humor.

"OK, but you're buying."

Dad shot Adam a meaningful look before following Pixie into an ice cream shop.

To my surprise, Adam looked intensely uncomfortable. "I think this is the point where I'm supposed to ask you out."

His declaration startled me out of my blue funk for a few seconds. "Oh, please—I'm not in the market, and besides, I didn't think you were . . . er . . . free."

"Nita isn't my girlfriend, if that's what you're thinking." He made a wry face. "She was a few years ago, but the relationship more or less fizzled out with me gone so much of the year. We're now what is ubiquitously referred to as 'just good friends.'"

"Ah. Well . . . I'm not looking for a romantic relationship, not that you're offering one. Just . . . er . . . so you know."

He nodded, resignation evident in his face for the few moments it took to walk to my car.

"Oh, come on, Karma, you should be celebrating," he suddenly said in a disgustingly cheerful tone.

I glared at him as I unlocked the door. "Celebrating? I was looking forward to a nice quiet jail cell, where I could spend my time reading and making license plates, and not having to work for the Akashic League anymore. *You* can celebrate; you're sitting pretty with the League confirming your ownership of the house. But for me . . . *double wergeld*, Adam.

Double wergeld is unprecedented in the League! It's never been bound to anyone before!"

Tiny little laugh lines appeared next to his eyes. "Yes, but you're free. And I know the involuntary manslaughter verdict rankles, but it's a hell of a lot better than murder. So they slapped another wergeld on you; it's not like you're unused to it."

I looked upward for a moment, praying for patience. "Oh, no, it's not a big deal. It just means I am going to be at the beck and call of the League for the rest of my life. I get to spend long, endless years doing whatever they demand."

"Ah, but you won't be alone during those long, endless years." The laughter in his voice was rich.

I banged my forehead a couple of times on the roof of the car. "I was sure the League home would take Pixie back. I never thought they'd insist that she stay where she is. . . . I killed my husband, for Pete's sake! I can't be a good model for an impressionable girl to be around!"

Adam laughed at the sob that accompanied my words, his hand warm on my shoulder as he gave it a sympathetic squeeze. "They seem to think your experiences make you the perfect person to handle Pixie. I have every confidence that you'll handle both Pixie and the double wergeld with aplomb. Besides, I'll be here to help when you need it."

"I have a horrible feeling you're going to regret uttering those words," I said, straightening up to rub my abused forehead. Despite my glum warning, I felt a little spike of hope. I'd coped with a lot in my life. . . . How much trouble could one teen and jobs every now and again for the League be?

Famous last words, people. Famous last words.

KATIE MACALISTER

EVEN VAMPIRES GET THE BLUES

Paen Scott is a Dark One: a vampire without a soul. And his mother is about to lose hers too if Paen can't repay a debt to a demon by finding a relic known as the Jilin God in five days.

Half-elf Samantha Cosse may have gotten kicked out of the Order of Diviners, but she's still good at finding things, which is why she just opened her own private investigation agency.

Paen is one of Sam's first clients and the only one to set her elf senses tingling, which makes it pretty much impossible to keep their relationship on a professional level. Sam is convinced that she is Paen's Beloved— the woman who can give him back his soul...whether he wants it or not.

Available wherever books are sold or at
penguin.com

Penguin Group (USA) Online

What will you be reading tomorrow?

Tom Clancy, Patricia Cornwell, W.E.B. Griffin,
Nora Roberts, William Gibson, Robin Cook,
Brian Jacques, Catherine Coulter, Stephen King,
Dean Koontz, Ken Follett, Clive Cussler,
Eric Jerome Dickey, John Sandford,
Terry McMillan, Sue Monk Kidd, Amy Tan,
John Berendt...

You'll find them all at
penguin.com

*Read excerpts and newsletters,
find tour schedules and reading group guides,
and enter contests.*

Subscribe to Penguin Group (USA) newsletters
and get an exclusive inside look
at exciting new titles and the authors you love
long before everyone else does.

PENGUIN GROUP (USA)
us.penguingroup.com